The Thin Gray Line

The Thin Gray Line

A Civil War Novel

Michael Kenneth Smith

To my readers: You are the reason I write.

Chapter 1

The pain woke him, an excruciating agony like the searing of his own flesh that went all the way up his spine. He opened his eyes and tried to focus. The room spun round and round in a maelstrom with his bed in the middle. A wave of nausea crept in like a slowly rising tide. He blinked, trying to stop the whirling. Sunlight shone through a window onto a muslin sheet. He brought his hand to his face and felt the coarse stubble of a week-old beard and wondered what possibly could have happened since his last shave.

The image of a burned farmhouse slid into his thoughts. The image kept spinning, fading in and out. Then he was riding a horse...a fast-moving horse. There was a shot. The horse went down and threw him hard into a patch of briars that stung his face. The impact of his fall forced all the air out of his lungs and everything went black.

Now, his mouth felt like it was stuffed with cotton. He blinked hard again, and the room slowly stopped spinning and came into focus. His hand went to his chest, finding the locket and clutched it tightly in his fist. Looking down for the source of a stabbing pain he saw only the outline of one foot under the sheet. When he tried to move the other foot nothing happened, except the pain shot up worse than before. He raised his head up to see more clearly and pulled the sheet up. Slowly, the realization came to him. He had only one leg. He screamed. A blood-curdling scream. A flock of cowbirds darted from a tree just outside his window.

His hand went back to the locket. A gray darkness crept in from all sides until only a small circle was visible. It stayed that way for a few seconds then everything turned black.

Chapter 2

Clyde yelled "Gee" as his six-horse team approached the turn-off to his homestead. He didn't really have to, considering the hundreds of times he and his team had come home. Even though the freight wagon was empty, the wheels churned a red cloud of dust that rose lazily behind in the late afternoon air, creating a plume that he hoped Joanie or the twins would see. He had driven his team hard all day to be home for supper and he was hungry. The team sped up as they neared home, they were hungry, too.

He pulled the team up to a halt in front of his barn. When he jumped off the wagon, Joanie, the twins, Timmy and Tommy, two dogs and Nanny, their goat, rushed to greet him.

Only ten days before he had arrived home with a special cargo, a young soldier so close to death that he had second thoughts of even trying to save him. He had originally given the soldier a ride to the nearby town of Crossville, Tennessee, and the soldier had insisted on walking the short distance to his parent's farm. The young man's leg was bent at an unnatural angle and his trousers were stained red with blood. Using crutches, the soldier hobbled away and Clyde drove on. But Clyde doubled back, thinking his passenger might not make it without help. The drover found him prostrate in a burned-out farmhouse that he surmised was his parent's place. He was unconscious, lying in a puddle of his own blood. Clyde found his pulse extremely fast but weak. He carefully laid the body in the back of his wagon and hauled him to his place. The soldier's pulse continued to be weak and his wounds reeked of gangrene.

As no doctors were within a fifty-mile radius, Clyde, with the help and guidance of Joanie, his wife, amputated his leg mid-way between his hip and knee. Joanie had cut the flesh around the bone, and then Clyde had used a bucking saw to cut through the bone. He still remembered the squishy sound of the saw. He winced every time he thought about it. After they had finished they still didn't think the soldier would make it, but Joanie's mother was a nurse and had taught her how to handle deep lacerations and other emergencies. Joanie tied off Luke's severed arteries and sutured the skin together over the stub. By keeping the patient hydrated and the sutures clean with frequent bandage changes, he slowly recovered.

After hugging Joanie, Clyde sat on their front stoop and said hello to the rest of his family. The twins and the dogs all sought Clyde's attention. Nanny playfully head-butted anyone or anything that got between her and Clyde. The boys, ten years old, talked at once trying to tell their father about their adventures while he was gone.

When Clyde could get a word in, he asked. "How's the patient?"

"Our new one gets a little stronger each day," Joanie said. "His stitches are holding nicely and we'll be able to take them out in a couple of days. He's in a lot of pain, though. I think we made the right decision to amputate ourselves. He would never have survived the fifty-mile journey bouncing around in the back of a wagon."

"Wouldn't want to do it again," Clyde said. "You were great. Neither of us could have done it alone. I'll go up to see him after supper. Anybody nosing around?"

"Nothing since the three Yankee stragglers came last week and I don't think they'll come back."

Clyde didn't think so either. He'd taught the Yankees a lesson in good manners with the help of two barrels of buckshot into their back-sides as they fled.

"Do I smell ham hocks?"

"With fresh beans...and a little surprise afterward," Joanie replied with a smile.

Clyde put the twins, one on each shoulder, and walked back to his rig. Setting the boys down, he let them struggle to push the barn doors open by themselves. Then Clyde guided the team in and unhitched the freight wagon. He removed the harness from the horses and carefully treated the leather with saddle soap. Then, with burlap bags, he laboriously wiped each horse down and turned them out to pasture. Just when he had finished with the last horse, Joanie rang the bell for dinner. Clyde smiled. She seemed to always know when he was about to finish his chores.

After supper, Clyde climbed the stairs, softly knocked on the second door and entered the room. The young man was sitting up propped against a pillow. His eyes closely followed Clyde as he approached the bed.

"Do I detect a smile?" Clyde said.

"Nothing to smile about," Luke said.

"You're alive, aint ya?" Clyde said.

"I guess so."

Clyde pulled up a straight-backed wooden chair and sat next to the bed. The chair creaked under Clyde's weight. "I just came from Nashville. Drove past the train station. Must of been thirty or forty fellas on the train platform waitin' to go somewheres. They all had arms and legs missing…several had both arms gone…they had no food, no shelter and no special care."

"All I know is I'll never be the same. Never ride a horse. Never walk. Never anything."

The young man winced, then looked down at his foot.

"How's the pain?" Clyde asked.

"The pain comes from the leg that's not there. It feels like someone is stabbing me in the bottom of my foot with a dull hunting knife. The blade goes in, and then it feels like someone is turning it around and around, like they're boring a hole in my foot."

The description made Clyde grimace. "You taking some of that?" Clyde asked pointing to a half empty bottle of laudanum standing on the bedside table. "I've got more if you need it."

"It makes the pain go away, but then I fall to sleep and when I wake up, the pain is back again."

"Maybe you could read a bible. Might get your mind off your suffering," Clyde suggested.

"Not much into religion," the young man said. "Never went to church when I was a kid."

Clyde told him more about his recent trip. He wanted to give the soldier a little more time before he asked him about his home and family. From the appearance of the place where he was found, the young man had lost his home, his leg and probably his family. Clyde suspected his recovery would be long and painful, if he recovered at all.

The young man flinched again as he reached over for the bottle and took a large gulp.

Chapter 3

A blue jay sounded an alarm from the windowsill just before Joanie entered Luke's room two days later with his regular morning breakfast. For the first time, the young man smiled as he watched her approach his bed carrying a tray with his breakfast.

"My friend out there can hear you coming," he said, "even with all this rain."

"He's my friend, too, and he told me you were awake," Joanie answered, also smiling. She sat the tray on his bed. "We were going to church this morning, but Clyde decided it was raining too hard…lucky us."

Clyde and the two boys came into the bedroom before Luke finished his breakfast eggs and grits. Clyde sat in the chair and Joanie and the twins sat on the bed, being careful not to cause much movement. Sensing the timing might be favorable, Clyde asked the young soldier how he got injured.

"My horse got shot out from under me," Luke answered. "Just before Gettysburg."

Joanie took the tray and set it on a table that was nothing more than an old, well-used, salt barrel. As she did, the slight movement of the bed caused Luke to flinch with pain and he reached for the laudanum. He took a swig and every one stared at him expectantly hoping he would talk.

The two boys were leaning toward him. "Gettysburg?" One asked.

After a short pause, the young man took a deep breath and said, "My full name is Luke Pettigrew. I was at Shiloh, then rode with Stuart…"

"Jeb Stuart?" Both boys said in unison, one jumping up.

"Yep," Luke said chuckling, then wincing from the movement of the bed. He reached again for the laudanum.

"Boys, don't shake Luke's bed," Clyde said.

One of the boys made a sword slashing gesture at his brother. "You're dead!" He said.

Luke smiled at Clyde. "I remember that age," he said.

"What did you do at Shiloh?" Clyde asked.

"Was in the Ambulance Corps. Took care of wounded soldiers…like me." His voice started to trail off. "Met Colonel Forrest…".

"You met Bedford Forrest?" One of the boys asked in near disbelief.

Luke eyelids closed then opened. "Yep," he said, then his eyelids slowly closed and he fell into a drug-induced sleep.

The next morning Luke was not entirely surprised to see the two boys, Timmy and Tommy, sitting on his bed when he opened his eyes.

"What is Jeb Stuart's horses name?" Asked Timmy.

"Does Forrest carry one side arm or two?" Asked Tommy.

"Is the story about Fallen Timbers true?" Asked Timmy.

"Whoa. Wait a minute. One at a time," Luke said trying to fold his pillow so he could sit up. He used his elbows to carefully slide up on the pillow without moving his stub. He pointed to Timmy and said, "Virginia", then to Tommy and said, "One", then back to Timmy and said, "Yes, it's true."

When the twins started peppering him with questions again, Luke held up his hands. "Now, hold your horses, boys, and I'll tell you the whole story," Luke said.

"I lived on a small farm with my folks. The land was poor and my father had trouble getting crops to grow in the rocky soil. I didn't really understand it, but money was always tight and my father had little funds left over each year for seeds to plant the following spring." As Luke talked he was reminded how he used to talk to his horse, Bonnie, when he was a kid. She always listened to him and never doubted a word he said, unlike his father who always found fault with whatever he said or did. Whatever he chose to talk to Bonnie about, she agreed…he was feeling that way talking to the boys.

"One day, it was time to milk the cows and my job was always to ride out into the woods, round them up and herd them to our barn. I saw a fox in the distance when we were about halfway to the barn." He told them how the cows usually kept going once they got started toward the barn and so he had decided to give chase to the fox. "The grass was wet and while we were chasing, the fox took a sharp turn, and poor Bonnie fell and hurt her leg."

"Did you catch the fox?" Tommie asked.

"No, but I had to walk Bonnie back to the barn. She was lame and my father was very angry." He told the boys how his father depended on the horse to pull their buggy and help with other work around the farm. "He said Bonnie would probably have to be put down, but regardless wouldn't be able to work again."

He told the boys how bad he felt about his poor horse. He had been irresponsible.

"I had never seen my father so angry," Luke said, "he told me he didn't need me anymore…that the farm couldn't feed us all. We always had plenty to eat, so I thought he just wanted to get rid of me. He told me I was old enough to strike out on my own."

"Did you cry?" Tommie asked.

"No. Not only was I losing my best friend, Bonnie, but I was losing my home. I wanted to lash out. I walked into town and enlisted…joined the Confederate army. I was bound and determined to make my father realize he was wrong about me. I would have done anything to make him ask me to come back. I thought I would go to war and become a big hero or something. That would make him sorry he kicked me off the farm."

"After I signed up, my sergeant found out I was good at working with wounded soldiers. I could stitch up cuts, apply bandages, all the simple stuff. Guess I learned that working with farm animals. The sergeant recommended me to the ambulance corps and I became a medic at the Battle of Shiloh, and that's where I met Bedford Forrest. Forrest led a charge of about six hundred of his cavalry against the advancing Bluecoats. The bravest thing I ever saw. That was on the day after the Battle of Shiloh. They called his charge the Battle of Fallen Timbers."

"Is that when he was wounded?" Tommy asked.

"You know your history, young man," Luke said.

Tommy stuck out his chest and glanced over at his brother with a superior attitude.

"The Union forces over-ran our little field hospital and I was taken prisoner. They took me to a prisoner of war camp in Columbus, Ohio. After several months, I was able to escape with the help of a prominent local citizen. I stayed in his house and there I met the love of my life, Carol." He reached up to his chest looking for the locket that had her picture inside and held it for a moment. "After promising her I would come back after the war, I became one of Jeb Stuart's scouts because I could ride so well." Luke looked down at his remaining foot. "Guess those days are over."

The boys were in awe. A wave of pain hit Luke just as Clyde walked in with a pair of crutches. Luke reached for the laudanum and took a swallow from the bottle. The liquid felt warm going down his throat and the opiate almost immediately numbed his senses and the pain became tolerable.

"Let's give these a try," Clyde said, "I got them from a young fella in Nashville earlier this week." His voice dropped off. "He won't need them anymore. Infection. Poor man. Well, as I told you before, you're in much better shape and we won't let that happen to you." He leaned the crutches against the wall and reached to help Luke get up.

Luke felt Clyde's huge hands go under his shoulders and in one single motion he was standing with seemingly little effort on Clyde's part. Luke was thankful it was Clyde who had found him in the burned-out farmhouse. A man of lesser strength would have had difficulty lifting him in and out of the wagon. A thought flashed in his mind that he would never want to get on the wrong side of the big man. Clyde helped him up and as Luke leaned on him, the boys gave him his crutches and he stood. The room was going around and around from the effects of the laudanum. Luke fought off the dizziness, trying to maintain his balance. The boys and Clyde moved away and Luke was standing by himself. With all his weight on his crutches, he swung his leg forward to take a step, but his crutch slipped and he fell, knocking over the salt barrel and slamming his head against the wall. "Whoa there, young fella," Clyde said, "take smaller steps until you get the hang of it."

When Clyde reached down to help him up, Luke said, "I think I can get up on my own, let me try." The barrel sat next to his leg and Luke noticed the curvature of the calf muscle on his good leg looked similar to the curvature of the wooden barrel staves. An idea flashed through his mind...*a wooden leg...instead of crutches, an artificial leg...maybe it could bend like a knee...*but the pain was too great to give it much thought. He accepted Clyde's help and, exhausted, he got back into bed.

"Must feel strange to walk with only one leg," Clyde said.

"I feel like I still have two legs," Luke said. "It's like the old diving board we had on the farm, only each step feels like the last, before you go into the water. I feel like I have to learn to walk all over again."

Clyde left, and Luke's mind flashed back to a field hospital at the Battle of Shiloh, where he had helped so many amputees such as himself. He had treated each one with care, but after he finished stitching them up, he moved to the next patient and forgot about the one he had just treated. Each patient had taken his total concentration as he attended to one after the other. So many wounded soldiers needed help, some on the verge of death, that he never gave much thought to the one he just had worked on. Now he was that patient. The one he had forgotten about before. Each one of them had to go through what he was now going to have to do himself... learning to walk again...learning to live again.

Within days, Luke was able to move around in his room. The hardest part was getting started. He began by sitting on the edge of the bed; standing up from there with his crutches required some training. When he fell, he had to get back onto his bed and start over. Slowly his coordination and balance improved. But his movements were limited to the second floor, where, the McCallister house had only a hallway for him to practice. He would start from his door at the end of the hallway, walking to the staircase and back, passing a door that was always closed. The stairs were steep, with narrow steps, and no one believed he could use his crutches to go down.

They thought he would have to sit on the top step, and then ease himself down one step at a time. Luke intended to prove them wrong.

Joanie had been a schoolteacher before she married Clyde, and because of the chaotic conditions in Tennessee schools caused by the war, she conducted the boys' schooling at home. When the boys were not being schooled, they frequently came up to Luke's room. If they weren't questioning him about the war, they would play war games on the floor using small pieces of wood for soldiers.

Watching them play, Luke reminded himself he was only eight years older than they were. It seemed like a very short time ago he was that age, almost like yesterday. He had been happy on the farm, riding, fishing, swimming in the river. His childhood had ended when his father told him to leave.

Luke, having seen countless amputated limbs, had a good understanding of the mechanics of how a leg worked. He asked the boys to bring him a length of four-by-four lumber and a sharp knife for whittling. He didn't want a peg for a leg. He sat on his bed and studied his stump and tried to visualize the mechanism he would use to attach the artificial leg. He admired the job Clyde and Joanie had done with his flap, the piece of skin that covered the bottom of his thighbone. He thought he couldn't have done it better himself.

He whittled the wood, forming it into a long tapered peg. His amputation was just at mid-thigh. He thought he would secure the peg to his thigh with a leather strap, like many he had seen before. But as he whittled on the solid piece of wood, he began to imagine what it would be like to walk with a straight-legged peg. Because the peg would not be flexible and bend at the knee, he would have to swing the peg out to the side each time he took a step. Not only would the peg make it difficult to walk normally, but climbing steps would be extremely cumbersome. More importantly it would be very conspicuous. People would know he had a peg leg.

He eyed the barrel table again and made a drawing with a pencil on the piece of wood he was whittling. The hinge could be made of leather. Then he thought of another problem: if he hinged the knee to avoid having to swing the leg out with each step, how would the hinge lock when he put weight on it and equally important, how would it hinge back when he wanted to step forward. Then, he foresaw a problem with friction. To keep his lower leg from swinging freely back and forth, he needed something to restrain its movement and the best way he knew to do that was with a tight fit between the upper and lower components.

His wooden peg had become covered with pencil drawings, so many in fact that he had to study it hard to figure out which were the most current. As he leaned his head against the back of his bed, tracing each pencil line, he realized he hadn't thought about his pain in the past several hours.

In addition, he had forbidden himself to think back to his escape from Chase Prison near, Ohio. Those thoughts always led to Carol, the girl whose uncle had helped hide him when the whole city was looking for the escaped confederate soldier. He remembered the first time their eyes met and felt that warm glow all over again. When they were alone, he remembered her touch and while he wanted her desperately, he feared she could never return his love. She would reject him, like his father had.

Over the next several weeks, Luke carved and whittled his pieces of wood. The two boys helped by bringing him scraps wood from discarded barrels and Luke made them promise not to tell their parents what he was working on. He thought if it didn't work, then they wouldn't be disappointed.

Chapter 4

A loud thunderclap awoke Luke from a laudanum-induced sleep. The curtains were being blown nearly horizontal by a strong gusting wind. Luke tried to get up to close the window but something was in his bed. He moved to the other side just as another bolt of lightning lit up the bedroom. Then, he saw her.

"Paul, can I stay with you? I'm scared." The woman's voice was pleading.

Luke stared. He thought he might be dreaming. He rubbed his eyes. And stared some more.

"Please, Paul, this is where I belong."

Another bolt of lightning lit up the room and Luke saw the woman in his bed. It was Joanie.

"Joanie, what are you doing here?" He asked incredulously.

"I'm not Joanie," she said.

"And I'm not Paul," Luke said.

"Of course you're Paul, why would you say you're not?"

More distant lightning lit up her face. Her hair was disheveled, but even though her blue eyes had a wild look, he was sure it was Joanie. She had nothing on. There was a very bright flash immediately followed by a horrendous crack that rattled the whole house. Luke shook his head trying to awake from what he thought must be a bad dream…but it wasn't. The light shining on her face on and off again made her look like she was moving in slow motion creating an eerie ghostlike image…but Luke couldn't take his gaze away from her body. He had never seen a totally unclothed mature woman before and his eyes devoured her even though he didn't want them to. He felt drawn by a rousing desire and, at the same time, repulsed by something he knew was wrong. Then he thought of Clyde. What if he walked in?

"Joanie, this isn't right. You should be in your own bed," Luke said.

"I am," she said softly. She slid over and reached her arm across Luke's chest and pulled him close. He could feel her bare skin moving next to his.

"Listen, Joanie, or whoever you are calling yourself, I'm not Paul. He gently tried to pull her arm off but she nestled even closer. He felt her bare breasts on his arm and her nakedness rubbing on his hip. "This is wrong," he said. He was to the edge of his bed. He would fall if he tried to move any farther away from her. He glanced at the closed bedroom door. If Clyde walked in, the big man would kill him.

"Paul, you always play hard to get," she cooed, "I love that about you." She raised her knee slowly over his mid-section, moved it back and forth, and giggled. "That's the Paul I know."

Luke was becoming more aroused and he knew it was wrong. He felt trapped...being drawn in. He tried to repress his emotion. "How many times do I have to tell you? I'm not Paul. I don't know anyone named Paul. I do know that you are married and this is totally wrong."

He thought he would just slide onto the floor but she hung on and continued to stroke him with her leg. "Oh, Paul, its been so long," she whispered. "You can't imagine how I have dreamed of this." She tried to kiss him, but he turned his head.

He smelled her sweet fragrance. The odor was familiar, but he couldn't place it. He felt her warm breath against his ear. He realized the hair on his arms was standing. "You're probably twice my age," he murmured.

"Be quiet and nobody will hear us," she whispered.

Lightning lit up the sky followed closely by the roar of the thunder and the woman threw down the blanket and straddled Luke. This could not be happening. He saw her clearly then and felt her moving against him. Luke saw her unkempt beauty. Her hands went to his chest as she moved and his hands went to her hips as he yielded to her rhythm

Luke opened his eyes. The sun had already begun its daily climb and cast shadows on the rumpled sheets of his bed. Then, he remembered. Any hope that what had happened in the night was a dream vanished in the telltale signs left on his sheets. He pulled a blanket up to cover the evidence. He cursed himself. How could he have let this happen? How could he have so easily tossed aside virginity when he had so many times promised himself he would wait for Carol? It had all happened so fast. And Joanie…why had she come to his bed and insisted she was somebody else? And if Clyde found out he'd be a dead man.

Just then, Joanie came into the room with a breakfast tray. Smiling, she asked if Luke had slept through the storm.

"I didn't sleep well at all," he said. "How about you?"

"I heard a couple of thunder claps, but that was about all…slept pretty well, actually."

Luke looked for a hint in her face. A smile. Or embarrassment. He saw nothing. She noticed that he was staring and stopped.

"Who's Paul?" Luke asked pointedly.

Joanie looked up abruptly. "Why do you ask?"

"I think you know."

Joanie took a moment like she was collecting her thoughts. "You've met Janie, haven't you?"

"Janie?"

"My twin sister. She lost her husband at Fort Henry and after that hasn't been the same. She's been living with us ever since. Did she come to your room? She's in the room next to you."

"She thought I was Paul," he said nodding.

"Paul was Clyde's brother. My sister and I married brothers. It's common in these parts…anyway, Clyde took Paul's death very hard, too. They were close. Afterward, he hasn't been the same. He has bouts of anger that he never had before."

"This war is effecting everyone," Luke said.

"What happened with Janie? She gets crazy sometimes, but she didn't bother you, did she? Her room is down the hall. We never know what she's going to do when she has one of her spells."

Luke hesitated. He thought he understood her concern, but wasn't going to say such in front of the lady. "When I woke up this morning, I thought it had all been a dream. No, now that I understand, I feel sorry for her."

Joanie accepted Luke's answer and left. Shortly the boys came in. Luke retrieved his carvings from under the bed and while talking to the boys, resumed his project. After they had left, he reflected back to Janie. Now that he understood, he felt guilty and cursed himself for yielding.

Chapter 5

September 2, 1863

While Luke was carving the upper part of his artificial leg that would serve as the thigh, he inserted some rubber from a pair of Clyde's discarded boots in the hollowed out portion where his stub would fit. As he held the piece up toward the window to see more clearly, he spotted a line of horsemen on the ridge nearly a half-mile away. He could only see them as they passed through an opening, but the line was long. He suspected the worst as the riders crested the wooded ridge and came closer. They were Union. Riding two-by-two, the line snaked for almost a mile heading to the southeast. Luke estimated the line would pass within several hundred yards of Clyde's homestead.

As the forward riders reached the closest point, two horsemen peeled off and headed toward the house. Luke's window was facing the back, so he could not see the soldiers approach, however he could hear their sabers rattling as they dismounted near the front gate.

"Hello, the house," someone hailed.

Joanie, who had been teaching the twins their lessons, opened the front door half way. "What do you want?" She asked bluntly.

"Where's the man of the house?"

"He's away," Joanie said stepping out onto the porch.

"Yankee or Rebel?"

"Neither, he's a drover and he hauls Yankee freight between Nashville and points east." The two soldiers walked closer. "Mind if we look around?" one asked.

"Do I have a choice?" Joanie said.

"Just doing our duty, ma'am," one said.

One of the soldiers walked toward the barn. Luke could hear the other's spurs as he stepped up on the porch, and then come inside the house. Luke followed his progress as he walked around the first floor. Luke deduced that the soldier might be limping because of the irregular rhythm of his footsteps. Jing-ka-jing, jing-ka-jink, jing-ka-jing, jingka-jink. He searched methodically. A door would open, then steps around the room, then to the next room. Luke felt helpless. He had no way of protecting himself…or Joanie. He had heard stories of how Union soldiers would pillage farmhouses such as the McCallister's, and then rape the women. He cursed himself for not being able to defend the house. Silently he set his jaw and promised himself he would never be caught helpless again. An image of his father flashed in front of him…smiling at him in his mocking way, shaking his head as if to say *you've failed again.* The soldier ascended the stairs. Slowly he walked down the hall that led to Luke's room. Luke's door opened and a tall soldier filled the threshold. From his stripes, Luke could see he was a lieutenant.

"What have we here?" the lieutenant asked approaching the bed, his hand touching his holstered side arm. "Are you wounded?"

"Lost a leg."

"You're a Johnny Reb, ain't ya? I can tell by your accent."

"Yep."

The soldier pulled the blanket off Luke to verify. "Where'd it happen?"

"Gettysburg."

"Not long ago, I see. You from these parts?"

"Yes, near Crossville."

The officer carefully put the blanket back. "I got a slug in my leg at Shiloh," he said. He pulled up his pant leg and showed Luke the deep scar on his upper calf just above his boot line. "Damnedest thing. I got picked up by the Rebs." He stood next to the bed, rolled his pant leg back down and seemed to relax. "Threw me onto a wagon. Hauled me to a field hospital where they tried to decide if they could save the leg. The next day, our boys overwhelmed the whole area and took over. Guess I was a prisoner for about twenty-four hours. Them Rebs were nice to me though…saved my leg."

This man is no threat, Luke thought as he relaxed. "Do you remember which field hospital?" Luke asked.

"No, but it was toward the end of the third day. You boys were on the run."

"About the time of the Battle of Fallen Timbers?"

"You know about that, boy?"

"I was there."

"Well, don't that beat all." The lieutenant looked at Luke with a hint of admiration. "What were you doing there?"

"I was a medic in a small field hospital. I was taken prisoner."

"If I recall, there were only two doctors and a medic…" He stopped and looked at Luke as if he was looking for a sign of familiarity. "You were the medic? You might've been the one who helped the doctors decide not to amputate. Do I look familiar?" He pulled up his pant leg again. "Couldn't have been many like this…it was you, wasn't it?"

"It's a bit foggy. There were so many." Luke could not remember ever treating this officer. He was fairly certain he hadn't, but it could be to his advantage if the man standing in front of him thought he owed a favor. "But I do remember treating a Union officer…we treated quite a few regular Union men…yes, I do recall. Our docs were moving fast. Sometimes it was easier to amputate a limb rather than try to keep it. We could amputate in about ten minutes but trying to save a limb with a complicated wound might take longer. The doctors just moved on to the next patient. Now that I think about it, I seem to remember you…your wound didn't damage the bone substantially…didn't feel right to take it off when there was a good chance you could keep it. I might have said something to the docs."

The lieutenant pushed his campaign cap back with his index finger. "I'll be damned," he said shaking his head.

The officer looked out the window. His whole unit had passed by. He glanced at his watch. "Look, son, I gotta go and catch up. I wish we could talk more." As he started to leave, he stopped and pulled out a piece of paper. "This is not a friendly place for Rebs to be out and about." He wrote something on the paper, and then handed it to Luke. "Here take this, it might get you out of a tight squeeze. It's the least I can do."

He walked to the door and turned, "What's your name, son?"

"Luke Pettigrew, sir, and thank you."

The lieutenant saluted and left. Then, as the lieutenant's footsteps faded, Luke looked at the note: This soldier saved my leg. Please afford him safe passage. Signed: Lt. Gus Hillenbrand, Army of the Cumberland.

Joanie walked in. "I couldn't help but overhear your conversation. Quite a coincidence."

The boys followed and Luke found himself telling them about the field hospital where Hillenbrand thought he was taken.

When Joanie left, Luke thought of her sister and the lightning flashing on her unclothed body. He felt ashamed for yielding…he should have resisted the temptation. He felt like he had betrayed the McCallister's trust. Most of all, he feared Clyde's wrath if he found out. He cursed himself, the loss of his leg and his whole predicament…he had to do something to help himself.

He sat up and brought out his leg carvings. Luke tried on the upper part of his new leg. He tied it on with a six inch wide piece of leather tacked onto the thigh section. It had a strap that could be tightened around his stub. With the piece firmly attached, he matched the length of the artificial piece to his good leg. He was satisfied with the length, so he took it off and started to assemble the calf to the thigh using a dowel rod as hinge serving as his new knee.

Having worked out all the dimensions, he had a firm idea of how the wooden leg would work. The more he thought about the mechanics of walking, the more he was amazed at how complicated such a simple process could be. To take a step, one foot is raised and put forward. Then the body's weight is transferred to the forward leg and the rear foot is raised and put forward and so on. The raising of the artificial foot was the problem. He needed a mechanism that would keep the foot from dragging on the floor as he took another step. He had considered a spring but discarded the idea because it would add too much bulk to the back of the leg. But he had another idea that might work instead.

He cut a long strip of left over rubber and attached one end to the wood just above the knee in the back. The thigh piece mated with the lower leg using a curved hinge resembling a mortise and tendon joint built on a curve. The knee hinged on the dowel rod. To the upper end of the lower leg, he attached the other end of the rubber piece, just above where the calf would be, and adjusted it so that the leg would lift whenever his weight was on the other leg.

A key to his design was modeled after the hinging mechanism of the hayforks his father used to hoist hay up to the loft. More than a hinge, it was a knuckle that bent two ways, opening and closing the forks.

Getting everything adjusted properly took two days. When he thought the leg was ready for trial, he asked the boys for help. He swore them to secrecy until after he learned how to use it. The boys looked dubious as Luke showed them how it worked.

He strapped it onto his stub and tried to stand. The leg fell off and Luke had to put it on again, this time drawing the leather strap much tighter around the stub. He stood again. The foot would not straighten because of the rubber piece holding it in a bent position. Having anticipated this, Luke threw his leg forward and as the leg straightened, he planted the foot onto the floor. Luke smiled. So far, so good. The leg had straightened because of the forward momentum of his foot. The boys watched in amazement.

Using his crutches, he took a couple of steps. The timing of when to throw his foot forward was difficult, but Luke knew he was on the right track. Staying inside his room, he took more steps, and the rhythm required to move forward became more familiar. The timing was much different than normal walking. He had to be very careful not to lose his balance as he shifted his weight to his good leg so he could swing the prosthesis forward. But with each try he got better.

Finally, he stopped and sat on his bed, nearly exhausted from the effort. He took a deep breath and smiled. He had actually walked. Something he thought he would never do again. While he was unstrapping his new leg he made the boys promise again that they would not tell until he was ready. They agreed, knowing their mother and father would be very surprised, and Luke told them he thought he would be ready to show it to them in a couple of days.

Chapter 6

That evening, Luke listened to Clyde coming up the steps. He felt himself tense up until he saw the smile on Clyde's face "How's the patient?" Clyde asked walking in with a bag under his arm.

"Pain comes and goes…"

"Here's some more medicine for the pain," Clyde said as he pulled two new bottles of laudanum out of the bag.

Luke thanked him and told him he was trying to take less of it than before. Clyde asked more about the cavalry lieutenant. He questioned Luke about what information he might have given about where such a large force was going. Luke said the officer said nothing about that, but the whole unit was headed to the southwest toward Chattanooga.

Clyde leaned forward in his seat. "I hear a lot about this war from other drover's. The Union wants the rail yards at Chattanooga. They figure if they can take them, then the road will be clear all the way to Atlanta. The Union army under General Rosecrans has a superior force or so they say, but Braxton Bragg's Army of the Mississippi may have a trick up his sleeve. Our boys need to hold Chattanooga or all of Tennessee will be lost. If only they would send Longstreet and his 1st Corps to back up Bragg at Chattanooga…."

"Where is Longstreet now?" Luke asked.

"He gave up the siege of Knoxville and now he's up at Russellville… getting ready to move though, but who knows when. Bragg wants Longstreet with him and of course Lee needs him desperately. My guess he goes to Lee."

"I'm surprised you have Confederate loyalties considering you live here in eastern Tennessee," Luke said. " Seems like most of us lean toward the Union, 'cept me and you." He also wondered if some of the freight Clyde was hauling might be something besides bales of cotton. He looked at one of the laudanum bottles. It read *Tincture of Opium, Samuel Duffield, Detroit, Michigan.* He had seen that same label on a bottle at Shiloh over a year ago.

"You have any family besides your mom and dad?" Clyde asked changing the subject.

"Just me...why?"

"Just wondering about your place. If, heaven forbid, your parents are gone, I was thinking about your farm. The property would go to you under Tennessee law," Clyde said.

"Haven't thought about that," Luke said, "It's hard for me to accept they are gone...but, there's really no law here in Tennessee right now with the state nearly taken over by the Yanks. Anyway, the farm has a lot of rocks," he looked down at his leg, "farming would be tough."

After Clyde excused himself, saying he had some work to do in the barn, Luke thought about what he had said. Even if his artificial leg worked as well as he hoped, farming would be nearly impossible. Thinking about farming, making a living and supporting a family brought Carol to mind. After the war, he could sell the farm. He would have something to offer. But then his leg...how could she love him like that. He was still only half a man. He felt a deep emptiness. He reached for his laudanum bottle and took a big gulp.

He picked up his knife and continued to fine-tune his wooden leg. The thigh section was solid wood, nearly eight inches in diameter at the thickest part, and probably weighed about ten pounds. To make it lighter, he carved out holes, decreasing the weight without compromising the physical integrity of the thigh. He made the holes go all the way through, except in the thickest portion where his calf would be, because his knife would not reach half way through. As he studied the holes, he thought they could make a great place to hide something. A secret compartment nobody would know about.

He reamed one hole slightly bigger so the knife and handle would fit into it completely. He carved a plug from a small piece of the same wood to fit into the end of the hole. He thought if he ever needed a knife for whatever reason, he would have one and nobody would know about. To keep the knife from rattling, he stuffed some cotton around it making it snug. Once the plug was inserted, he rotated it so the grain of the thigh matched that of the plug, then sanded it smooth. It blended perfectly. He held up the thigh piece and admired his work. The plug was nearly invisible save a tiny indentation that allowed him to pry it open with his fingernail when he had to.

He donned the apparatus, and noted how the now-lighter weight felt more natural. Standing took a great deal of practice. When he tried to stand, his artificial leg could not help him. He also practiced walking. The lighter leg was much easier to propel forward. Before, when he took a step, the leg would swing past the natural stopping point. Now, it felt more normal because it had less momentum.

He practiced walking up and down the hallway. He wondered about Janie each time he passed the door next to his that was always closed. He wanted to knock on her door, but he couldn't find the nerve. On the fourth time, he stopped near her door to adjust the strap around his thigh. As he leaned over, he heard a soft moan. He lightly tapped on the door. There was no answer and so he tapped again, only to hear the moaning continue. He pushed on the door and it opened slightly. "Janie?" Luke said in a low voice.

He only heard the soft moans, so, thinking something might be wrong he pushed the door open. Against the wall was an unmade bed with a cushioned chair next to it, but Janie was not there. Luke took a couple steps in and the moans were coming from behind a door on the opposite side of the bed. He walked over and put his hand on the doorknob and slowly opened the closet door, letting light into the darkened space. Janie was sitting on the floor with her arms around her drawn up knees. She wore a full-length sleeping gown. Her head was down, her disheveled blonde hair hung down over her legs, and she did not look up. Her moaning continued and Luke could see her lips moving.

"Janie?" Luke said almost whispering.

She looked up. Her eyes were blank, unseeing, almost glazed over. Then she put her head down again and continued her soft moaning.

Luke left the closet door open, hobbled through the bedroom doorway and quietly closed the door behind him.

Chapter 7

Sunday evening suppers were always special meals at the McCallister's. Joanie would cook a ham or a chicken, Clyde would carve and the boys knew the meal would end with a fruit pie. The aroma from the stove would spread through the whole house and everyone's appetite would thoroughly whetted in anticipation of the big event.

The kitchen in the McCallister house was the biggest room in the house. On the outside wall there was a immense wood stove that Clyde had found abandoned in a burned-out plantation house in western Tennessee. Two turkeys, side-by-side, could be roasted in the oven. On top were six burners. Next to it was a wood bin, that when closed served as a comfortable bench. But Joanie's favorite was the hand pump above the sink. She could pump fresh water without having to go outside. In the center of the kitchen was a table and chairs where the family took their meals. The stove also served as the source of heat for the whole house on cold days, but whether it was cold or not, the kitchen was the gathering place for the family.

Joanie's specialty was her pies. She made the crust using lard rendered from butchered hogs. The pie fillings were made from apples or cherries, fresh, if available, or from the jars of fruit she put away every year. She preferred to use beet sugar rather than cane. Her mother had always used it and Joanie shared her belief that it was more pure than cane sugar because it was whiter.

The twins particularly enjoyed Sunday suppers because their dad was always home. He planned each week in such a way that guaranteed his return. His trips might be shorter and he would arrive Thursday or Friday, but never later than Saturday evening or Sunday morning. After church, they were free to do the things they enjoyed most, like identifying every squirrel's nest in the woods so they could show their dad where to find them. Clyde would always make a big fuss over the twin's ability to find game, and made sure their mom knew about it. When Joanie cooked up the squirrel, the boys would get all the credit.

On this particular Sunday, Joanie noticed the boys were especially wound up. They stayed inside the house even though it was warm and sunny outside. They kept coming back into the kitchen asking how soon until dinner. They even washed up before they were asked to. Joanie just shook her head. The boys never failed to amaze and entertain her. She thought whatever they had up their sleeves, it was catching. When she took up the tray to Luke, he hardly ate anything and roasted chicken was his favorite. She knew she could count on Clyde, however. He would eat anything she put in front of him.

"Supper's on!" Joanie announced. "Come and get it." When she carried the chicken platter into the dining room, the boys were already seated as if they had been there for a while. After grace, Clyde carved and passed the platter around. When the boys took very little, murmuring something about not being very hungry, Joanie had had enough.

"Okay, you little rascals, I worked all day to cook this meal and you're not eating. I know something's up and, as your mother, I demand to know what it is."

Just then they heard a hollow 'clunk' coming from the stairway, then another and another. The boys looked toward the staircase and stood up, smiling. Joanie quickly looked at Clyde with a questioning glance and he just shrugged.

Clunk, clunk, clunk. The mysterious sound was getting closer. Joanie was frozen in her chair. She felt like she was waiting for an apparition to appear. Clyde stood. "Joanie, I think our upstairs guest is about to make an appearance," he said.

Luke appeared in the doorway. His arms were extended to each side to keep his balance as he slowly took a few steps forward. He didn't have his crutches and he hobbled his way into the room with no assistance. Joanie and the boys stood also. All had their arms out as if they expected Luke to fall.

"Better get me a chair before I fall down," he said breathlessly.

Clyde set a chair down behind Luke while putting his arm around his waist, but Luke pushed his arm away and took a few steps toward the kitchen as if modeling a new wardrobe, then turned around and came back to the chair using his hands on the chair back as reassurance.

"I need some practice and maybe this thing needs some adjustment, but I feel like I'm gonna be closer to normal again," Luke said. Then he sat and both knees bent at the same angle. He had no shoes on and Joanie could see two feet. They were roughly the same size and the wooden one had little toes drawn on with a pencil.

"I've been wondering about the sawdust," Joanie said, "I was beginning to think we had mice."

"Get another plate," Clyde said, "looks like Luke'll be eating down here with us from now on."

"A special thanks to the boys," Luke told him. "They helped me by getting me all the materials I needed. Plus they're good at keeping a secret. Well done, boys."

The boys were giddy. They peppered him with questions. "Will it wear out? Will you take us hunting? Can you ride? Why doesn't it fall off?"

Luke tried to answer each question, but finally Clyde told the boys to give Luke a chance to eat. And he did…several helpings, making Joanie smile.

After the chicken, Joanie served apple pie. Clyde tipped his chair back on two legs and said, "Luke, I had no idea you were a wood carver. How did you figure all of this out?"

"As I mentioned," Luke answered, "I was involved in a lot of amputations at Shiloh and got to study a lot of knees first hand. When I saw them boys with one little stub like mine, I always thought there had to be some way to make life easier for them. Never thought it would be me, but I had an added incentive. I knew I couldn't ever even think about seeing Carol, my girl back in Columbus with only one leg, and I had promised to come back to her. I felt like I had to do something."

"I'm sure she's a wonderful girl," Joanie said.

"And I expect to do something about that," Luke continued, "once I get better with this thing…and the war is over."

"You're welcome here until then," Joanie said. "We like having you around."

"Very much appreciated," Luke said, "but maybe a couple days more to get used to this thing and I'll take my leave. I'll be forever in your debt."

"What will you do, if you leave?" Clyde asked.

"I've been pondering on that…probably head on down to where the action is…I'm sure I can assist in a hospital. There are a lot of wounded soldiers who don't get enough care." He took a deep breath. "Would you mind helping me back up the stairs? I haven't had so much exercise in a long time. I'm feeling a little weak."

"I'm leaving in the morning," Clyde said, "don't you dare leave 'til I get back." He reached into his pocket and pulled out a flat, curved metal flask. "Take this with you. It's full of laudanum. You can take a pull on it anytime the pain gets real bad."

Luke thanked him and slid it into his rear pocket.

The boys were told to go to bed and, shortly after, Luke again said he was tired and Clyde helped him climb the steps.

They both tucked him in. Joanie said, "Luke, I'm so happy for you" and kissed him on the cheek. They closed the door softly behind them.

Chapter 8

Five days later, Luke was ready to leave, waiting only on Clyde to return. He had tweaked his new leg and could walk at a slow pace without losing his balance. He tacked a short strip of rubber from his artificial calf to his thigh so the leg would bend slightly when he brought it forward for the next step. The rubber enabled him not to have to sling his wooden leg outward when he stepped forward. His steps were much more even, and with practice he hoped to walk so normally that nobody would guess he was an amputee.

It was Saturday and Joanie looked worried. Clyde was late. She sat on the front stoop anxiously looking down the lane. Luke came out and sat beside her. "Could be anything," Luke said. "A lame horse. Broken wheel. Bad axle...anything."

Joanie ran her fingers through her hair. "I have a bad feeling. Something must be wrong," she said.

Luke sensed that whatever he would say would not console her.

"These last few weeks Clyde hasn't been himself," she confided. "He's been on edge. And he's been getting up in the night and pacing. He never had trouble sleeping before."

Luke waited.

"You know he sometimes carries things in his wagon that, if he was found out, might give him problems."

"Oh?"

"I'll tell you because you are our friend." She took a deep breath.

"You mean guns? Ammunition? That kind of stuff?"

"No. Nothing like that. Medicine. Hospital supplies for the Confederate wounded. Ether. Bandages. Stuff like that."

"Laudanum?"

"Yes."

Luke saw a cloud of dust, then a fast approaching rider. The early afternoon sun went behind a cloud as the rider pulled up in front of the porch. The man had a gray beard and long hair topped by a western style hat. His jacket was dust covered, but Luke could see that the shoulders had once had epaulets sewn on. His sorrel horse was blanketed in lather.

"Are you Mrs. McCallister?" He asked with a heavy drawl. His horse, though winded, nibbled some grass making a hollow chomping sound.

Joanie could only nod to the question.

"Clyde's been taken. Damn Yanks caught him crossing the Tennessee. Took his team and wagon, too. Just before they took him away, he asked me to let you know. Told me to tell you not to worry. He'd be a little late getting home."

"Where'd they take him," Luke asked walking towards the rider.

"Believe they took him to the stockyards, next to the rail depot. Not sure, though."

"You mean the Chattanooga stock yards?" Luke asked.

"The same. They converted a part of it into a stockade. Gener'l Bragg has the whole cottonpickin' Yankee army pinned down. I heard that Grant has taken command."

Luke thought a minute, and then looked at Joanie. "I know exactly where the stockyards are," he said. "My dad used to go there once a year for breeding stock."

Joanie looked puzzled.

The rider wheeled his horse around and told them he had to get moving. "Promised Clyde I would tell you," he said and spurred his mount into a gallop and left.

Joanie started to cry. "I knew this would happen," she said, "I told him not to do it anymore. What do you think they will do to him?"

Luke looked towards the barn. "Mind if I borrow your mule?"

"What could you do?" She asked glancing down at his leg, then feeling sorry she did.

"Got an idea," was all he said as he walked toward the barn.

———————

By mid-afternoon the next day, Luke was on Signal Mountain, looking down at the sprawling city of Chattanooga with the Tennessee River meandering through, and Lookout Mountain looming behind. Smoke rose from smokestacks. From the distance the city looked peaceful. On closer observation however, he could see little white dots and small wisps of smoke on Lookout Mountain. To the east, more little dots extended from north to south along the entirety of Missionary Ridge. They were the campfires of the Confederate army. The city itself looked like a busy ant colony with thousands of people scurrying to and fro. These people were soldiers and they wore blue. The only thing that separated the two armies was the Tennessee River.

He had left Joanie and the twins, riding the mule he had promised to return and telling her he thought he might be able to help Clyde. Joanie had been reluctant to let Luke go with the mule, not knowing if Luke could ride, but she was desperate to do something.

Luke, dressed in some of Clyde's old oversized clothes, hoped he wouldn't draw attention. The pants had a large rear pocket that was perfect to carry the flask with the laudanum. He thought that this was one time when his wooden leg might be an advantage because he would appear to be just another soldier with an amputated limb.

Even though he was riding a mule, having a mount under him again felt good and he had quickly learned the nuance of riding with a wooden leg. He nudged his mount forward and they descended into the city. As he got closer, he could see more distinctly thousands and thousands of bluecoats.

Amid the din of yelling, cadence calling, rumbling caissons, and the neighing of horses, the Union Army of the Cumberland was preparing to launch an attack on the dug-in forces of the Confederates under

General Braxton Bragg. Little noticed in the melee, Luke guided his mule toward the rail depot located near the intersection of Broad and Ninth Streets. He was surprised when he got there to see the terminal had been converted to a hospital. The unforgettable odor of ether reminded him of the field hospital at Shiloh where he had spent three days working over twenty hours per day. He recalled the sweet smell of blood and the foul odor of a wounded man with a gut wound. His hands would be sticky from drying blood as he stitched closed incisions made by the surgeons who were operating on the next soldier. He heard the moans of soldiers dying and their pleas for relief. Relief, that might only come from death. Strangely, he thought he belonged in that hospital, helping those that needed help.

"You got business here, son?" A grizzled old sergeant asked.

Luke broke out of his daydream. "Yes, sir. I'm looking for the stockade. I've a friend who is being held there."

The sergeant looked down at Luke's leg with a questioning look. "You lose a leg, son?"

"Yes, sir. Gettysburg."

The sergeant reached down and pulled up Luke's pant leg. "Mighty fine job. You do that?"

"Yes, sir."

"The stockade is just over there," he said pointing to an area behind the hospital. "What's your friend in the stockade for?"

"Don't know," Luke replied, "but he helped me when I really needed it."

"Good friends are hard to come by these days," the man said. "C'mon, I'll take you over there. The lieutenant who's in charge is my boss."

Luke dismounted and as they walked together, Luke saw Clyde's freighter off to the side. The horses were gone. The sergeant asked the name of Luke's friend as they walked.

"We have a Clyde McCallister here?" the sergeant asked the lieutenant.

"Yep, the big man...why?"

"He's a friend of this young man's," the sergeant said.

"Well, he was caught trying to cross the river with supplies to help the Rebs. He's going to be here for quite a while."

Luke pulled out the note of safe passage given to him by the cavalry lieutenant and handed it to the lieutenant in charge who read it. "You a doctor?" He asked.

"No, but I'm asking you to let Clyde go."

"This note just asks to give safe passage and I assume it applies to you. Doesn't say anything about letting a 'friend' out of jail."

"It's a stretch, I know," Luke said, "but he has a wife and two kids just north of here and they'll starve without Clyde being able to provide."

"He shoulda thought of that before," the lieutenant said.

"If I'm not mistaken," Luke said, "the 'supplies' you caught him with were medical supplies and had little to do with waging war. You might say those 'supplies' were for humanitarian use. You surely can't blame a man for wanting to alleviate a man's pain even if it's an enemy."

The lieutenant read the message again. A mule brayed in the distance. The screech of a red-tailed hawk could be heard overhead. Luke, seeing him waiver said, "let him go and his wife and two kids won't be on your conscience, especially tonight when you're trying to sleep."

Luke and the sergeant both looked at the lieutenant. He shrugged. "I gotta go get some chow," he said to the sergeant. Then he tipped his head toward the stockade and said, "maybe he won't be here when I get back," as he walked off in the other direction.

Ten minutes later, Clyde was following Luke back to where the mule had been tied up. "You gonna tell me how you arranged all of this?" Clyde asked.

"No need. Just consider it a partial repayment for saving my life," Luke said. "You take the mule back to your place. Joanie and the twins will be glad to see you. Be sure to thank them for everything they did for me...tell them I'll come back after this confounded war is over."

"What'll you do?"

"Tomorrow at this time, I'll be up there," Luke said pointing toward Lookout Mountain.

Clyde tipped his hat back with his forefinger. "And, I have no doubt you will. We won't forget you, boy…er, Luke. And, don't forget, when this war is over, we'd love to see you." He started to walk away. "Maybe you'd need some help getting your old homestead rebuilt…be glad to help." Clyde reached into his pocket and pulled out a small roll of Confederate notes. He took two five dollar bills and handed them to Luke. "This isn't much," Clyde said, "but you're gonna need it."

Luke hesitated, embarrassed.

"Just take it," Clyde said shoving the bills into Lukes's pocket, then as he walked away he said, "Don't forget us."

"I won't," Luke said then whispered to himself, "I won't."

Chapter 9

November 23, 1863

As evening approached that day, Luke slowly realized that something big was going on. Troops were marching east toward the river. Thousands of them. His clothing and limp made him look like a previously wounded soldier and he moved around unnoticed. He wondered how Grant would get his army across the Tennessee River to attack the entrenched Confederates on Missionary Ridge and Lookout Mountain.

He followed the movement of the soldiers while staying in the shadows. As he neared the river, the line of soldiers backed up as if they were in a queue, waiting for something. Some of them sprawled out on the ground and tried to sleep. A few started small fires and cooked a meal. Luke smelled coffee and was reminded he hadn't eaten since early morning. He took a chance and approached a small group of men dressed in blue encircled around a campfire.

"That coffee smells mighty fine," Luke said coming into the light of the fire.

"What do we have here?" a soldier asked. "You a deserter?"

Luke pulled up his pant leg. "Do I look like a deserter?"

"Well, look at that," another said. "C'mon over here. Let me see."

Luke stepped up still holding his pant leg up.

"Where'd you lose it?" Another soldier asked while he took a skillet of coffee beans off the fire.

"Gettysburg," Luke said taking a seat on the ground.

"Look at that," the first one said, "it bends and everything."

The man had a tone in his voice and Luke could not figure if he was mocking him for being an amputee or he was really admiring the craftsmanship. He decided to shift the subject and take a guess. "You gents gonna cross the Tennessee tonight?"

"Yep, they say we'll start around midnight," a soldier from the back retorted.

The man with the skillet picked up his rifle and Luke thought he was in trouble. However, the soldier started to mash the coffee beans with the butt of the rifle. "Coffee'll be ready in a few minutes, care for some?"

When Luke nodded, the soldier said, "you're hungry ain't ya." And as he said it, he reached into his haversack, pulled out a can and tossed it to Luke with a smile. The can had a paper label that said *Underwood Canned Lobster,* and the men all chuckled.

Luke looked at the can then up at the laughing faces in wonderment.

"Nobody wants that stuff, but if you're really hungry, it'll fill you up. It's better when unheated," the coffee man said as he detached the bayonet from his rifle and handed it to Luke.

Luke punctured the can with the bayonet and using the same blade started to eat the lobster. It tasted bland, but Luke ate hungrily and the conversation switched to the upcoming attack. He learned that Grant was sending Sherman's army over the river that same night to surprise the Confederates in the morning. A pontoon bridge was being built and the men expected to move out as soon as it was ready.

Luke thanked them for the food and coffee and left heading for the river. When he reached the riverbank, he was just below the confluence where the Chicamauga Creek dumped into the Tennessee. A large side-wheeler steamboat, the Dunbar, was moored at the river's edge and men were loading pontoons onto it. The soldiers, Union military engineers, worked frantically to load the last several pontoons. Most of the engineers were unarmed and paid no attention to Luke as he approached the boat. Two gangplanks led from the shoreline to the vessel, one forward and the other aft, and Luke saw that only the aft gangplank was being used. He took a deep breath and walked up the forward plank. Once aboard, he hid among some barrels on the forward deck. He only had a short time to wait. Within minutes, the steamer's big wheel started to paw at the water, the vibrations from which caused the barrels to slide together pinning Luke's wooden leg between a barrel and the cabin wall. He didn't know what was in the barrels, but pushing with all his might could not free his leg.

In desperation, Luke disconnected his leg and was able to stand, however, he was still unable to free his prosthesis. The only light available was from the helmsman's cabin just above him. He felt around the barrel and found a cork on the other side and using his pocket knife he freed the cork and the contents of the barrel came spewing out onto the front deck of the steamer. It was water. Luke was then able to move the barrel enough to free his artificial leg that he managed to re-attach. Just then a soldier noticed the streaming water from the barrel and walked over and saw Luke hiding.

"What the hell...?" He yelled.

Luke froze.

"You a stow-away?" He yelled up to the helmsman, "Hey, Captain, look what I found."

Luke stood, speechless. The soldier could see only Luke's face. The soldier pulled out his revolver and aimed it directly at Luke's head. "Captain, I got him. He's a spy sure as looking at him." He cocked the hammer back. "Don't move or you're a dead Rebel spy."

Luke heard the sound of men running, coming nearer. Just then he heard the steam engine surge as the captain reversed the water-wheel. The steamer swerved hard to the right as the prow of the steamer turned away from shore and caused the soldier to fall against the forward rail. Luke braced himself against the barrels and saw his chance. He quickly stepped to his left, lifted his good leg over the rail, used his hands to help lift his prosthesis and jumped. The last thing he heard before he hit the water was, "shoot'm before he...".

The sensation of hitting the water felt like somebody had hit him hard in the stomach, shocking his whole body. He tried to find the surface but the water was so roiled from the side-wheeler being in reverse, he didn't know which way was up. He kicked but he only had one leg that worked.

The prosthesis was useless in the water. He stopped kicking, trying to let his body rise naturally, but nothing happened. His normal frog kick was useless. He used his arms frantically, but he wasn't sure what direction he was moving. Then he heard a 'thwump, thwump' sound and realized he was being shot at. He looked up and saw the bright lantern light of the helm through the last several feet of water. Then he saw the bubbled line of a Minié ball fired from the steamer. The line was at an angle that told Luke the direction from where the shots came, and he instinctively swam toward the shooter, knowing the hull of the steamer offered his best chance. With his lungs bursting, he lifted up and gasped for breath just as he broke the surface. The prow of the boat was just above him and the shooters could not see him…but they heard him. They could hear him gasping for breath and one leaned over the rail and Luke saw him shouldering his rifle.

"There he is, git'm," the man yelled, but leaning over the rail and trying to shoot back toward the water line of the boat was difficult. If Luke moved toward the back of the boat, the overhang of the prow would not protect him. To stay where he was would be suicidal. He took three deep breaths, submerged and propelled himself away from the steamer. He tried to be smooth in the water because he knew panicky strokes were inefficient. He swam submerged as long as he possibly could, using his arms to make powerful strokes. He surfaced and looked back. The steamer was behind him and he thought he was probably out of eyesight. He felt the cold water stealing his body heat. He rotated in the water trying to get his bearings. When he saw the dim fires from the top of Missionary Ridge, he headed that way, but it seemed a long way away.

As he stroked toward the Confederate side, he realized he had no feeling in his good leg. The water was not only robbing him of heat, but also was stealing his will to live. He shook his head to clear his thoughts and tried to focus on the far bank. Was it getting closer? He desperately pawed at the water, stroke after stroke. He couldn't feel anything below the waist and he knew he had to get out of the water. He could feel his lungs constricting and his breaths getting shorter. The thought came to him that even if he made the shore, he would not be able to walk because he couldn't feel anything. Then he thought of Carol. If he didn't make it, he would never see her again. Then he thought what a stupid thought that was. How could he see her if he was dead?

With a light breeze behind him, he swam on. Stroke after stroke. One at a time. He tried to find the will to keep going. Giving up and sinking into the water would be so easy. He could just quit and maybe it would all be over. He desperately stroked the water. Hand over hand, he kept reaching out and pulling the water toward him, but each stroke was getting shorter and shorter.

His right hand hit something. Was it something floating in the water? His hands had no feeling. He reached out with his arms and pulled it into his grasp. It did not move. As he held on to it, the current pushed against his body trying to pull him away and break his grip. He refused to let go. He sensed this was his last chance. To release his grip meant drowning. He realized he had hold of a small tree. He hooked his arm on a limb and pulled. Then, he found another limb. His foot hit something firm. It was the bottom. It was the other side.

He pulled himself to the bank. He looked up from the river's bank and saw the light of campfires. With little energy left he dragged himself out of the water onto the muddy river's edge. The cool air felt like an arctic blast through his wet clothing. He had no energy left and could tell he was on the verge of losing consciousness. Luke thought it couldn't end like this. He tried to yell out but only a hoarse sound came out of his throat. He thought he heard vague voices and everything went black.

Chapter 10

Luke was lying in a patch of clover when he awoke. A blanket covered him and a pillow was under his head. Men with stretchers streamed past carrying wounded soldiers. The moans of the wounded were a cacophony from hell. Insects buzzed around a pile of discarded arms and legs. A canvas tarp, held up by six poles, sheltered doctors working on wounded soldiers at two tables. A man screamed, and under his screams Luke could hear the sickening sound of a saw cutting bone. A man lying next to him saw that Luke was awake and pleaded with him to tell his mother she would be proud of him. He had a huge hole in his abdomen.

Luke's hand went to his back pocket and he felt reassured when his flask was still there. He reached out to a passing soldier. "Where am I?" Luke asked.

"You're on top of Missionary Ridge," he said, "and we're being overtaken. Them Yanks are running through a cover of fog and we can't see 'em to shoot 'em 'til it's too late. We got orders to move south into Georgia." The soldier left in a hurry.

Luke was all too familiar with forced evacuations. He remembered the third day at Shiloh when his field hospital was taken over by Sherman's men as Beauregard fled back to Corinth. He didn't want that to happen again. He sat up. A man in a white, bloodstained smock approached from behind.

"You doin' better now?" he asked. "We put you out here because we had no room under the tent. You were suffering from exposure. All of us are interested in that thing." He pulled up Luke's blanket and pointed to his artificial leg. "Not that we have time now."

"Wow, I thought I had lost it. The water was so cold I couldn't tell if it was still attached."

"Do you need help? I'm not a doctor, just an orderly."

"I think I can manage," Luke said and the orderly moved on.

Luke's prosthesis was covered with mud and grit from the river. He unstrapped it and used the blanket to clean it up, especially where his stub fit. He then strapped it back on and tried to stand. It took him a while but he eventually got his good leg under him and he was able to heft himself up. When he stood, everything else came back to him. He had been placed in a row with dozens of other wounded. He already knew the drill.

At Shiloh he was the one who determined whether a soldier's wound was treatable or not. Usually a gut wound or any wound to the torso was not treatable. Even if the bleeding vessels could be tied off, the damage to vital organ tissue would not heal, become gangrenous, and ultimately be fatal. The soldiers who had wounds on their extremities would be treated, and most of them had a good chance of making it, provided infection didn't set in. The poor men lying in the rows where he had been laid would be the last to be evacuated. Most of them knew it. Some just lay there waiting, maybe even hoping to die. Others moaned and pleaded in their delirium.

He walked back toward the medical tent. A man reached out and grabbed his leg as he passed. His grip was like iron "you got a gun?" he asked. The man had a hole in his side and some of his small intestine had spilled out of the rupture.

Luke felt the desperation in the man's grip. "Sorry, soldier, I don't have a gun," Luke said, "but I'll be right back." The soldier's grip loosened and Luke walked toward the tent. A doctor was sawing off an arm at one table while another soldier was being stitched up. There were two bottles on a side table, one was a half full bottle of whiskey and the other was a small bottle of laudanum. He grabbed the whiskey and after staring at the laudanum bottle briefly, unscrewed its cap and took a large swig, and put the bottle back. Then he returned to the soldier, held the whiskey bottle to the dying man's lips and told him to drink as much as he could.

The soldier with a hint of understanding in his eye, drank the bottle dry.

Luke pulled his blanket up around his neck and softly told the soldier he would feel better in a few minutes. Then he put his hand on the soldier's cheek and thanked him for being so brave.

A captain rushed into the tent ordering everybody to move out and that they would be over-run within ten minutes. One doctor, who just finished sawing off the arm, said he wouldn't be able to sew him up in time and that if he left him, the patient would bleed to death. The captain told him he had no choice, with thousands dead or dying another didn't make much difference. The captain ran out faster than he had entered.

Luke went over to the operating table. "Doc, I know how to sew this flap shut, you get all your stuff packed and we'll make it."

"Who the hell are you?" the doc asked.

"I've done this a hundred times before…trust me," Luke said, as he picked up a needle and sutures.

The doc watched Luke as he expertly folded the skin flap over and started to stitch, then, somewhat satisfied, grabbed his bag and loaded his tools.

"We'll have to leave him here," Luke added.

"He'll probably be better off," the doctor said.

Moments later, shouting could be heard as the last soldiers began to retreat. The doctor, having packed his equipment, looked at the patient's arm just as Luke tied off the last stitch. He glanced over at Luke, faintly nodded and told the few who were still there to get out immediately. The doctor put his hand on Luke's back as if to make him go faster when he saw that Luke was an amputee himself. They hurried to a departing hospital wagon and grabbed the last two seats on the tailgate as the teamster cracked his whip.

"They brought you in last night," the doctor said, "you were unconscious. They said you swam across the river. Is that true?"

"Not quite, doc, I jumped off a side-wheeler when the Yanks discovered me. I wanted to warn everybody of the surprise attack, but I fell a little short. The water was so cold, my muscles quit working, I guess."

"You were suffering from exposure and you could have frozen."

"Yeah, and my brain almost got a Minié ball," Luke answered with a smile.

Once they got past the Confederate rear guard, the pace slowed as the word came that Sherman was not pursuing them. The wagon contained three wounded officers, and Luke noted one was a cavalry officer dressed in a long gray cavalry coat with a black sash wrapped around his waist. The soldier had been shot in the arm just below his shoulder.

"What about that cavalry officer?" Luke asked. "He looks like he's bleeding. Probably opened up when he was moved."

"Yes, it appears so," the doctor said, "I fished a Minié ball out of his shoulder. He hasn't come to yet.

"Mind if I have a look?" Luke asked.

"Might be a good idea."

Luke pulled himself next to the officer, a captain, who had started to come around. When Luke moved the man's arm slightly to get a better look at the wound, the captain winced in pain. The doctor threw him some additional gauze and Luke wrapped it tightly around the already existing bandages. Then he made him a sling to immobilize the arm.

"You're gonna be just fine, Captain," Luke said softly, "we'll be stopping as soon as we put some distance between us and Sherman."

"We being chased?" he asked.

"No, but they routed us. Couldn't see them because of the fog. We're headed toward Atlanta. Who were you with?"

"Forrest."

"Forrest? How's he doing? Haven't seen him since Shiloh. Some thought the shot he took would kill him."

"He's too cussed ornery to die," the captain said with a hint of a smile.

"What's your name, Captain?"

"Milner. Henry Milner. Alabama."

"Rest easy, Captain, we'll be stopping soon," Luke said as he crawled back to the tailgate.

"You have a nice way with the wounded," the doctor observed, "tell me about Shiloh."

Luke explained how he helped a field hospital handle the hundreds and hundreds of wounded especially the amputees. He told the doctor how they were able to move patients through faster by dividing the procedures so that doctors could do the amputations while he did the closing.

The wagon lumbered on, traveling only a little faster than the retreating foot soldiers could walk. After several hours, Luke heard the sound of horses fast approaching from over a rise to his left. A large contingent of Confederate cavalry snaked two-by-two into sight and turned towards Luke's wagon. As they neared, Luke could make out a bearded leader riding a huge iron-grey gelding followed by two flag bearers. He wondered, could it be?

The officer was Nathan Bedford Forrest, himself, and he sat in the saddle effortlessly as the giant horse ate up the distance between them. When he drew abreast of Luke's wagon, the general pulled back on his reins and the horse came to a sudden stop leaving deep ruts in the soft clay from his skidding hooves.

He dismounted and Luke broke into a grin, climbing off the end of the wagon and saluting. The officer ignored Luke and looked over at Milner, the wounded officer. He walked over to the side of the wagon where he was lying. "Captain, we've been looking all over for you. Get the hell up and let's go. We got Yankees to kill."

The captain broke into a sheepish grin. "Give me a day or two. Got a hole in my shoulder." The general took his hand and briefly bowed his head and said a silent prayer after which he whispered something in the captain's ear that caused a broad smile. He saluted and walked toward his horse passing in front of Luke. He glanced at Luke's face and stopped. "Do I know you?" He asked.

Luke saluted again, "Shiloh, sir. I guess they call it the Battle of Fallen Timbers."

A gleam of recognition registered in Forrest's eyes. "You were there. The white coat," he said. "Now I remember. God-damnest thing I ever saw. My boys still talk about it. Hey, Milner. You should have seen this man. It was after Shiloh. Our charge was stopped by Yankee infantry, and our colors were laying on the ground. This man, dressed in a white coat came barreling down the hill, riding like his pants were on fire. He sweeps into the befuddled Yankees, picks up our colors and rides back to our lines. Hell, them Yanks shot a thousand times, but he rode like the wind." As he stuck out his hand to shake Luke's, he glanced down at his foot. "What's that?"

"My new leg, sir," Luke said pulling up his pant leg. He then took a couple steps showing how easily he walked.

"Hell, boy, you could ride with me," Forrest said, "where'd it happen?"

"Gettysburg, and I think I can better serve wearing a white coat."

"He any good?" he asked looking at the doctor.

"Seems pretty handy," the doctor replied.

Forrest glanced back at his captain, waved in a partial salute, and mounted his gelding with easy, swift motion. Then, addressed Luke. "Well, when you get tired of this namby-pamby stuff, come and see me." Then he pulled back on his reins just enough for his big horse to rear slightly, and by leaning forward and touching his horse's flank with his heel, left at a full gallop.

Luke smiled, thinking Forrest was almost as good as he used to be.

When the din of the rattling sabers of the cavalry faded and the wagons resumed their slow pace south toward Atlanta. "What's your name again, son?" the doctor asked.

"Luke Pettigrew, Tennessee."

The doctor looked at Luke's leg. "What happened?"

Luke gave him the now familiar explanation of how he lost his leg and fashioned a new one.

"I've seen something like this before. Man named Hangar, I think, James Hangar. Close friend of Jeff Davis." Changing the subject, the doctor asked, "where'd they take you after you were captured?"

"Chase Prison, just outside of Columbus, Ohio. Didn't take me long to get out though…." Luke said wistfully. "Got out with the help of a young woman. Name's Carol."

The wagon rocked and creaked as they went over small cross-rut in the road. The doctor asked, "Is she waiting for you?"

"Sure hope so," Luke said. Something in the back of Luke's mind bothered him. He kept coming back to it. He felt like he had cheated on Carol.

Almost unworthy. He cursed himself for his weakness that stormy night and reached for his flask.

"You don't seem so sure."

"She probably wouldn't want me…like this," he said motioning toward his leg.

"Well, I can't help you on matters of the heart," the doctor said, "but my guess is that a few more months practice with that contraption and a tweak here and there, she'll never be able to tell."

They passed a broken caisson. The doctor asked, "What do you want to do in this war? You could rightfully go home and leave it all behind you. Nobody would find fault with that."

"Not ready, Doc. I gotta work this out. But while this damnable war is going on, I think I can be of service."

The doctor pushed his campaign cap back. "You could go to Richmond, show Hangar what you've done. I'm sure he could use you. Richmond's hospitals are over-flowing with amputees that you could help."

Luke liked the idea. Technically, after he had been discharged to go home, he was no longer a Confederate soldier and could do anything he wanted. Richmond was a long way, nearly five hundred miles he guessed. The war would slow down during the coming winter's months and traveling would be safer, he thought. He had a little money and could take his time to get there. He decided he would go to Atlanta and hopefully find a train northbound. Almost automatically, his hand went to the flask. He took a big swallow and put the flask back in his pocket.

Chapter 11

Early Spring, 1864

As the morning sun rose above the trees near Richmond and the terminus of the Richmond and Danville Railroad, the hoar frost melted in a stubbornly yielding shadow that portended fair weather. Luke approached the terminal and the cold air caused his leg to clack and drew the attention of the dozens of ambulatory soldiers who had sought shelter for the night. Luke needed to get to Staunton, Virginia, where Hanger was making artificial legs.

The trip from Atlanta to Richmond had taken nearly four months, partially because he had to rebuild his prosthesis. The hinging mechanism that worked as a knee became loose and required a new dowel rod, that in turn required a new lower leg. He decided to make the new parts out of teak wood to resist the effects of moisture. Finding the right materials had taken a lot of time, but he finally found some in an abandoned furniture shop in Atlanta. The teak had a natural oil that helped lubricate the joint and seemed to work well.

The railroad tracks from Richmond to Staunton had been torn up by marauding Yankee cavalry. They would build huge fires, heat the rails to red hot, and twist them, rendering the rails unusable. The marauders were led by General Phil Sheridan, the general who had brought the Union cavalry up to the standard set by Confederate cavalry generals such as Stuart and Forrest. The delays caused by these raids were proving costly for the Confederates because new rails had to be brought up from Richmond, consuming valuable resources and interrupting the flow of much needed food and supplies to Lee's army.

Not knowing when the rails would be replaced and the next train to the north might depart, Luke began walking to the edge of the city, hoping to catch a ride with a supply wagon heading toward Staunton. The exercise warmed him as he got into the rhythm of walking.

The gloom of the wounded soldiers at the train station extended into Richmond. Many stores were closed and boarded up. A few horses and buggies were parked along Broad Street, the main street of Richmond. The horses were gaunt, with their heads hanging down. A wagon with "Richmond Daily Dispatch" printed in large red letters on the side was returning to its home office after delivering the morning edition. An old black man wielding a wheelbarrow and shovel was picking up horse manure while he sang a mournful, melancholy song, in a thick accent that Luke did not understand.

Luke walked over to the news wagon and paid two cents for one of the last remaining copies. He asked the driver for the latest news on the war and was told that everything worth knowing was in the paper. The driver did not go into detail, but talked instead about Lee rising above all the disadvantages he had suffered and claiming ultimate victory. Luke wondered if the man really believed what he was saying.

He had the sense that a lurking shadow or pall hung over the city and an inevitable end of the war was hidden ominously behind closed doors and mouths. The few people who walked the streets had their heads down, shoulders slumped. When they talked to each other, it was in whispers as if the enemy was listening. They seemed to fear an ignoble end that nobody wanted to admit. He scanned the front page. Almost everything was about the war. One headline stated: *LEE READIES VETERANS FOR FINAL PUSH*, another spoke of a Stuart raid into Maryland.

Luke had only reached the outskirts of Richmond and already he could feel blisters forming on his stub from the chafing of his artificial leg. He rested, sitting on the side of a small bridge. A freight wagon pulled by four mules came to a stop and Luke could feel the bend of the bridge planks under him.

"Look's like you could use a ride." The drover was a young man about Luke's age.

"Headed toward Staunton. You going that way?" Luke asked.

"Sure thing, hop on." As Luke climbed up, the drover could easily see Luke was an amputee.

"Where'd you lose it?"

"Gettysburg," Luke said. Even though the drover was young and slight of build, he handled the team like he had been doing it all his life. The wagon seat, supported by two leaf springs, one on each side, leaned toward Luke when he sat.

"Looks like somebody is handy working with wood," the drover said slapping the reins against the rumps of the rear two mules.

"It's a work in progress," Luke said pulling up his pant leg, "which is the reason I want to go to Staunton. I hear they make artificial legs there. A man named James Hangar. You ever hear of him?"

"Can't say that I have, I'm not originally from around here. Originally from Ohio. Dad came down to start this hauling business, but when the war came on, he went back to sign up for the Union. He was killed at Manassas, the second one."

Luke thought about his father. If he was dead, why didn't he feel remorse? Maybe it was be cause he couldn't accept that he was dead.

They rode in silence. After a while, Luke asked, "If you're from Ohio, why are you hauling for the Confederate side?"

The drover eyed Luke nervously. "Just trying to keep the business going."

Luke sensed he might be asking too many direct questions. The drover shared some hardtack as they rode through the day. By late afternoon, the mules were tired, so they pulled off the road near a clump of pine trees and a small stream.

"This is where I usually overnight," the drover said jumping down. "There's fresh water for my boys and we can sleep under the wagon. The mules were unhitched, led to water, and then tethered on a long rope that allowed them to munch on grass.

Luke made a fire using some kindling that had been left by other drovers passing through. While the fire was getting started, the drover gave Luke some more hardtack. The drover took off his gloves and Luke could see his hands were fine boned, but tanned as if they had been exposed to the sun. He remembered when he had stepped down off the wagon that the young man's ankles were the same way. He thought the drover must be even younger than he originally had guessed. His eyes were dark, deep set and shifted constantly like he was looking for something unexpected. That night while they were sleeping under the wagon, Luke's phantom pain woke him and when he glanced over, he noticed he was alone. Luke took a gulp from his flask. Some time later, the drover returned and almost immediately broke into the light rhythmic breathing of sleep.

Back on the road the next morning, the wagon was over-taken by a fast moving Confederate cavalry unit heading northwest. Luke wondered if they might be more of Forrest's unit but Forrest wasn't with them. The drover had pulled off to the side of the road and seemed intent at watching each of the riders go by, riding in the customary two by two formation.

"Looks like we'll make Staunton around noon tomorrow," the drover said pulling off the road for the evening. Heavy clouds to the west had formed and Luke reasoned the drover wanted to set up camp before the rain came, and, as expected, just after they had crawled under the wagon for the night, the rains started. A steady rain and Luke was pleased to be warm and dry. The drover claimed he was tired and rolled over to sleep. The next morning, the rain had stopped but the young man's clothes were wet. When Luke noticed, the drover smiled and off-handedly commented that it was the call of the wild.

The sun came out and Luke felt the warmth on his back and they relaxed as they rounded a hill that led to Staunton. "I don't even know your name," Luke said, "we've come all this way and I would at least like to know who I should thank for carrying me."

"They call me Cuff," the drover replied.

"How old are you?"

"How old are you?" The drover asked defensively.

"Nineteen."

"I'm the same."

"Why don't I believe you?"

"You should believe me because it's the truth...I swear."

Suddenly, six riders bolted from a thick copse of trees and came directly toward them. Luke saw that they were Confederate cavalry and as two of them stopped in front of the mules, the drover was forced to pull back to a sudden halt. The other four riders surrounded the wagon two on each side.

The sergeant, who wore no patch signifying his unit, dismounted and said, "you two are under arrest for spying against the Confederacy."

The drover appeared to be nervous, actually scared, as he slowly climbed down off the wagon. Then, two more riders came out of the copse; one was a Union lieutenant and the other an officer dressed in a gray uniform. The soldier in blue had his hands tied behind him and his horse was being led by the officer. Luke walked over and stood next to the drover who was visibly shaken.

"Is this the other spy?" The officer in gray asked the lieutenant pointing at the drover.

"What the hell is going on here?" Luke asked.

"He's a spy," the sergeant said pointing first to the drover. Then, as he pointed to the lieutenant he said, "he's been reporting Confederate troop movements to this man and he has confessed. In these parts we hang spies...or shoot 'm. No trial needed."

"I had nothing to do with this," Luke said, "The drover was just giving me a ride to Staunton."

The officer dressed in gray said, "if you hang around spies, then we hang you, too." He laughed at his own joke.

Luke put his hands in front of him. "Wait a minute. First of all, I'm no spy. I was shot at Gettysburg and lost my leg." He pulled up his pant leg showing his artificial limb. "I rode with JEB Stuart and—"

"And my mother's Varina Davis," one of the other riders said laughing.

One of the rebels tied Luke's hands and when he attempted to tie his feet together, he hesitated never having hog-tied an amputee before. He tied his two legs together anyway and as he did, Luke noticed the poor condition of his uniform that had frayed sleeves with buttons missing replaced by twine to hold it together. He smelled of sour sweat and wet cedar tobacco that was so strong Luke had to hold his breath.

"You know what's worse than a god damned spy?" he sneered looking at Luke.

When Luke didn't give him the satisfaction of an answer, he said, "Nothin'." Then he laughed a raspy deep laugh, and put him into the back of the wagon next to the drover. They drove off toward Richmond with Cuff's rig in tow.

Chapter 12

The wagon carrying Luke and the drover finally came to a bumpy stop. For the last ten minutes of their long journey, they had been bounced and jarred by the cobblestone streets. The steel banded wheels of the wagon slowly ground over each stone that had created a eerie hollow clacking sound. With their feet and hands bound, they were unable to see over the sideboards of the wagon, but they knew they had to be in Richmond because of the gas street lamps atop poles, indicating they were in a city.

The driver got off, lowered the rear wagon gate, cut the ropes around their legs and told them to get out of the wagon. Four guards with rifles at the ready watched them as they stretched. They were in front of a large brick three and a half story building with an old sign hanging by one nail above the main door that read *Greanor's Tobacco Warehouse*. A nearby street sign said *Carey Street*.

The faint sound of a fast approaching horse drew the attention of the guards. They immediately formed a line facing the street with their rifles in port arms position. The beat of metal horseshoes on cobblestone grew louder and the hollow timbre left no doubt that the yet to appear steed was a huge animal. On and on the unseen horse came, the sound echoed off the walls of buildings and amplified the noise causing Luke to wonder if there might be more than one animal. The front door of the building opened and more soldiers streamed out, formed a line and held a salute.

Just when the noise was so loud and the source seemed upon them, a giant black stallion turned the corner onto Carey Street in full view and running hard. The rider was dressed in black, black shirt, black jacket and black hat. His long black hair, blown by the wind, flew behind him as did his equally long black beard. He sat leaning forward as to urge his horse even faster with his face just above the steed's neck. The long flowing mane of the horse blended with the rider's long hair and beard. The rider was laughing, and the contrast of the black with his white teeth created an image like something evil and straight out of hell. They headed toward Luke and the drover. The thunderous noise was almost deafening and Luke could see the white behind the man's black eyes. The rider was reveling in the other men's fear. The stallion's nostrils flared as he gulped air and the white surrounding his huge black eyes matched his rider's. Immediately behind the huge horse was a magnificent black hound, about the size of a small horse, running hard with its black tongue waving to his side from the exertion.

Just when Luke thought it was time to crawl under the wagon to avoid being trampled to death, the man yelled a deep resonant 'whoa' and pulled on the reins as he leaned back in the saddle. The black steed put all four feet in front of him as he skidded to a stop and Luke could see sparks as the iron scraped the stone. The horse stopped only a few short feet from where they were standing. Luke felt the steed's labored breath against his face.

"What have we here," the big man roared. His horse pranced nervously, his huge hooves clacking on the street. Nobody answered, so the rider yelled. "What have we here?" This time even louder.

"Spies, sir. Caught 'em nearly in the act. They're guilty as sin, sir," said the head guard.

The big man dismounted and stood in front of Luke and the drover appraising them. The horse was taken away by one of the guards, but the hound stayed at the big man's side. "Spies, huh," he said while he rubbed one of the dog's ears. "Caught them in the act? You say?"

"Well, er, almost, sir," the guard replied.

The man turned and walked into the main door of the building. He turned and faced Luke and the drover. "Welcome to Castle Thunder," he said. "Only the chosen few enter my castle and even fewer leave." He laughed a belly laugh that showed his white teeth and the contrast with all the black again reminded Luke of the devil himself. "You may wonder why this nice prison is called by the horridly euphonious name of *Castle Thunder*. Well, gentlemen, you are about to find out that my prison is much more hideous than it sounds. Bring 'em into my office and we'll see what their future might be." As he walked away Luke could see the man's trousers were buckled at the knee, under which he wore black stockings. It was the uniform of a provost marshal.

A sign on the office door said, *Captain Alexander*, and the captain motioned for Luke and the drover to stand in front of his desk as he sat behind it. On a wall of the office hung a pair of leg irons, and several sets of handcuffs. One was larger, for a male and another was smaller, presumably for a female, as well as a truncheon and a horsewhip. On his desk was a strange knife that looked to be very sharp with a curved hook on the end. When the captain saw Luke staring at it, he said, "That's what I do to liars. Just a flick of the wrist and his tongue comes off. Haven't used it in a few days…hope to soon, though." He bared his teeth in a broad sneer. He leaned back in his chair, put his feet up on the desk and, looking at the drover who was staring at the wall, said with a continuing smile. "Tools of the trade…Name?"

"Er, Cuff," the drover uttered.

"Cuff? Just Cuff? That's your name?" He asked.

"Yes, sir. That's what my daddy called me."

"Cuff…seems like I've heard of that name. Where're you from?"

"These parts. Daddy was killed in '61. I'm trying to keep his haulin' business alive."

"By 'hauling', you mean stuff to help the Yankees?" The captain asked. His feet were crossed, and he clicked his toes like he was keeping a beat to some unheard song.

"No, sir, nothing like that, sir."

"And you?" He asked turning to Luke.

"I'm a Confederate soldier, and proud of it. Lost my leg at Gettysburg," he said pointing to his prosthesis. "I am not a spy."

"We'll see about that," the captain said. "Guard, did you thoroughly search these two?"

"Not yet, thought we would hang 'em first," he said with a grin.

"There'll be no hanging…at least not today," the captain said standing. "Take them up to the cell on the third floor. The same cell used by our friends who left this earth yesterday. Oh, and search them."

After they were searched and pockets emptied, including Luke's flask, the guard escorted them up three floors to their cell. It was a small room with a high window on the far end, boarded up from the outside. The room had a wooden floor and it smelled of old tobacco, an odor Luke found mildly attractive. Near one wall was a bucket that was empty but not cleaned. The guard, who appeared to be in charge of the whole floor, was old and while he did not say much, he seemed apologetic for the lack of facilities. "Haven't had a chance to clean this up much," he said, "hope to later."

"Your captain seems like an interesting fellow," Luke said hoping the guard might be talkative.

"He's one tough son of a bitch." The guard pushed the bill of his campaign hat up with his little finger—the only finger he had on that hand. "But, as you saw, he's an actor. A real life 'actor'. He performs at the Richmond Theater sometimes. He even wrote a play. Likes that sort of stuff I guess. But he does have a mean streak. Those two who were in this cell yesterday, he decided to hang 'em, just like that. No trial. No nothing. Just hung 'em." Luke looked at Cuff and shrugged with his eyes rolling up.

The guard walked out the door. "We'll give you some grub 'bout six," he said as he locked the door.

Cuff and Luke stood by the window looking through a slit between the boards that sealed the cell. It looked out onto the backside of the prison where a high fence enclosed an exercise area. Nobody was exercising. A dilapidated set of steps went down from the third floor to the second and then to the ground. Luke could see that the steps were not in use. Guards were posted on each of the back two corners with their rifles at the ready as if they would shoot without hesitation.

Luke wondered how he could get out of the fix he was in. He was no spy and had done nothing wrong, but nevertheless, he was in prison. He thought about asking for a private meeting with Alexander to explain who he was. But that would leave the drover alone and at the mercy of the commandant who appeared to be ruthless. He felt an obligation to the drover because he had given him a ride and fed him.

"Is Cuff your real name?" Luke said casually. Luke suspected Alexander was right about him being a spy.

"Yep," Cuff replied.

"What about the lieutenant? Were you reporting Confederate troop movements back to him?" Luke asked.

"Many I was and maybe I wasn't," Cuff said with his hands on his hips.

A mule brayed in the distance. "Well, Cuff, we're in here together and like it or not, we have to work together if we're going to get out of this place. From what we just heard about the captain, we need to get out of here and the sooner, the better."

"Any ideas?"

"No, but I think our guard might be a little sympathetic."

They considered different ways to escape. They could pry a couple boards loose on the back wall of their cell and lower themselves down to the ground after dark, but the steely-eyed guards might hear or pick up their movements in the moonlight. If they had exercise walks, they could sneak away, but they thought to be too dangerous because the guards were probably doubled during these periods. They strongly considered faking stomach cramps from the poor food and being transferred to the prison hospital, but the one they thought might actually work was for them to overpower the guard. Cuff, without the guard seeing, would get down on all fours behind him, then Luke would push him over. It was an old trick, but they liked its simplicity. Luke would then don the guard's uniform, and both would just walk out as if the guard was escorting Cuff. Once clear of the prison building, they would run for it, although both knew Luke could not go very fast.

Their plans were foiled, however, when the food came. A large Negro dressed in rags unlocked the door and slid a tray of food in with a tin pitcher of water. Luke asked him what happened to the guard and the man answered in only garbled mutterings. Luke wondered if the big man had his tongue cut out by Alexander. He visualized the 'flick' of the captain's blade. They ate the food and Luke was curious when Cuff did not touch the water.

They lay down on the floor as darkness closed in. Luke pretended to sleep, and was aware that Cuff was not sleeping either. After an hour or so, Cuff, who evidently assumed Luke was asleep, got up to use the bucket. Luke had always suspected something strange about the drover. He recalled the fine bones and the way the drover got on and off the wagon. Now he was convinced. Cuff was a woman.

Chapter 13

Early the next morning, a guard entered the cell, slowly circled the room, and stopped in front of Luke. "You. Come with me," he said, and herded Luke outside and back into the captain's office.

The captain looked like a different man. His wild hair was combed back and Luke could see he had a ruddy complexion and handsome face. He motioned for Luke to sit in a chair while he remained standing. The captain had removed his coat, revealing a black sleeveless vest with a brass star inscribed *PROVOST MARSHAL* pinned onto the right side. Under the vest was a crisp white shirt with a black string tie done in a bowknot. Two Colt black powder revolvers in matching black holsters hung from his belt, one on each side. On the wall behind his desk was a very large portrait of General Bedford Forrest mounted atop his loyal horse, Roderick. Bedford was standing in the saddle with a sword in his hand, as if he was issuing a command for his cavalry to charge.

"You say you're a Confederate soldier? Can you prove it?" He asked in a conciliatory tone.

"I don't have any papers proving I was mustered out, if that's what you mean. They aren't issuing them these days because they lack personnel, however, I served at Shiloh, later rode with Stuart and was wounded just before Gettysburg. I think they sent me home to die, but I managed to live somehow."

"What did you do at Shiloh?"

"Worked in a field hospital. Mostly amputating arms and legs. Met that man in the picture behind you."

The captain laughed. "You telling me you know this man?" he asked turning in his chair to look at the picture. "I find that hard to believe. You being some kind of medic…"

"Believe or not, sir, makes little difference to me, but I was there when he took a bullet that lodged in his spine during the third day and the Battle of Fallen Timbers."

The captain leaned forward in his chair as if he was studying Luke's face for the first time. "If you were there, tell me how he was shot," he asked in a tone that made clear he knew the answer but was testing Luke's honesty. His hand went to the curved knife.

"Forrest had three hundred cavalry from the Third Tennessee. He led the charge with some added Texans right into the center of Sherman's infantry. That's where he was shot. In the spine, but he managed to get back to his own lines."

"You say you worked in a field hospital? How did you see all of this?"

"The hospital was up on a ridge and we could see it all, plain as day."

"You like to ride horses?" The captain who seemed to know where he was going with the question.

"Almost born on one."

"You're that crazy son of a bitch that swept down and rode into that bunch of Yankee infantry and picked up our colors, ain't ya," the captain asked pointing an accusatory finger at Luke.

Luke relaxed a bit and smiled. "You could say that…don't know about the 'crazy' part."

"Seems crazy for a medic working in a field hospital, if you ask me," the captain said leaning back and putting his feet on his desk.

"That's how I learned to make this contraption," Luke said pointing at his leg.

"Why did you choose to fight for the South? You said you were from Tennessee. Many boys from your state fight for the North."

Luke wondered why he asked the question. He decided to be perfectly truthful. "We lived on a farm. My dad never had any slaves and I don't have an iron in the fire about that. I am not quite sure why I signed up for the South in the beginning, but I'm sick and tired of all these Northern soldiers down here invading us. We got as many rights as they do and I wonder how they would feel if we invaded the heartland of the North. I was asked the same question when our field hospital after Shiloh was taken over by the Bluecoats and I was taken prisoner. An officer asked me why I was fighting and I told him 'because you are here'."

"This note was found when my men searched you. Looks like it got wet, but your story jibes with the other things we know about you. Do you still want to be of service to the Confederacy? What do you want to do?"

"There's a lot of amputees who could use an artificial leg like I have, I was thinking I might be able to help."

The captain leaned back in his chair. "What do you know about the spy you were caught with?"

"I've been with him for almost a week now." Luke looked around to see if anybody could hear him. "I think he is a she. I suspected it when we were traveling in the freighter, but last night when she thought I was sound asleep, she got up and used the pail, I'm convinced."

"One of the duties of the Provost Marshal's office to is apprehend spies. I make it my business to know every Union spy that comes across our lines. The name *Cuff* is an alias and alerted us who she might be. You're exactly right. We think she is Emma Edmonds, a Canadian turned spy. She has infiltrated our lines many times posing as a nurse, a black man…you name it, then crossing back over with valuable information. She may be one of the most notorious spies in this whole war."

Luke could hear guards shouting at a prisoner on the floor above. "Why are you telling me this?" He asked.

"Because I think you can help us win this war or at least convince the Northern residents that the cost of this war is too high. There are a lot of people up there who are strongly against the continuation of this war. They want peace and are willing to negotiate an immediate end of hostilities."

Luke listened attentively. He had no idea why Alexander was telling him these things. Alexander continued, "There is a Yankee election this fall and if by chance Lincoln were to be defeated, his replacement would surely represent those who oppose this war. They call them Copperheads or Peace Democrats and if one of them were elected president, we are convinced the war would be soon over with favorable conditions for the South." Alexander leaned forward in his chair and spoke in a softer tone. "I saw how the girl, Cuff, looked at you. I think she respects you...hell, she may even be sweet on you. Imagine this...we release the two of you with instructions to join Lee's army. I'm sure she would relish that. With your help we could convince her to give misinformation back to the Union army."

"Meaning no disrespect, sir, but that doesn't make sense. How could we give her the wrong information when she can see it right in front of her?"

"You'll have to be clever. With the cooperation of some of our commanders, the army could appear vulnerable when it's not. Maybe give the impression to be stronger on the left when it's really stronger on the right or something like that. Do you see what I mean? One mistake on Meade's part. That's all we need to land a crushing blow."

Luke saw Alexander's point. They decided an escape would be more convincing than a release because to release them might make Cuff suspicious. Alexander told Luke of a suspected spy for the North named Elizabeth Van Lew who lived in Richmond. She hadn't been apprehended because she had Alexander's superior officer, Provost Marshall General John Winder, wrapped around her finger. Winder was unwilling to prosecute her for spying saying that there was not enough evidence. Privately, Alexander said he suspected Winder was having an affair with Lew. So did many who lived in Richmond.

Alexander gave Luke Lew's address with directions for him to go to Lew's house with Cuff. He explained that, as Cuff had crossed the enemy lines so often, Lew might already know her.

"Imagine this," the captain said, "a big battle is looming and Meade is planning an attack, suppose Meade thinks the right side of Lee's defenses are stronger than his left, when really it's just the opposite. Meade attacks the left and Lee surprises him turning his whole flank...that's what I'm talking about. As I said, you're gonna have to be clever." Alexander leaned back as if the conversation was coming to an end. "I know this is a difficult and vague assignment, but I think if you get out there and up close to our lines you're smart enough to figure out an opportunity.

The spurs on the captain's boots clanked when his feet went from his desk to the floor. "Luke, you can see how important this might be. You can do it, son."

When Luke got up to leave he asked, "Can I have my flask back? Helps with the pain." He pointed to his artificial leg.

"Of course," the captain said.

Later, after Alexander told Luke how to escape and find Lew's house, two guards escorted Luke back into his cell, where they tied up their arms and legs, then left. The door was again chained and locked.

Cuff asked, "What happened. What did you say to them? Why are we tied up?"

"Captain Alexander's a real bastard. He thinks we're both spies. We all know what they do with confirmed spies. He said that as soon as General Winder gets back from a trip to the Camp Sumter area, he will ask permission to execute both of us…said it would be a firing squad…if we're lucky."

"Are you a spy?" Cuff asked thoughtfully after a few moments.

"No, but I can't prove it. Are you?"

"Do I look like a spy?"

They heard the sound of a guard's footsteps in the hallway outside. He stopped at the door and listened, and then in a low menacing voice said, "Looks like the two of you will meet your Maker. Around sunset tomorrow. You're gonna hang."

"We're going to have to get out of here…somehow," Luke said, "not sure how, but we're goners if we don't."

"Must be why we're tied up…they know we'll try," Cuff said.

Luke bent forward and removed the wooden plug from his artificial leg and took out his small knife. He explained that he carried the knife to make adjustments when the knee started to rub too hard from wear. He showed Cuff the knife, and then cut them both loose.

"Now, all we have to do is figure a way to get outta here."

Cuff studied Luke's face. "You seem to have things pretty much figured out."

They discussed ways to escape. Cuff suggested they overpower the guard when he brought them food. Luke said he was comfortable with that idea but wasn't sure if it was the best one. He suggested they bribe the guard and asked if Cuff had any money secretly hidden and the answer was negative. They discussed boring a hole in the floor big enough for them to slip through down to the next floor, but decided as all they had was the little knife, it would take too long. Eventually, they decided that Cuff's original idea of over powering the guard was best, with one of them wearing the guard's uniform. Together they could walk out.

Later that evening Cuff became restless, getting up to walk around, then sitting down on the floor only to get up again. Luke thought he knew the problem. He got up and walked to the door as if to inspect the hinges and security of the latch. Cuff immediately took the opportunity and used the pail. Several minutes later, Luke returned and sat where he had before.

"You know, don't you," Cuff said.

Luke looked at Cuff with a questioning look.

"When did you figure it out?" Cuff asked.

"The way you cross your knees when sitting. Sometimes your hand goes to your hair as if you're worried how you look."

"You sound very experienced with the ways of the fairer sex," she said.

"Does it bother you that I know?" Luke asked.

"If it doesn't bother you, it doesn't bother me. Nothing is different. We still have to get out of here right away. I don't think the likes of Alexander will change their mind about hanging a spy just because I'm a woman."

Chapter 14

Pain in his amputated foot kept Luke awake that night. It was raining heavily outside and it roared on the building's metal roof. His pain seemed to be always greater when it rained and he remembered how his father's arthritis would flair up on humid, rainy days. He drained the flask of its remaining contents.

Luke remembered those first days after he signed up for the Confederacy. All he wanted to do was to accomplish something that would make his father proud. Now that his father's death was almost certain, he wondered if he was still trying to impress him. Or maybe he was trying to prove to himself his self-worth. He wondered why he wasn't sad about his father's probable death. Maybe it was because his memories of him were still so vivid.

He looked over at Cuff, sleeping in her corner of their cell, her head propped up against the wall, breathing softly. He had had a vague attraction to her ever since he figured out she was female. Now, nearly certain she was a spy, he still wanted her to like him. But he could never have a relationship with her. He didn't know exactly why he wanted her to like him. Other than his mother, the only females he'd ever been around were Carol, who he had fallen in love with, and the crazy woman in the thunderstorm to whom he had lost his virginity. He knew he liked women, the way they walked and talked and smelled. But he knew he didn't feel about Cuff the way he thought about Carol. Thoughts of Carol excited him and flooded him with warmth…Cuff didn't do that, but there was something. Something he couldn't pin point. If she was a spy as Alexander said, then she was duplicitous and conniving. She was the enemy, even though Luke couldn't quite see her that way.

His hand went to his chest almost by habit before he realized Carol's locket was still not there. He had left it where he threw it in his bedroom at McCallister's house. So much had happened since that glorious night he had spent with Carol almost two years ago. He pictured her face. Her brown hair and mischievous eyes. Were they blue?

The sound of distant yelling of the guards woke Luke as a dim light started to penetrate the boarded-up cell. He looked over at Cuff who was already awake and watching him. Luke propped himself up against the wall, brought the knee of his good leg up to his chin, then reached down and did the same with his artificial leg. With his arms around both legs, he told Cuff the details of how they were going to escape.

An hour later, an old, bespectacled guard entered their cell with a tray of food that only had two bowls of watery soup. "How did you get untied?" He exclaimed.

Luke was near the door and drew his attention. "Wasn't difficult. We just cut the ropes."

With the guard facing Luke and the door, Cuff went up behind the old man and quickly got down on all fours behind his legs. Luke, seeing that Cuff was in position, snapped his two hands up and pushed hard on the guard's chest. The guard's eyes got big as he fell backward. He yelled, "what the...", then the tray went up in the air spilling the soup. His head hit hard on the floor, causing his glasses to come loose, and the soup landing on top of his head. He lay there unconscious, with beans from the soup dripping off his chin and down his cheeks and his glasses hanging by one ear. Cuff looked up at Luke and started to laugh.

"Hope he likes our soup," Luke said.

The humor quickly vanished when the old man moaned. Luke quickly undressed the guard while Cuff readied ropes to re-use. The old man's uniform had a rank odor and Luke wondered when the old geezer last washed. However, the uniform fit him reasonably well and when he posed in front of Cuff, she held her nose.

"Must admit. That was pretty easy," Cuff said.

"Perfectly planned. Perfectly executed," Luke said sweeping his hands back and forth. "Now the tricky part."

With Cuff's hands tied behind her, Luke pulled his cap down to shield his eyes and with Cuff in the lead left the cell and walked down the hall and rapped on the door for the attending hall guard to open. When the door opened, Luke said, "Alexander wants to see the spy."

The guard motioned them through as if nothing were out of place. As they descended the stairs, Luke clamped his hand onto Cuff's collar and led her out the front door past two more guards who hardly gave them a second look. They marched the full length of the building toward the front door of the prison's offices where Luke had met with Alexander the day before. But instead of entering the office door, Luke marched Cuff straight ahead onto a cobblestone street. At the end of the prison building was an eight-foot wooden fence surrounding the exercise yard for the prisoners. Luke could hear the scraping sound his artificial knee joint made as they approached a corner where the fence made a right angle. When they got to the corner, three Confederate soldiers were loitering, having casual conversation. They looked up when they saw Luke and Cuff, but resumed their talking.

Luke didn't know where they were exactly, but he knew where the James River was, and he knew the heart of Richmond was north of the river. As they approached the commercial center of the city, the hour was too early for the start of the business day. He guided Cuff into a space between two wood framed buildings and untied her. He straightened out his cap into a more normal position, and they resumed their walk this time casually and side-by-side.

"I can't believe it was so easy," Cuff whispered glancing behind, looking for anybody who might be chasing them.

"Me either."

Cuff looked at Luke with admiration. "I never expected to just walk out of there. You had it all figured out."

"Must have been the uniform, I was surprised myself."

The morning sun broke through a low cloud and cast a bright light behind them as they walked down Main Street. The slow cadence of an emaciated mule pulling a wagon echoed off the cobblestone street. The wagon, carrying the morning newspapers, stopped in the middle of the street and the driver pitched a bundle right ahead of them. Luke could easily see the headlines: *LEE CROSSES RAPIDAN*. That meant that Lee was retreating to the south toward Richmond. If Meade couldn't be stopped, Richmond would inevitably fall, as would the whole Confederacy. Alexander was right. The battles in the west had been decisive, and with Sherman freely wreaking havoc across the deep south, Lee's army was the only hope. Something had to be done that would allow Lee to strike a decisive blow.

"Where are we going?" Cuff asked, breaking Luke's train of thought.

"We're heading to Grace Street. There's someone there who might know you," Luke said quickening his pace.

"Wait a minute," she said trying to keep up, "how do you know all this?"

"Tell you later," Luke said as he guided her across the street, "we need to get off these streets before we're reported missing and somebody spots us." Luke admonished himself for not being ready for Cuff's question. It was such an obvious hole in Alexander's strategy. As they walked, he tried to think of what he would say. He decided that if she asked again, he would say he really couldn't tell her the answer. If she persisted, he would say that Alexander was a spy and that was how they got out so easily and that Alexander made him promise not to tell anybody. It seemed plausible but he hated to lie.

They found Grace Street, lined on both sides with flowering Linden trees. The scent reminded Luke of his mother, who would drink tea made from Linden blossoms. She claimed the tea was an elixir that could prevent just about everything, and drank a cup every day.

The houses were large, mostly brick federalist-style, two story structures surrounded by lush lawns. Wide brick walks lined with lupines led to gracious front entrances. Between the houses were flower gardens, now turning green and ready to flower.

Shortly, they came to the house Alexander had described to him: a three-story brick mansion, surrounded by a short iron fence, with two sets of steps leading to the front door. As Alexander had instructed, Luke took Cuff around to the back of the house and lightly knocked on the door. They heard the sound of footsteps and the door was opened by a tall, thin, middle-aged woman dressed in a long black dress with a white collar. Her fair white face was ringed by curled black hair and Luke immediately saw kindness in her deep-set gray eyes.

"May I help you?" She asked.

"Madame Lew?" Luke asked.

"Why yes," Lew replied. She looked from Luke and his uniform to Cuff and seemed to sense the two people in front of her were not the usual beggars. "Please come in," she said as she looked out into the back yard to see if anybody had seen them.

Lew led them through a narrow hallway that led to the main foyer in the front of the house. There she stopped and said, "I'm Elizabeth Lew and with whom do I have the pleasure of speaking?"

Luke looked around the foyer. A tintype hung on the wall showing a store in a large brick building with a sign that said, *JOHN LEW HARDWARE*. A tall man stood in front, smoking a cigar, and Luke thought he might be Mrs. Lew's husband. A circular stairway with ornately carved balustrades led upstairs. The walls were rich dark wood with raised panels. Luke thought back to the old modest farmhouse in Tennessee where he had been raised. The opulence of the polished hardwoods with hand-carved finials was something he'd never experienced before.

Lew coughed lightly to get Luke's attention.

"Oh, I'm sorry," Luke said. "I'm Luke Pettigrew, from Tennessee, and this here is Cuff." Lew's eyes quickly went to Cuff. "Do I know you?" she asked. "You look familiar...or maybe it's your name."

Cuff glanced at Luke as if she was about to say something that Luke didn't know about her. Then she looked back at Lew. "I've heard of you many times. My real name is Emma Edmonds. I think we are in the same business."

Lew invited them into her library and asked if they would like some tea. A huge painting of Union General Benjamin Butler hung on one wall of the room. On another was Union General George Thomas. When she left to prepare the tea, Luke said in a low voice, "Emma Edmonds? You are full of surprises. First, I find out you are not a man, but a woman. Then I learn you are not Cuff, but somebody else. My gosh, Cuff...or Emma...or whoever you are...what's next?"

Cuff put her hand on Luke's shoulder. "I'm sorry for the deception," she said, "however, I think we are both interested in the same thing... ending this war as soon as possible."

The room had bookshelves on three walls and while Cuff looked out the window onto Lew's manicured back lawn while Luke scanned the shelves. On one shelf, next to a tome titled *The History of Ancient Civilization,* by Gustave Ducoudray, were several bottles containing medicine. One bore a label of laudanum. Luke saw that Cuff was still occupied looking the other way, and he grabbed the bottle and took a long swig. He took a deep breath and remembered how good it felt. Then he wondered why he did it. He remembered the guilt he felt when he would steal a cookie from his mother's cookie jar. He could never resist those cookies and usually he had more than one. But this was more of a need than want. He pulled out his flask and filled it from the large bottle.

Luke stood in front of a painting of Northern General Benjamin F. Butler. It showed a balding man, and the hair he did have was long and stringy. His round pudgy face made him look like a Saint Bernard. When Lew returned with a tea set, she explained, "that's my friend, Benjamin. He's the reason I'm doing what I'm doing. Very handsome isn't he?" she said smiling, then pointed to another portrait. "Oh, and that's my friend and fellow Virginian General George Thomas. They call him the *Rock of Chickamauga* for his bravery there. He valued allegiance to his country over allegiance to his state...a mighty fine man."

She expertly served the tea. "Now where were we..."

Cuff looked back at Luke, "We're here to ask you if you would consider helping us with a plan we have in mind, that might help the Union win this war more quickly."

"Yes, I would. Please tell me more," Lew asked.

Cuff and Luke explained to Lew how they hoped to gather information about the Confederate lines and feed it back to Lew who they hoped could get it promptly back to Union authorities. They gave her the full details of their plan.

When they were finished, Lew told them that if the information they uncovered was important, she could get it to Grant himself by the next morning. Luke thought if she could in fact do what she said, she must be a very powerful and well-connected woman.

Chapter 15

Luke and Cuff left the Lew house via the back door after dark. Mrs. Lew supplied Cuff with a gray Confederate uniform, albeit two sizes too large. Luke snickered at her rolled up pant legs and the extra material flopping back and forth when she walked. Considering the severe shortage of uniforms, it was the best Mrs. Lew could do and she made every effort to convince Cuff that she would not stand out much because many soldiers had ill-fitting uniforms for the same reason.

The streets were eerily quiet and nearly empty as they made their way to the Richmond train station, walking back the way they had come. Grace Street, where Mrs. Lew lived, was quiet, and most houses were dark. A mangy dog crossed in front of them under a street light. They could see that the dog had little to eat, as his ribs and spine stuck out grotesquely. Seeing the two approach, the dog cowered and slinked off into the darkness.

As they neared the center of the city, a light fog rolled in and created a misty halo around the street lamps. No horses or carriages traveled the streets. Only a solitary cleaner pushing a cart over the cobblestones could be heard. The cart would stop and then the shovel would scrape up a pile of horse dung then move to the next one. As they neared Main Street, Luke could hear soft noises, almost moans. Then they saw vague shapes in the darkness. They were soldiers. Wounded soldiers. The moist air became thick with the smell of sweat and decaying flesh. The moans became louder as they neared the station. Hundreds of men, some either dead or near death, lay near the street. As Luke and Cuff walked by, some of the wounded saw them and pleaded for water or help.

One wounded soldier put his hand out and grabbed Luke's pant leg. "Help me," he said in a pitiful voice.

Luke squatted down next to the man who was under a lamppost and could see he was lying on his side. "Where are you hurt?" Luke asked, "I can't see your wound."

"Back side. I think I gotta Minié-ball back there," he said gesturing toward his rear mid-section, "it feels like it's on fire. Luke glanced up at Cuff and held up a finger meaning he wanted to take a moment to help. He then rolled the soldier over on his stomach. His uniform pants were soaked red and he had been lying in a small puddle of half coagulated blood. When Luke ran his hand over the man's buttock, he screamed. Luke gave him the small flask he had taken from Lew's library. "Here, take a sip of this, it'll ease the pain."

Luke took the knife he had hidden in his wooden leg and ripped a hole in the soldier's pant's seat. With the wound exposed, Luke thought the Minié-ball had not penetrated very far into the muscle. "This is going to hurt," he told the soldier, "bite down on the bottle cork and I'll get this piece of lead out. Shouldn't take long."

Luke felt the soldier flinch as he probed the wound. Then he felt a click on the end of the blade as it touched the bullet. "Found it," Luke said, "now bite hard." He pushed the knife passed the Minié-ball and pried it upward. The soldier screamed in agonizing pain.

After a few moments, Luke held the bullet in his hand. "Got it," he said, "You may not be able to sit for a few days, but you'll be as good as new."

Lacking any kind of bandage material, Luke tore the soldier's pant leg into two strips and tightly bound the wound. He took the Minie-ball, held it up and said, "I'll keep this as you won't be needing it any longer." Then he put it in his pocket.

The soldier took another sip from the flask, returned it to Luke, nodded at Luke started to walk away. Cuff spotted a watering trough and suggested Luke could wash his hands there. As he was doing so, Cuff said, "Nice job with the soldier, but he didn't seem very appreciative of what you did for him."

After Luke had washed, he took the Minie-ball from his packet and held it up. "He knew," Luke said.

"Knew what?"

"He knew that I knew. See this bullet? It has two rings around the base. This piece of lead was made somewhere here in the South. If it were a Northern Mini-ball, it would have three or four rings."

"So?" Cuff asked.

"So, that soldier was shot by one on his own side trying to run away. He was deserting, probably in the heat of battle. That's why he didn't say much, he was too embarrassed…or scared."

Luke suspected there were many more like him, who had run under fire. It seemed to be an indicator of the health of an army. Lots of runaways and deserters meant the general spirit of Lee's army was low. From what he was able to gather, the North had nearly unlimited resources to wage war both from recruiting men to producing war materiel. He felt all was not lost, but he would have to act quickly.

Mrs. Lew had suggested the best way for the two of them to get close to Lee's camp was to ride in one of the supply trains that carried food and war materials, routed through Richmond. The beleaguered army was only a short distance to the north. She told them that once they arrived at the camp, an ex-slave by the name of Rogo would find them and he would pick up any messages they might have around midnight each night.

The train station was over-flowing with people. On one side of the large station room were women and children with their bags piled all around them. It was easy to determine these families were vacating Richmond. Their husbands were probably at war, so the ladies were headed south to safety. The women wore elaborate hats, colorful dresses with full crinoline petticoats that ballooned out when they sat, and each carried a parasol. Many had their servants with them. The children were dressed in what looked like their Sunday best clothing and each had their hair perfectly combed. Black patent leather shoes for the girls and light jackets for the boys.

On the other side of the station room were soldiers, most of who were in transit away from the fighting. Almost all had wounds of some sort, and those who didn't simply sat with blank expressions, seemingly unaware of their surroundings. One soldier had only one leg and the stump of the other had a bloody bandage sticking out through his dungarees, which had been cut short. Beside him was a pair of crutches that looked like they were lopped off limbs of a tree. Luke went over to him and stood in front and pulled up his own pant leg exposing his own, thinking the soldier would be encouraged. But the soldier did not focus on what was in front of him. He said nothing, continuing to stare ahead unblinking.

Luke asked the man at the ticket window when the next train north was scheduled. The man looked at Luke as if he were from a foreign land. "Mister, I don't know where you've been, but our trains don't have a schedule. They come and go and we have no idea when or how. Been that way for weeks."

Luke and Cuff decided to wait for the next supply train heading north. They found a narrow, cramped place to sit and there they waited. Later, Cuff fell asleep and her head found Luke's shoulder. Her short curly hair had a sweet, smoky odor and Luke wondered what she would look like in a dress. He felt her soft shoulder against his and he cautioned himself that sometime in the future, possibly near future, she would not consider him a friend.

The shrill, high-pitched whistle of the supply train approaching the station woke Luke with a start. The same squeal always reminded him of a fox in distress and his mind went back in time to the day he would always regret and never forget when he gave chase to the fox that led to his father kicking him out.

His body ached from sleeping on the hard floor, so he got up and walked around trying to loosen up. He asked a soldier, who appeared to be a member of a squad assigned to protect the train from the Yankee cavalry, where it was headed. He told them it was bound for Gordonsville about sixty miles north. Cuff had awakened and together they walked toward the loading platform to board.

Chapter 16

April 29, 1864

It was almost mid-day by the time the train finally departed Richmond for Gordonsville. Luke and Cuff found a place on the floor of the rear car. It was filled with corn silage to feed the Confederate army's vast herd of horses. A grizzled old soldier who had worked with the railroad all his life sat with them. He had long gray hair, white beard and a soiled black patch over his left eye. Not shy about talking, the old man said he lost the eye in the Battle of Buena Vista in '47. Feeling free to talk because Luke and Cuff both wore Confederate uniforms, he said he had been in Gordonsville just six days before. Lee's army was not getting enough food and the hope was Meade would not move until early crops farther south could improve the situation. As the train slowly made its way north, vast herds of horses could be seen munching on early spring grass.

"A month ago, them horses were starvin'," the old man said. "If them Yanks woulda attacked back then, Lee would've had no way to deploy his artillery. All General Meade had to do was move around our right flank and we'd been a goner. But, maybe that's why old Abe replaced him with Grant. Meade was a stumblebum…much too cautious. Well, it's all different now. Plus, Ole General Longstreet, Lee's right hand man, is due up from Tennessee any time now. Lee's gonna whup 'em…just you watch."

The train stopped at Hanover Junction, where it was joined by a column of cavalry riding along side. They would escort them to Gordonsville. As they approached Mechanicsville, a huge expanse of green pastures extended far to the west, and in the middle was a sea of thousands, possibly tens of thousands, of gray soldiers lined up in double columns with batteries of cannons on their sides.

The train came to a stop and a military band could be heard. An officer riding a magnificent grey horse rode through two large gateposts onto the field and between the columns. The officer had a large hat with gold braid, and as he neared his cheering men, he took it off and held it low to his side. His gray hair blew in the light breeze. The soldiers, unable to hold back their demonstration of love for the general broke ranks and engulfed him.

The old man jumped to his feet. "That'd be General Lee hisself right there, gentlemen," he yelled. "Yessir. And that would a military welcome for his ole warhorse, Longstreet. Back from Tennessee. Yippee. Now Lee will really whup 'em."

Luke stole a glance at Cuff. She was frowning. Inwardly Luke was thrilled.

Rebel yells spread over the men like waves, back and forth. Hats were thrown into the air and a line of one hundred cannon all roared in a deafening tribute to the returning Longstreet as Lee reviewed the thirty-thousand, battle-hardened men of Longstreet's 1st Corp.

An hour later, the train made its customary back up before it went forward. Cuff wrinkled her forehead. "Why does this train always go backwards before it goes forward? Is the engineer confused?"

"Ah ha," the wizened old soldier said, "good question. The train could never start forward and move all the cars at once…the load would be too heavy and the engine would just spin its wheels, iron on iron. You see, there's some play…about three inches…between the hitches on each car, so the train backs up taking all the play out of each car. Then, the engineer puts the engine in forward gear. When that happens, the first car moves three inches before the second car starts moving, then the third, until the whole train is moving forward. Simple as that!" He smiled, proud of himself.

Cuff sighed and rolled her eyes. "Sorry I asked," she said, "next time I need to know something, I'll look you up."

Not to be put off, the old soldier shrugged his shoulders. "You sound like my long deceased wife. She would've said the same thing…

women," he said, "after my sixty-five years, I still don't have a clue…
reckon I never will."

Cuff laughed.

The small station at Gordonsville was the end of the line for all
Confederate train traffic and where trains disgorged their freight. Because
the station had no roundhouse in which train engines could be turned
around, the engines would simply run backwards to the closest round-
about, just north of Richmond.

Luke and Cuff said goodbye to the old man and walked from the
station toward the center of town. Luke's prosthesis was chafing and he
stopped to make an adjustment to the strap. As he did he noticed a black
man behind them. The man had scar tissue on the right side of his face that
covered part of his eye. When they turned a corner onto the main street
of Gordonsville, he was still behind them, but when Luke feigned another
strap adjustment, he was gone.

Soldiers were everywhere, with horses and wagons slowly trying to ma-
neuver through chaotic traffic. Men yelled and cursed. Whips cracked. Horses
neighed. All trying to get someplace as if their lives depended on how fast
they got there…and size mattered. Four dappled grey Belgians pulled a huge
freighter that had wheels taller than Luke. The drover steered a path through
the center of the chaos as if he dared something or somebody to get in his way.
When a small buggy with a load of grain had to back up to avoid a collision
with another wagon, the rear wheel of the buggy was hit by the front wheel of
the freighter. The drover casually glanced down as his big wheels crushed the
little buggy into pieces and kept going as if nothing had happened.

Luke and Cuff stopped in front of a large, white building where officers
and white-coated men were intermingling in excited conversation. Luke
determined the building was a hospital and he asked one of the men in
white what was happening.

"Lee and Longstreet just rode through," the man answered. "On their
way to Clark's Mountain. It's the best place to watch Meade's army on the
other side of the Rapidan." Luke knew that he and Cuff needed to go to
Clark's Mountain.

"Why have you switched your allegiance," Cuff asked abruptly as they made their way towards the mountain, "You signed up over in Tennessee, right?"

Luke had known the question would come sooner or later. "There were two posters on our home town post office windows. The Union poster said something about saving the Union and the Confederate poster headlined, *Wanted: 100 Good Men to Repel the Invasion.* My father had just kicked me off the farm and I felt like I was a rebel myself, so I became a Rebel." He smiled at Cuff. "It was as simple as that. I believe my folks leaned toward the Northern position. We had no slaves."

Cuff studied Luke's face. "You lost your leg because of a Yankee bullet. You were imprisoned in a Yankee prison. They've treated you like dirt, I'd say, so why switch sides now?"

Luke hesitated. He wasn't prepared for this pointed question. "Because ending this war is the most important thing," he said, "And because of you."

A small company of cavalry rode passed them, heading in the opposite direction creating a dust cloud. Cuff's features softened. "Because of me?" She asked after the dust and noise settled.

"When you came back that second night we slept under your wagon. I remember because your clothes were wet, and I could tell you were a woman. You are always gentle, kind, and very passionate about what you're doing. My mother was like that sometimes.

"So?"

"So, I knew you were somebody special."

The conversation was interrupted again, this time by four teams of horses pulling cannon and caissons toward the mountain, a short distance ahead. Clark's Mountain was a steep hill that rose south of the Rapidan River, and Cuff and Luke made their way up. Both felt the exertion from the climb. "About a year ago, when Hooker was the Yankee commanding general, they were also camped on the other side of the Rapidan," Cuff told Luke. "Lee climbed this same hill and saw what Hooker was up to." She stopped to catch her breath. "He could see all of Hooker's movements, so when the Yanks crossed the river, Lee attacked and the battle of Chancellorsville ensued. Lee's right hand man, Stonewall, flanked Hooker and the Rebel army chased the Yanks back across the Rapidan with very heavy losses."

"Were you there?' Luke asked.

"Yes, on the other side. It was humiliating. Lee split his forces and caught most of Hooker's army in that wooded area over there," she said pointing to the northeast. "Those woods are so thick, the advantage of numbers is nullified."

"What do you mean...'nullified'," Luke asked.

"In those woods, the visibility is a very short distance. A larger army loses its advantage over a smaller army because the shots can only be fired at close range plus maneuverability is limited. Cannons are useless. Cavalry cannot be effective. Many of the advantages we had were gone."

"You talk like you were actually right there in the middle of it," Luke said.

"I was probably too close," she admitted, and then added, "It was a frustrating battle, if it were not for those thick woods, this war might already be over."

They gazed down from the top of the hill to the opposite side as the sun set. A mile away, the Rapidan flowed lazily, snaking its way to join the Rappahannock, eastward toward the Chesapeake Bay. On the north side of the river, the smoke from hundreds of campfires rose straight up into the still air like columns holding up the sky finally flattening at the top, bent by upper level breezes.

South of the river, only the smoke from a few fires rose as a stark reminder that Lee's army had very little to eat, and what they had, did not need to be cooked. Mounds of dirt, resembling huge anthills, littered the banks and hillside where Lee's army had entrenched themselves in a formidable defensive position. Cannons were set above the entrenchments, all aimed at the river, the direction from which Meade's forces would inevitably come. Behind the cannons, protecting Lee's left was the thick wooded area, almost a square mile, which had stymied Hooker a year before.

The view was better than any map and as Luke and Cuff surveyed the area, they saw the strength of Lee's position. Grant could either attack Lee's left or right flank and because attacking his left would leave a clear path for

Lee to march on Washington D.C., both Cuff and Luke expected Grant would cross the Rapidan to the east and attack Lee's right.

Darkness had come by the time Luke and Cuff got back to Gordonsville and only a few soldiers remained, most of whom huddled in small numbers, likely talking about the attack that all were sure would happen soon. Three doctors were talking in a group on the steps outside the hospital when Luke and Cuff arrived .They wore white smocks smeared with blood, but not stained nearly as much as they would be if an active battle were taking place. One of the doctors, with his back to them, was taller than the others, and Luke thought he looked vaguely familiar. "You, there," came a gruff voice from behind, "show me your papers." A Confederate soldier wearing a star on his chest approached Luke and Cuff with his hand on his holstered pistol.

"Who's asking?" Luke asked.

"I'm the Provost Marshal around here. Checking for deserters and spies…show me your papers," he said more emphatically.

Luke looked at Cuff, who drew closer to Luke and a bit behind. "We have no 'papers', officer," he answered. We aren't deserters and certainly not spies."

"Who's your commanding officer, then," the man bellowed.

Not knowing how to answer, Luke was about to say Colonel Alexander, but then the tall doctor came over. "Luke? Luke Pettigrew? Is that you?" He asked, drawing close to Luke so he could see in the dim light.

"John?…John Herbert?" Luke replied.

John thrust out his hand and shook Luke's vigorously. "How did you escape? Last I saw you, the Yanks had you hog-tied and took you north just after Shiloh. That was two years ago."

"Oh, that was nothing…," Luke said.

"You know these two?" The marshal asked.

"I know this soldier. I worked side by side with him in very busy field hospital." John said, "And I'll vouch for anybody Luke Pettigrew hangs around with."

"Okay, just doing my job. I've heard there are some Union spies around," the Marshal said, walking away in the direction of the train station.

Chapter 17

The lower level of the hospital where Luke's friend John took them late that evening was a large room with cots lined up on both sides. The room was dimly lit, and all but two cots in one corner were occupied by sleeping hospital staff members. An alcove at one end of the dormitory had a bucket and as Luke and Cuff glanced at each other when they saw it. Cuff shrugged and laid down fully clothed and pulled a blanket up over herself. Luke did the same. It was then that a racket of twenty or thirty snoring men got their full attention. From the other end of the room, he heard a lion-like sound as a man roared with each inhalation. Another sounded like a calf bawling. All blended together into one symphony of noise and Luke mused it sounded like a snoratorium if such a word existed.

Sometime later, Luke, unable to sleep glanced over at Cuff who peered over at him at the same time. "The problem is," Cuff whispered, "how will Lew's contact get in touch with us. Surely he won't be able to find us here in this…dormitory?"

"I was thinking the same thing," Luke responded. "Maybe he'll find us in the morning."

The next morning, Luke awoke. Cuff was sleeping soundly. He got up and walked outside. The air was heavy with a thin fog hanging in the cool morning. In the back of the hospital was a chow tent and Luke could smell food cooking. As he walked toward the tent, a man approached him and Luke recognized him as the Provost Marshall from the day before.

"Mornin'", the marshal said.

"Are you still looking for papers?" Luke asked.

The marshal looked around. Men were lined up for chow. Others were sitting under trees eating. "Where is your friend?"

"Sleeping."

"Alexander sent me," he whispered, "I'm supposed to coordinate with you.

"We're supposed to meet with Lew's contact," Luke said in a low voice. "Until we do, I don't know who he, or she is, so we best not be seen talking. Somebody could be watching us."

"Suppose you're right. She usually uses darkies for messengers. They can move around easily without being challenged...just too many of them. But I don't see any right now...I'll contact you this evening. Meantime, you should get a clear understanding of what's going on on both sides of the Rapidan." As he walked away, he said. "Don't look for me, I'll find you."

John picked his way through the hungry men and approached Luke, stopped next to him and lit a cigar. "That marshall giving you trouble again?" John asked exhaling a cloud of smoke.

"No. He's one of those men who you give a little bit of authority and they think they're really some kind of general officer. Seen those kind before and I'm sure you have, too."

As John took another long drag, he squinted like he was in deep thought. "You know there's a big battle coming. Sure could use an extra experienced hand when it happens. We're going to get flooded with wounded...may be worse than Shiloh. I don't know what your assignment is around here, but it sure would be a personal favor if you could help us out. Still remember how to suture?"

"Had some practice last night. Poor bastard had a Minie ball in his ass...had to pry it out with a pocket knife."

"Probably a Confederate Minié ball, right?"

"You see a lot of them?" Luke asked.

"More and more. Are you in?"

"We'll see, but I think so." Luke could see clouds of dust rising to the east caused by the stomping feet of thousands of soldiers on the move. Lee's army was estimated to exceed sixty thousand and they all seemed to be getting ready for action, causing everyone in the little town who wasn't a line soldier to understand something big was coming.

"When you hear the popcorn popping and the canon roaring, come a running," John said with a slight smile as he walked away.

Luke walked back toward the dormitory and met Cuff coming from another direction. "You're up," Luke said. "Did you have to wait until everybody left?"

"Nothing you need to worry about," Cuff said. "Do we have a plan?"

"We need to go back to Clark Mountain so I can get a better picture of what's about to happen," Luke responded. "Let's go."

During the hike to the peak, Cuff explained that she had been contacted by one of Lew's agents who, as suspected, was a freeman. She thought Lew would only use freed slaves because they had papers. "He bragged that General Grant would read first thing in the morning any important information she could give him," Cuff said.

"Madame Lew must have a powerful line of communication," Luke said.

As they climbed, Cuff reached out for Luke's hand to help her up some of the steeper areas. When Luke saw that the red dust from the horse traffic and the soldiers on the march had settled onto her black curly hair making her look like a red head, he laughed.

"What's the matter now," Cuff asked coquettishly turning her head and posing, "something wrong with my looks?"

Before Luke could answer, discharges from a Union line of cannon echoed from across the Rapidan.

Luke pointed across the Rapidan. "Let's see if I have this right. Those encampments? They stretch for miles. Meade has to have more than a hundred thousand soldiers ready to move." He swung his arm to the right. "Over there is Germana Ford, and further to the right is Ely's Ford. If Meade crosses, and he almost has to, he will use one or both of those fords."

"Sounds right, but we're going to have trouble explaining this in words. Maybe the easy way is for us to draw a map," Cuff said. "Show where Lee will be waiting and suggest how to avoid getting wiped out like Hooker did."

Luke glanced at Cuff. This was the moment he had been waiting for. The opportunity to provide Lew with tangible information, which once fed back to Meade would give the Confederates an advantage. All he would have to do is to make sure the Confederates knew they might come through the woods at night and the advantage would belong to them. He hesitated. He had grown to care for Cuff. He felt guilty just thinking of deceiving her. In essence he would be using her, betraying a friend. Would he feel differently if she were a man? Regardless of his father's unkindness toward him, his father had always been kind to his mother. But then Luke wondered what his father would do in this circumstance. Would he use Cuff and deceive her to accomplish something he believed in? Or would he confess that he really wasn't on the Northern side. Luke's mind went back to that day when his father told him to leave and the look in his eyes…almost remorseful. Maybe his father was just cutting the rope and turning Luke free.

"Hello," Cuff said, "where did you go?"

Luke snapped back. "Sorry. Your map idea is perfect," he said, "Grant may have to move at night to keep from being detected, but maybe moonlight would help. Anyway, it's a good idea. I'll draw it up."

"So, then I meet with Lew's contact and give him the map, right?" Cuff said. "Then we'll be done?"

"Exactly," Luke replied. Then I will give the Provost Marshall a copy of the same map to beware a night attack, and Lee will win the day with a decisive victory.

As they headed back toward Gordonsville, Luke felt awkward when she brushed against him. He had known that the time would come when he would have to lie to her and now that moment had arrived. He didn't like the feeling and almost hoped the battle that was about to take place wouldn't happen the way they had planned.

"Cat got your tongue?" Cuff asked when Luke hadn't said a word during most of their walk back.

"Just thinking I'm not cut out for this spying stuff," Luke said, "I'd rather work in the hospital and help people."

It was Cuff's turn to be quiet for a spell. Finally, she said, "I agree. After this is over, maybe we can quit. Maybe you could teach me to help with the wounded."

"You would do that?" Luke said. "You've been doing this for a long time, why would you stop?"

"Because it makes you uncomfortable," Cuff said, "and I want you to be happy."

"How do you know I'm uncomfortable?"

"Darn it, Luke, give me some credit. I just know."

Luke smiled. Whether he wanted to or not, he liked this woman more every day. She was different. She had an appealing manner, but his own realization that he was growing more fond of her made him more uncomfortable with his deception.

Chapter 18

When the travelers finally got back to Gordonsville, the last rays of the sun were filtering through the giant white oaks across the street onto the converted hospital. Luke admired the wide, graceful stairs leading to an elevated front porch. The staircase had white wooden balustrades on the side of the steps that wrapped around the porch and gave the building a warm, gracious feeling. The conversion of the building from a hotel to a hospital had made it the center of activity as soldiers, doctors, nurses and patients all milled in front.

They walked inside, and Luke asked a passing nurse if he could borrow a pencil and paper. He sat on a bench and sketched out the movement of Meade's forces should follow to avoid being caught in the dense undergrowth, the same brush and bracken that caught Hooker in the Battle of Chancellorsville. He gave the map to Cuff, who studied it. She then excused herself to find the man who would forward their information to Lew.

Luke made another copy of the map while she was gone, and then went in search of the provost marshal. As he left the hospital, Luke saw John in front of a tent with 'QUARANTINE STAY OUT' written in bold letters above the entrance.

"Why the quarantine?" Luke asked.

"Small pox. We have five new cases since last evening," John said with a sigh. "All the staff has been exposed. This could explode to an epidemic if we're not careful. We think it started with two Negroes who came into camp several days ago." He mopped his brow with his sleeve. Not sure what to do about it…except keep the affected in separate facilities."

"I'll be glad to help. I think I'm immune," Luke said.

"How in the hell are you immune," the doctor asked.

"This might sound silly, but when I was little, my father came down with it. My mother nursed him back to good health, and when his lesions scabbed over, she pried them off, let them dry and ground them into a powder."

Luke's attention was diverted by the provost marshal walking by. He motioned to Luke.

"So what then?" The doctor asked.

"I'll be right back," Luke said, "have to talk to that man." He ran after the marshal.

When Luke had caught up with him, the marshal asked, "You got anything for me? I've been hoping to hear from you."

"I think I do, yes," Luke said. "We think Meade will cross the Rapidan at Ely's and Germana Fords and…"

"Hell, anybody can figure that out," the marshal said. "The question is: *When?*"

"Hear me out," Luke said. "We all remember how Hooker was outsmarted when he got caught in the area referred to as the *Wilderness* and had to retreat to the north with his tail between his legs? Here's a map…it shows exactly what Grant's spies are telling him to do…and he's going to do it at night."

The marshal studied the map. "All we have to do is move into that area before they do. You got anything else?"

"I'll be working at the hospital if you need me. Looks like they're going to get busy…and soon."

Luke returned to find his physician friend, John, talking with another doctor. Luke sat on a nearby bench and began to take off his prosthesis. Naturally, that drew the attention of the doctors. "Starts to hurt if I walk or stand all day," Luke explained, massaging his stump.

"Luke, say hello to Jeffery Bushnell. He's an up and comer and has just joined my 'staff', such as it is."

The other doctor appeared to be only a bit older than Luke. After some discussion, Luke found out he was not a doctor as such, but was a second year medical student at Bowdoin College in Maine. When the war started he had traveled back to his home state of Virginia. The Confederacy had a severe shortage of trained doctors and they recruited anybody who had training even if it was only one year. They were all called 'doctor'.

"We were talking about our little outbreak of smallpox," John said. "You said you thought you were immune and were telling me why…"

"When my father came down with smallpox, my mother took some scabby lesions from him, dried them, then ground them into a fine powder. She then had me inhale the powder. Seemed to work. Never caught it even when our neighbors had it several years later and we had to help."

"You inhaled a powder made from dried pox scabs?" Jeff asked.

"Yep. Maybe, after inhaling the stuff, it's like getting a very light case of the pox. I've never heard of anybody that ever had it getting it again."

Jeff looked dubious. While he couldn't find any fault with Luke's reasoning, he seemed to doubt anybody without professional medical knowledge could have a theory that had any credence. However, John who knew Luke was a solid thinker.

"Did you get sick after inhaling that stuff?" John asked.

"No. But I did get a couple of faint lesions on my arms a couple weeks later," Luke said.

John said, "Luke, if you're immune as you say, then you're now in charge of the pox ward…at least until this battle starts when we may need you in the hospital. How does that sound?"

Luke quickly agreed, thinking the pox ward would take up his time while the armies moved.

He untied the front flap of the quarantined tent and the stale odor of sickness, vomit and diarrhea hit him like a wave and almost made him retch himself. Under the tent were fourteen cots, seven lined up on each side with a narrow walkway between. The tent was in an open area behind the hospital, and even though the temperature outside was mild, the sun beating down on the canvas roof had caused the heat to increase to sweltering levels. Each patient had a bucket and a jug for water next to their cots, and all but one of the jugs were empty.

Luke threw open the front tent flaps and tied them back, and then the two rear flaps, to let air flow through. The tent was pitched over raw earth, without a floor and the ground was not level, causing each cot to be slanted one way or another. Several of the patients moaned.

Luke decided to inspect each patient, starting on the left side. The first patient appeared to be peacefully asleep with his arms crossed on top. When Luke peered at his face, however, he saw that the man had scratched his lesions and his left side was covered in dried blood. He picked up his arm to check the pulse and discovered the man was dead. He went to the front of the tent and called for a stretcher-bearer to haul the body away.

The next patient was wet with fever and Luke soaked a rag in water and bathed his face and arms as well as he could. His lesions were starting to dry up and Luke guessed the worst was over for him. He worked down the line trying to make each man as comfortable as possible. When he got to the last cot in the row, he saw a black man nestled between the cot and the tent lying on the bare earth. He looked at Luke with panic in his eyes. He held up his hands as if to keep Luke away. "Please, Masa, don't tell," he whispered loudly. His face and the back of his hands were covered with pox lesions. Streaks of bloody sweat swept from his face to the back of his head and had dried to a crust that looked like red lightning on a dark sky.

Luke took his hand in re-assurance. The hand was huge and dwarfed Luke's, and it was covered with thick calluses that were rougher than a coarse rasp. Luke realized that this man was the first black man he had ever touched. It flashed through his mind that some thought the whole war was being fought for this man and tens of thousands were dying either to enslave or free him…this fearful, wretched, probably illiterate man.

As Luke hesitated, the black man pulled his hand away, turned over, lifted the tent canvas and tried to crawl out the way he evidently got in. Luke reached down and pulled the man into a sitting position. "Stay," Luke said, "we'll help you." He helped the big man to his feet and walked him over to the now empty cot and lay him down. The cot creaked under the heavy burden and the man lay there seemingly afraid to move.

Luke methodically checked the others. Another had died, possibly only a very short time before, his red, lesion-wracked body still warm, and his forehead still moist from sweat. The last one in the row was in an early stage of the pox with only faint red splotches. His head was propped up on his pillow, and as Luke wiped his forehead, the patient grabbed his wrist and pulled him close. "You get that god damned nigger out of here," he said, "I will not stay in the same tent with him. He's the reason we all have the pox. Those damn niggers brought it." He pulled Luke even closer. "Get him out, now, and if you won't do it, I'll shoot the bastard."

Luke saw the hatred in the man's eyes. He looked back at the black man who was staring at him with the same fear in his eyes as if he knew exactly what the older man was saying. Luke felt like he had two options: throw the black man out or throw the white man out. Luke stood. "You calm down and wait a minute. I'll be right back," he said.

Luke walked out of the tent and as he passed the black man, he held his finger to his lips asking him to be quiet. He walked straight to the hospital, looking for John. He found him on the back porch, explained his problem, and asked him what to do. John could sense the urgency. He threw the question back to Luke. "You're in charge of the pox ward," he said. "You're the boss. But maybe you should find another place for the black patient."

"Where? We don't have another tent for him. And he's much sicker than the other soldier." Luke was frustrated and getting angry. "This is bullshit," he said. "Remember Shiloh…when we had a Yankee soldier badly wounded and we were head over heels treating our own southern boys, you told me it didn't matter…Confederate or Union…to you they were all humans and you felt you had an obligation to treat them all the same. Are you telling me this black man isn't human?"

John stared at Luke with a grim face, then he softened and smiled. "You missed your calling, Luke. You'd make a wonderful doctor…better than me. It's your ward, go handle it as you see fit."

"But I have no clear choice. I can throw out the soldier…but he has a right to be there. This is a military hospital…or I could throw out the black man and if I did, he wouldn't make it without care." Luke stopped for a minute trying to weigh his options.

"It's a tough decision, Luke. And I don't know what I would do in your shoes, but whatever you decide, just remember it's your ward and I'll back you."

Luke thought about John's answer. Nobody had ever had enough confidence in him before to make his own decisions. As a soldier, his job was to take orders, before that, his father had always given him detailed instructions as if he did not have faith in him to figure it out for himself.

Luke turned and marched out of the hospital. He decided his decision did not have to be in favor of one over the other staying in his ward. He went straight back to the pox tent and approached the soldier who was still propped up on his pillow. When Luke approached, the man threw up his arms in a shrug and said, "He's still here," in a demanding tone.

Luke bent over the man, put his face close to the patient's ear and whispered, "You have two options: get the hell out of my ward and if you do, I'll make sure no other hospital in this county will take you. Or you can stay here and shut your big mouth. If you choose to stay here, you have a good chance of surviving. Outside, you don't. The choice is yours."

The soldier recoiled as if he was bitten by a snake. He opened his mouth as if to continue his argument, but didn't say anything. He stared at Luke defiantly.

Luke busied himself with the other patients. He nodded at the black man who seemed to relax. A while later the complaining soldier was sleeping. Luke went outside for a breather and a woman approached. "Doctor John asked that I help you out," she said, "I've had the pox so I think I'm immune. I'm a nurse."

Luke silently thanked John for sending the nurse. "We have to make our patients as comfortable as possible," he said. "We'll assess each one, then I have a very special job for you."

They visited each patient and the nurse noted the condition of each. When they finished she asked what the special job was.

"I want you to find some mature dried scabs on some of our patients who are in the later stage of this pox, then pick them off and grind them up into a powder using a mortar and pestle. You can find one at the hospital. Do you understand?"

The nurse turned up her nose. "Why would you ask me to do that?"

"We'll immunize those here that have not had the pox by having them inhale a bit of the powder," Luke said.

"I know you're not a real doctor," the nurse said, "so how do you know all of this?"

Luke answered by repeating how his mother had done it.

The nurse looked at him with tired eyes. "Okay, I'll do it. Doctor John thinks very highly of you and that's good enough for me."

Luke gave her a couple more instructions, and then went back to the dormitory where he quickly fell to sleep…but only after he had a swallow from his flask.

Chapter 19

An hour later, Luke was woken by Cuff shaking his shoulder urgently. "Meade is moving," she said, "we can't see him, but we can hear him."

Luke sat up and shook his head trying to clear his thoughts. He had been in a deep sleep and remembered a dream about Carol in which she had seen that he had only one leg for the first time. In the dream she turned and vomited. Her vomit was a pile of Minie balls. The Minie balls had two rings. He shook his head again trying to focus on what Cuff had said. "Which way is he moving, can you tell?"

"Unless it's a feint, he's moving to his left just as you suspected," she said.

Luke lay back down on his cot and put his arm over his eyes. "Aren't we going to do something?" Cuff asked.

"What do you want to do? If Meade is moving either to his left or right, we can't do one single thing. If we're right about him moving to his left, then our map idea is working. Nothing we can do but see what happens in the morning. Just calm down"

Luke thought about Meade's move. He was moving early, possibly crossing Germana Ford in the night. It appeared he was heeding the advice Luke had drawn on the map. Cuff had passed it through Lew to Meade. That part was fine. If Lee then moved into the wilderness area, he would be in a position to deliver a blow that would make the North think twice about re-electing Lincoln.

Before long, however, his thoughts drifted back to Carol and the horrible dream he was having when Cuff woke him. The thought of Carol's gross rejection made him feel like a failure. He tried to go back to sleep, but the image kept coming back. Finally he sat up. He had to tell her somehow. To warn her. To prepare for that first meeting. He went back to the hospital and found a pen and paper, walked out to a bench on the street near a lamp light and wrote.

My Dear Carol, Not a day goes by without thoughts of you. I am sending this letter in care of your uncle in Columbus in the hopes it will find its way to you. This war seems to be about to reach a conclusion with victory possible for either side. When it's over, I will find my way back to you wherever you are and I hope against hope you will be anxious to see me. This war has taken its toll on me both physically and emotionally and I hope the conflict has not bore its heavy weight upon you nearly as much. Please be safe and when it's all over, look for me because all the king's horses and all the king's men will not keep me away from your door. I will find you, Dearest Carol, I will find you.

Luke

Luke reread the letter and felt better. He had been hesitant to write to her before, because he didn't know what to say. He had a feeling she was becoming just a memory. His mental picture of her was indefinite. Not only could he not remember the exact color of her eyes, he forgot what the line of her mouth looked like. As much as he tried, the image of her would not come into sharp focus.

If his message found Carol, she might not be so surprised when she saw him. Maybe in another letter he would be more specific about his amputation. He walked back to the dormitory, stretched out on his cot and fell asleep.

The early morning light was starting to filter thorough the trees outside the dormitory door when Luke was again shaken awake. This time it was John. "We're going to get real busy," he said, "I'll need you in the main hospital."

Luke sat up. He heard mules braying and the shouts of ambulance drivers, and the cracking of whips urging the wagons back to the battle. The battle was on. Luke saw a clear sky above, and figured it was a good day for the battle from the South's perspective. Good weather meant Lee's army would not be slowed down by mud or other poor conditions that could hamper moving his army effectively. Of course, the same could be said for the North. However, Lee's force was smaller and Luke reasoned good weather was better than bad for the smaller force.

Luke washed his face and hands and went to his pox ward. "Any trouble with the older man in the back corner?" Luke asked.

"No, he's pretty sick. His lesions have flowered," she said. "The rest of the patients seem to be holding their own." She walked to a small table and brought him a small dish that had seven dry scabs. She turned her head in repugnance and gave them to Luke who told her to mash them into a fine powder.

"You're going to inhale the powder," he said, "and that will keep you from getting the pox."

"Inhale? Like through my nose?"

"Yep," he said firmly walking away, "and the rest of the staff should, too."

Luke went into the main ward where John hovered over a table, shared with his associate, Jeff. Lined up neatly were the tools of their trade: three different sized saws, knives, pincers, and scissors, all cleaned and ready for use. A basin of clear water was to one side. Mirror backed candle lamps were available to help illuminate each operating area. The beds were already nearly full and there was an air of expectation among all the doctors like the calm before a storm and the storm was a giant ominous black cloud heading straight at them.

"Luke, you prioritize," John said. "You've done it before. Leave the torso wounded outside the building." He pointed at Luke's leg. "Those with wounds to the extremities, line 'em up. We'll handle them first."

Luke knew the drill. It was counter-intuitive. The least serious were handled first, but it was the best way to save the most lives. Frequently, those who yelled the loudest were the ones who were taken last...if they were still alive. He knew he could do the job as instructed.

He went outside onto a large tree shaded lawn. There was cannon fire in the distance from the direction of the river. Cannonball wounds usually arrived before musket wounds, and Luke braced himself when a large ambulance wagon arrived. Several older soldiers in tattered gray uniforms approached to unload the wagon. Luke thought he was prepared to see the carnage, but he was wrong. The victims had been thrown onto the wagon like cordwood. Because the drivers were under fire, they had not taken time to place them in any kind of order. Blood was everywhere, and the air was filled with a disjointed chorus of moans, screams and pleading. One soldier was wheezing loudly, evidently from a Minié ball through his lung. Another, on the bottom of the pile, was laughing a maniacal laugh, as if he had lost his mind. The first soldier they unloaded had both his hands shot off. As they pulled him off of the man underneath him, a loose leg fell from another soldier and seemed to be unclaimed. As each man was removed, Luke would hold up one finger those who had a chance. Row One was for them. Luke directed all the others to row two. He dreaded passing by a gut-wounded soldier who would look at him with pleading eyes, knowing he was going to die. He remembered and dreaded the depersonalization of being the judge of who might live and who might die.

Luke glanced back as another wagon pulled up and saw the soldier missing two hands being taken inside on a litter. If he survived, he could never feed himself again, or even write a letter home. The inhumanity struck him hard. At Shiloh, two years before, there was similar carnage, but the war was young, and even though the South had been routed on the second day, the first day was a big victory and those victories were remembered. Now, the war in the west was lost and southern resources were depleted, while it appeared that resources of the North were infinite. He wondered why this killing should continue if the southern cause was lost? And, what were they fighting for? He thought of the black man in the pox ward. To Luke, the difference between a white man and a black man was color only. He thought about a war poster he had seen for the South: *Wanted: Good Men to Repel Invasion.* Was the war being fought for that? Because Northern armies came south to impose their will? Or was it only about slavery? If it was slavery, he had made a mistake.

Hours passed. The ambulance wagons kept returning with more wounded. Sometimes the victims were piled three deep. Hundreds and hundreds, and Luke knew the battle was fierce and possibly decisive.

John came outside and summoned Luke. "We need you inside." By now, the litter carriers knew which row to put the soldiers in before Luke could tell them. John looked over the rows of wounded, and added, "without more help, we're going to lose most of them before we even see 'em… and we're only half way through the day." He wiped his brow with his bloody sleeve leaving his forehead streaked red.

Inside the operating room, Luke watched Jeff sawing off a shattered leg just below the knee. The patient screamed and blood spurted. Jeff dripped more ether on the man's mask that covered his mouth, and Luke turned away fighting back the nausea that he frequently felt during an amputation. When the bone was severed, Jeff threw the amputated leg, it still wore a shoe, onto a pile, its muscle tissue still quivering.

Luke felt John's sense of hopelessness. The task of treating the wounded seemed humanly impossible. "If you have two doing the amputations, I'll do the flap work," Luke volunteered.

"Exactly what I was thinking, we'll get another table…just like Shiloh," John said with a sad smile.

While the work could be tedious, Luke preferred it to what he had been doing, as he wouldn't have time to think.

They set another table up with a complete set of operating tools for Luke. They had discovered at Shiloh that while two doctors did the actual limb amputations, a third person, Luke, could do all the closures. It would take Luke half the time a doctor normally needed to amputate, so he could close for two doctors and save a lot of time.

Jeff had just finished sawing another man's leg off below the knee. John told him that Luke would finish and he could start another. Jeff looked dubious about the arrangement as Luke approached the table.

Luke studied the patient's flap that Jeff had left. Normally, the doctor doing the amputation cut a generous flap of skin below the point where the bone is cut. Then the flap was sewn over the end of the limb, forming a natural way for the wound to heal. Luke looked over to Jeff and told him, "There's not enough flap here. There'll be too much tension on the sutures."

"That flap is perfect," Jeff answered, "don't tell me how to make a flap."

He said it loud enough for John to hear—prompting the lead doctor to look more closely at the flap. "Not big enough," he said, looking at Jeff, "make 'em bigger." Jeff glared at Luke, before he went to the next patient.

Luke took a needle and did the best he could with the flap. He knew from personal experience the patient's stub would forever cause him discomfort—assuming he survived.

Eventually, they settled into an efficient rhythm and processed as many as twelve patients per hour. The decision to amputate or not always favored removing the limb. Many doctors felt a clean cut was preferable because the incidence of infection and other complications was lower, making the survival rate higher. A nurse applied the anesthetic using a cone placed over the mouth and nose. The anesthetic put the patient under within a few minutes. Luke was thankful the supply of chloroform was adequate, as it eliminated much of the patient's pain during the actual amputation, and made the procedure easier. Recalling his agony when he initially woke up, he tried to minimize pain whenever possible.

Hours later, with all three men were exhausted, when a patient with a bad wound in his right buttock was placed on Jeff's table. The soldier lay on his stomach and evidently a Minié ball had passed through and had exited near the soldier's right hip. When the nurse started to administer chloroform, Jeff stopped her and told the orderly to move the patient out.

"Why not clean him up and stitch him back together?" Luke asked. "He'll die sure as can be if you don't."

Jeff glared at Luke and his face turned beet red. He slammed his fist on the table making a noise so loud it could be heard across the room. "You are telling me?" He shouted, "I've had enough of your ignorant, uneducated comments. This man is a deserter. He was shot in the ass trying to flee… leaving his fellow soldiers to do all the work. He doesn't deserve to live." He repeated his order to the orderly. "Get him out of here."

Luke stood his ground. "You might be right about him being a deserter, but then you might be wrong. Whatever the case, it makes no difference whether he's a deserter, a hero, or even a black man. He deserves medical care and if you won't give it, I will." Then Luke reached over and stopped the orderly from moving the patient.

John came over. "Look, we're all getting tired. We're doing good work here…saving a lot of lives, but we're under a lot of stress. Let's take a break one at a time." He looked at Jeff. "You're first. Cool off and come back in half an hour."

After their breaks, the team worked on for hours more. When the natural light grew too dim to continue they decided to take a breather, while lanterns were brought in. They men sat on a bench in front of the hospital. Any previous hard feelings were lost in their weariness. On his second cup of coffee, Luke heard his name whispered.

It was the pox ward nurse motioning for him to come over.

Chapter 20

Luke could feel the coffee trying to give him a boost over his extreme weariness. His back ached from the hours of leaning over the operating table. He opened and closed his fist because the fingers of his right hand ached from holding a stitching needle.

The nurse stood in front of the pox tent, and was very upset. "We have three new patients," she said, "and no place to put them."

He entered the tent where three soldiers showing advanced stages with red scabs on their faces and hands were lying on the ground. He looked to the left. The black man was gone, his bed occupied by another new patient who had evidently come in during the night. "What happened to the black man?" Luke asked pointing to the cot where he was the night before.

"They sent him away," the nurse said.

"They? Who's 'they'? I authorized no such thing."

"Two generals came through. I had to do as they said." The nurse was nervous and wouldn't look Luke in the face. She seemed ashamed.

Luke was angry, but he didn't want to further distress the nurse. He took a deep breath. "Okay, when did this happen and can you remember the general's name?"

"Last night, shortly after supper. He acted like he was in charge of the whole army. I had to do it. I was not told his name."

"Where did you put the patient?"

"I didn't put him anywhere. I just told him he had to leave and he got up and left."

Luke told her he would be right back and left seeking John. He found him checking some of the patients with amputations. When Luke approached red-faced and angry, John cut him off before he could say anything. "I've been waiting for you. I have no authority. He's the Surgeon General. Doctor Moore. Sam Moore. He's an okay man but doesn't care much for blacks."

Luke turned red. "I thought we treated everybody equally, John, this is more bullshit. You know where that patient went? He's contagious. He could infect the whole camp if we don't isolate him. Where do you think he is?"

"Probably just outside of town," John said. "There's hundreds of them camping. I hear the conditions are appalling. It's filled with very sick slaves who have nowhere to go."

"Sounds like a perfect place for pox to spread," Luke said. He hesitated for a moment, then added, "I'll be right back."

"Don't go," John said, "it's full of all kinds of disease. I need you back here...in good health."

But before John got the words out, Luke was gone. He knew just where to go, an area near the railroad tracks just south of town. The dust from the road drifted behind him as he determinedly walked through the village. He wasn't sure what he would do when he found the missing man with the pox, but he had been wronged and Luke wanted to help him.

A small stream meandered through a large grove of trees outside of the village. From a distance, the shaded area looked like a nice place for a picnic, however, as Luke approached, he realized his worst fears. The first thing was the odor. A strong sickening fecal smell made Luke hold his breath. As he rounded the knob of a hill he saw several hundred people, under the trees, most of whom were lying haphazardly on the ground.

Smoke rose from a few fires and hung lazily in the thick air. With his hand over his nose, Luke walked into the camp. Everybody, including the few who were trying to cook on the fires seemed to be infected with the pox. He started to work his way through some of the sick. The wary eyes of some of the patients followed him as he moved from one to the next.

Luke remembered from his childhood the disease had several stages. The ones with slight blotches on their face were in an early stage. Those that had fevers and reddish spots that had turned to pimples were the next stage. The final stage seemed to be when the red scabs turned to wet blisters. He passed a few who had blankets and rags pulled up over their faces and had succumbed.

He walked past a man who was lying on his side who, when he saw that Luke might be a doctor, raised his hand. "Masa doctor," he said in a weak voice, "please help."

The man had pox scabs on his arms and covered his entire face. Luke took his hand, "you're going to be okay," Luke said, "your disease is in a later stage. You will be okay."

"My family," he said. "They all have it. My two sons and wife…I fear for their lives. Please help."

"Where are they?" Luke asked.

"Last I saw them, they were near Barboursville down the road…they were too weak to walk so I came ahead to get help."

Luke looked over the camp and the others who needed urgent care and realized there was no way he could help the man. "I'll see what can be done," he lied. "But let's get you well so you can return to them." He patted the man on the shoulder and moved on.

Next to him was the man from the pox ward. He was dead.

The sheer magnitude of the misery and agony almost overwhelmed Luke. As he stood in the middle of the camp wondering what to do, a young girl stirring a pot of what looked like a watery soup, asked, "you a doctor?"

Luke, realizing that his white smock made him look like one, said, "No, I am not, young lady. Is your family here?"

"Yes, suh…I mean no suh…they're over there," she said. "Both gone early this morning."

She kept her head down as if to look directly at Luke would be some kind of sin. Luke reached down and put his hand on her forehead. Her hair was matted with filth but she was cool. "I got the pox when I was a kid," she said.

Luke almost smiled at the little girl, who was probably ten or eleven years old, thinking she had arrived at adulthood. *Maybe she had*, he thought. "Tell me, how long have you been here?"

"Five or six days…Mastah Manroe owns us and he was taken by Yankee cavalry three or four weeks ago. We had nowheres to go…ended up here… that's when everybody got sick."

Luke walked to the small stream that trickled through the campsite. The area around it had been used as a latrine and smelled foul. Upstream, he could see the water was clear and he walked back to the little girl. "I'll try to find some help," he said, "do you have any food?"

"Jus' this soup. Found some greens. Had some left over pork skin."

"Be sure not to drink any water unless you boil it," Luke said, "and I'll be back as soon as I can."

The girl kept stirring the pot, not looking up. "Not goin' anywhere," she said.

Luke took his time walking back to the hospital, trying to sort things out. He thought of all the wounded soldiers waiting for urgent treatment, and those who he knew would be coming. Those were soldiers needed his immediate help, but so did the blacks he had just left. He couldn't effectively help both. He believed his father would want him to do. Funny, he thought, he was still trying to please him. He also knew he was weary and possibly his reasoning could be flawed.

Luke looked for John when he got back to the hospital. As he walked through, he saw all the wounded men who were fighting a northern army bent on defeating them. Many of these men were dying just because they wanted to keep the Negroes enslaved. Even though he guessed that many of Lee's army were like him and had never owned a slave, the object of the war seemed to be for the preservation of slavery as an institution. Had he made a mistake with his choice? Then again, maybe he picked the South because he sensed his father was leaning the other way.

Luke found John , who had a fresh white smock on. He offered a clean one to Luke. "Here. Put this on. Somehow a clean smock always makes me feel better."

Luke took the smock. "This war's getting to me," he said. "I just came back from the camp south of town where there are well over a hundred people, all Negros. Most of them have pox and they are dying. They have no care, no water, no food…no nothing. I feel like I have to do something to help them…but there's nothing I can do. We have no room and no facilities. The Surgeon General made it clear he doesn't want any resources taken away from our wounded soldiers. You're a part of the Confederate Ambulance Corps and you have to obey what they tell you. But, I'm a volunteer and have no such obligation."

John put a hand on Luke's shoulder. In a fatherly tone, he said, "Luke, you've got your heart in the right spot. When the Surgeon General threw your black patient out of your ward, I was pretty sure you would be pissed off…really pissed off." A pair of vultures circled above. "You're right. You don't have any superior officer to tell you what to do, all you have is your conscious, but may I suggest to you that you cannot expect yourself to do everything. You can only do so much. I'm not going to tell you what to do, you'll have to work that out, but I do know you'll make a good decision. Until you decide, we could really use you back in the hospital. I have to go, the wounded are coming in faster than ever. Good luck," he said patting Luke on his back.

As John walked away, Luke heard the telltale sounds of ambulance wagons approaching the hospital, mixed with new groans of pain and pleas for help. He smelled fresh blood mixed with the putrid odor of offal from soldiers with gut wounds. He saw John standing at his table, saw in hand, ready to begin his first amputation of the morning. Jeff was doing the same. Luke's worktable was vacant. He felt a surge of energy sweep through his body, the same feeling he always had when emergencies arose. He looked back in the direction of the Negro camp, then at his worktable where he sutured. He tore off his dirty smock and put the clean one on and walked up to his table. John looked over at Luke and nodded, neither smiled.

Chapter 21

Luke never thought suturing a man's skin could become boring, but after an intense six hours, he was not only bored, he was bone-tired. The stub of his leg ached from the standing, and his phantom pain came back. The pain was never quite the same from one time to the next. This pain was in his toes and he felt like somebody was trying to bend them around double. It hurt so bad tears came to his eyes and he kept wiping them with his sleeve. He broke out in a sweat from his head to his toe. Finally, he told John he had to take a break. He walked outside. He breathed deep, the cool fresh air filling his lungs in a welcome reprieve.

The sounds of the battle continued. The thud of cannon discharges echoed through the trees and became so regular nobody gave it special attention. It had become so expected that when it stopped briefly, the silence was deafening. Periodically, thousands upon thousands of rifle discharges would ring out in what seemed like waves, from sporadic shots to crescendos of concentrated fire, rising and falling as if driven by some unseen wind. *A wind from hell*, Luke thought. He imagined each shot being aimed at a human. Could half of them find their target and tear into soldier's flesh? Even if it was less than half, the carnage would be incomprehensible. Both generals were leading their men into a slaughter for which Luke could see no justification.

He sat down on a grassy part of the hospital lawn that had not been trampled by horses and wagons. After slipping off his wooden leg, he rubbed his irritated stub trying to get the blood circulating again. Soldiers, most of whom had minor injuries, were gathered in several small groups discussing the ongoing battle.

As Luke absentmindedly scanned ahead, he saw a young black child peering at him through the legs of a soldier. She was looking intently at him and he realized it was the same little girl who had been stirring the watery soup and had talked to him that morning. She continued to stare at Luke with sad mournful eyes that held his gaze. He beckoned her with his finger to come. At first she didn't move, possibly because she thought she was hidden and Luke couldn't see her. He beckoned again.

She looked around wondering if the signal was meant for somebody else, then, realizing Luke was motioning to her, slowly approached walking as if she thought each step was a forbidden act and she would be punished. She stopped when she was ten feet away and steadfastly refused to come closer. She wore what looked like a gunny sack with a slit in the top for her head. Her hair stuck straight out giving the impression her head was over-size. She was shoeless and Luke guessed she never owned a pair. Her skin was mahogany and hid her soiled face, but her alert big brown eyes showed intelligence. Her little shoulders were slumped forward as if she were trying to be smaller than she was. She stood with her wrists crossed in front of her as if she wanted to hide behind her arms.

Her eyes went to his prosthesis and grew bigger as if she realized he needed help, too. Maybe she thought that Luke was vulnerable also and that made him more trustworthy, or maybe realizing Luke had suffered, made him a kindred spirit. For whatever reason, she came forward and squatted down by the artificial leg and felt the wooden foot with her tiny fingers. She studied them for a moment then looked up and gazed at Luke with pleading eyes almost squinting. Luke realized she was asking him for help. She may have been too proud to ask or afraid to ask verbally, but he thought she wouldn't have looked for him unless she thought he was her only hope.

"What's your name, young lady?" Luke asked.

"Posey."

Luke put his leg on and got up. "Posey, I'll be right back," he said and he walked into the hospital where he saw that John was taking a break and also had seen the little girl. Luke took off his smock, folded it, and returned it to John. John took it and nodded his head resignedly knowing well that Luke had just made his choice and felt he was more needed somewhere else.

"Stay in touch," John said, "I'm in your corner. You may need supplies and you can have whatever I can spare."

"Thanks, John. This battle is probably about over. It's probably another battle in which nobody wins a decisive blow. However it goes, we should have time to catch up a little. Hope to see you in a couple days." They shook hands and Luke walked outside, taking the little girl's hand and heading for the camp.

The afternoon sun was warm on their backs as they walked through the little village. When they neared the edge of town and the camp, Cuff appeared and Luke assumed she had been waiting for him to be away from any Confederate soldiers so they could have a private conversation. The little girl's grip tightened on Luke's hand when she saw Cuff as if she thought her a threat by taking him away from her.

"The battle's about over," Cuff said in a low voice not paying any attention to the little girl. "It's another battle that thousands have died and nobody wins. Appears Meade got confused in the darkness and missed the opportunity...but he had 'em. Right in his grip. The war could've ended right then and there..."

"What happened?" Luke blurted out.

"Longstreet's First Corps arrived. Turned around the whole battle. Nobody could've figured he'd get here so soon."

"Meade's retreating?" Luke said in a deadpan voice trying to suppress his satisfaction.

"Won't know til morning...look's bad though. Maybe we should talk in the morning."

Cuff left, walking back toward the village to try to seek more information. Luke and the girl walked in the opposite direction toward the camp, the little girl was pulling his hand.

The little girl had lost her parents and was alone. He remembered his own hurt of being cast out alone…the empty feeling. It was worse than nausea. Maybe it was like losing a best friend, but when he thought about it, he realized he didn't have a best friend. Actually, he had had no friends at all. Luke left home hating his father and was determined to prove him wrong. After his heroism at Shiloh, he dreamed about his father finding him and asking him to come back to the farm where they would work together and make a go of it. Slowly he realized that wasn't going to happen and when he woke up at the McCallister's with only one leg, the harsh reality of the situation hit. And now, his father and mother were surely dead and he was on his own. Just like this little girl.

The little girl pulled on his hand again and he realized they were at the camp. Two men and an older woman were leaning against a large sycamore next to the stream. They had faint red marks on their faces where smallpox scabs had once been. He counted the patients lying haphazardly under the trees…fifty six. The campsite was littered with refuse, and wreaked of urine, feces, vomit and sickness. Most of the sick were lying on the ground without blankets or other means to keep them warm. Some were softly moaning, while others just stared blankly into the sky.

"You're going to make everything okay, right?" Posey asked.

"We can give it a try, but we have to work together. Okay?"

Luke thought the best way to proceed was to move the camp to a clean area with fresh water. The little stream flowed in a northerly direction on its way to the Rapidan, and one hundred yards south, there was another large copse of trees. Upstream and upwind, the copse would be an ideal place to re-settle the sick.

He approached the same people under the tree who looked at him fearfully, but didn't run. "We need to move these people over there," Luke said. "Will you help?"

"We'll help, suh, but we don't want to get sick again," one of the men said.

"Don't worry about that," Luke said. "Once you get the pox, you'll never get it again." They looked at each other, their eyes betraying doubt.

"I got it when I was a kid," Luke said as he pulled up his sleeve to show a faint old scar. "Trust me, I'm sure I'll never get it again."

The woman peered at the old scar, then glanced back at the other two, who might have been her sons. "We have nowheres else to go, what you want us to do?"

Luke introduced himself. The woman said her name was Maude. The men were Isaac and Jupiter. Luke asked Isaac, the smaller of the two, to dig a hole. He pointed to an open area about fifty paces from the new camp and explained that the hole needed to be dug about an arms length square and just as deep. With no shovel, he instructed the man how to use a strong stick. Then he told Jupiter to start carrying the dead up to the area just outside the hospital where all the dead soldiers were waiting to be buried.

"Masa, they might not allow," Jupiter said.

"Allow what, Jupiter?"

"Allow niggers next to dead white folk."

They could hear the 'clump, clump' sound of Isaac digging the soil with a stick.

"Go see Doctor John Herbert at the hospital. He will tell you where to put them," Luke said.

The dead from the day before were still there and Luke told Maude to cross their legs so he would know who was dead. He remembered Shiloh and the thousands of soldiers lying on the ground, some dead and some alive, and John telling the orderlies to identify the dead the same way.

He and Maude then made the rounds, stopping by each sick patient to evaluate the stage and severity of the pox. Luke knelt next to each patient, with Maude standing close by. Posey would squat on the other side of the patient and look up at Luke with hopeful eyes, as if she expected him to perform a miracle and the patient would get up fully cured and walk away.

Most of the patients were ambulatory, and after Luke made his appraisal, he asked them to walk to the new camp area. Those who couldn't walk were left until all the dead were carried out, and then the young men would carry them.

Luke was surprised by how similar the patients' cases were. The disease had very distinctive stages. First, using the palm of his hand, he checked their foreheads for fever. He remembered from his childhood that fever and nausea went together. His mother had nursed him through his pox and had told him about each stage of the disease as he went through it. If there was fever and no pox sores, then the indications were for an early stage. Next came the rash. Luke always checked the mouth where red spots and sores would usually appear before anywhere else. Then the sores would appear on the forehead, face and extremities. The sores would gradually fill with pus. Luke didn't know for sure, but he suspected a patient was most apt to die during this period. Later, the sores would dry up and at that point full recovery would ensue.

Luke and Maude approached a man and woman lying close together. As they did, Posey quickly ran away. As Luke watched her go, the woman told him they were her mother and father. They were holding hands and had evidently died nearly the same time.

Luke crossed each one's legs. "And your husband?" Luke asked Maude. "Dead."

They approached the next patient. "How did it happen?" Luke asked.

"He escaped back in '61. Promised to come back and get me and the boys…" She hesitated, trying to collect herself. "He did, too. Came back last year. Had gone all the way to Boston where they paid him money to work. Came back all dressed up…white shirt, trousers with a crease…"

Luke gave her time. He knew what was coming.

She looked up with tears in her eyes. "They hauled him in with his hands tied to his feet around a horse. Brought him right up to our quarters and hung him…" She wept. "They found two dollars in his pocket. They took that, too."

Posey rejoined them, and they worked through the remaining patients. When they had finished, the sun was setting. Luke's next job was to find food, blankets and utensils. He remembered John had said he would help in any way he could, so he started to walk back to the hospital. He asked Isaac and Jupiter, to go with him, as he knew he'd need help carrying what supplies could obtain. Before they had gone ten steps, Posey came running up and tugged his hand. Luke looked down at the little girl. She looked distressed.

"Don't go, masa, we aren't finished yet."

"We'll be right back. We need food and blankets."

"I can help you carry."

Luke scooped her up and set her on his shoulders. "Okay, Posey, you're going with us. That way you'll know I'll come back." Luke felt her little legs grip his shoulders and they walked back toward the hospital.

Chapter 22

Supplies for food and bedding were scarce, with most of the Confederacy's resources going directly to Lee's men, who were nearly starving. Supplies for the hospital were funneled through the local quartermaster, who guarded his dwindling stash like a mother hen. Standing with Jupiter and Isaac, Luke appealed directly to the quartermaster. But when he found out it was for a camp of sick slaves and former slaves outside of town, he flatly refused to give Luke anything. Instead of walking away, Luke took a more aggressive approach. "I would remind you, sir, that keeping the pox infected ex-slaves away from the hospital, and other soldiers will stop the spread of the disease to our soldiers."

The quartermaster, a grizzled old man who looked like he'd caused the food shortage all by himself by eating everything in sight, retorted, "those niggers down there are not 'former' slaves. They are property. Property of many of those out there who're fighting, and as such, they are escaped slaves and we hang escaped slaves on sight…that is, if we don't shoot 'em first." He spat yellow fluid at Luke's feet, but some of the fluid added to the brown streak on the front of his jacket. He looked up at Luke to see the effect of his words.

"You're wrong," Luke said flatly. "If those Negroes were escapees, they would have fled north. But they didn't. Every last one of them was displaced by Federal forces. Their homes have been burned to the ground. Their owner's mansions destroyed. They have no where to go."

"Can't help that," he said and started to walk away.

"You said they were property, didn't you? What would happen when this war is over, and some of those 'property' owners out there fighting found out you were the direct cause of their 'property's' death from starvation? All because you withheld food and supplies. My guess would be you'd be on the wrong end of a noose, standing on a gallows in front of all your fellow soldiers. And I might be the one who pulls the little lever that drops the floor from under your feet. They say white folks kick a long time after they're hung."

The quartermaster stopped. He slowly turned around, his defiant gaze replaced by a resigned look. "If I gave you everything I have, it wouldn't be near enough, but I'll give you whatever the three of you can carry in one trip."

The camp was totally dark when the three of them returned. They carried five large cooking pots, the kind used for making soup, each containing food. One was filled with ham hocks, two others with dried beans and rice and another with corn. Luke, himself, had carried the fifth pot, which was filled with as many blankets as it would hold.

With Maude in charge of cooking. Isaac and Jupiter carried water from the stream, made fires and, using the big pots, started to boil water for a rich soup of the ham hocks, beans and rice that could feed the patients for a couple days.

Luke decided Maude, Jupiter, Isaac and Posey could manage without him, at least through the night. He was bone tired and realized he had not slept significantly for the past forty-eight hours. When he turned to walk back to his dormitory, Posey ran after him grabbing his hand and tugging again. He could not see her face in the darkness, but he didn't have to. He knew she feared he wouldn't come back. He leaned over and gave her a hug. "Please don't leave," she begged, "stay."

Her arms were wound around Luke's neck and he was surprised by her strength. Her grip seemed to be driven by shear desperation. He could feel her convulsive sobs and the moisture from her tears on his cheek. He didn't know what to do, so he held her tight. Maude came over and wrested Posey from him telling her that the kind man needed to sleep and reluctantly, Posey's grip loosened. Luke promised to return in the morning.

While he walked back to the hospital, he couldn't get his mind off the little girl. He pictured the little girl, alone, without her parents, nobody to take care of her. What future would she have? He felt himself being drawn to the girl, like a whirlpool on the edge of a raging river. Sucking him in. Consuming him.

When he got back to the dormitory, Cuff was asleep. He lay down, his body feeling heavy from exhaustion, but sleep was slow to come. He wondered if anybody ever felt about him when he was very young like he was feeling for Posey. Maybe his mother…but she never expressed it. He reached under his cot for the comforting feel of the laudanum bottle.

When Luke awoke the first thing he noticed was the silence. No musket fire. No canons belching. No wagons with dead and wounded, with men shouting, and whips cracking the air. The din of battle was gone. He sat up and noticed he had forgotten to take off his leg before going to sleep.

Cuff was gone. The entire dormitory was vacant. With its low ceiling and bare walls, it looked like an empty tomb. The cots were gone, with only his cot, Cuff's, and a few others remaining. The morning sun that normally shone through the front opening had risen above it and Luke realized it was nearly mid-day. He trudged outside. Far from feeling refreshed from his much-needed sleep, his body felt heavy and sore. He saw work still going on at the hospital…*probably working on the gut shot wounds*, he thought. He stretched, and then heard his name being called. He looked up and saw Cuff on the hospital building's widow's walk motioning for him to come up. The old man from the train was with her. Luke entered the house and hobbled up the stairs. He remembered just a short time before when he had climbed stairs for the first time at McCallister's. Walking and moving with his artificial limb had become second nature to him.

The widow's walk was a flat rectangle on top of the roof and it had a white picket fence around its perimeter. Cuff and the old man were gazing to the southeast. "Ya hear that?" the old man asked.

Cuff and Luke listened. The faint sound of singing. Soldiers singing. "Who's singing," Cuff asked.

"Jus' listen," the old man said.

Then they heard the distinct words, *Tramp, tramp, tramp* from the song about a Union victory.

"That's a song we don't want to hear" the old man continued. "The Yankee army is on the move and they ain't movin' north like they normally do after a big battle. They're movin' south."

"But, why are they 'singing'?" Cuff asked. Luke was equally perplexed.

The old man shielded his eyes with his hand. "I know why they're singing and it's a sad day…mighty sad."

"Would you care to share the reason?" Luke asked.

"And I thought you were a smart kid," he said. "The reason they are singing is because they're happy. They're happy because every other time Lee beat 'em, they would retreat…to replenish their supplies…lick their wounds. This time, with ole Grant in charge, they're trying to flank Lee's right. Grant smells an end to this war, and it's not the end we were lookin' for. He thinks he can go right around him and attack Richmond. So they're singing."

"Lee won't let him, will he?" Luke asked.

The old man was quiet for a while as he stared off in the distance. Finally, he pointed to the southeast and said, "if I remember right, 'bout five or ten miles on the other side of that ridge is a little place called Spotsylvania… Spotsylvania Court House. There's an embankment that would give perfect cover for an army to repulse an attack. That's where Lee and Grant are goin', sure as green apples. Yessir."

"How do you know all this? Seems like pure speculation to me," Cuff said.

"I was right about yesterday, weren't I? Longstreet came up and kicked their ass in them woods…jus' like I said…and mark my words, the first army to get to Spotsylvania will win. The thin gray line will stretch and break…and them Yanks will flood into Richmond like a giant blue wave."

Luke asked, "But why is Grant so hell-bent on marching around Lee's right? He could wait, get reinforcements, rest up, and then move in another month our two."

"Remember what I told ya, it's all about the election…Grant loses, then Lincoln loses, and the North will stop fightin'. Simple as that. Now then, I gotta go. See you around." The old man disappeared down the steps.

"It's true, Longstreet did arrive in time yesterday," Cuff said. "He stopped our boys from claiming the day. It's always something, but if what the old man says is correct, we might be able to help from this side. I see you're involved with the poor displaced blacks. I admire you for what you're doing. By the way, how do I know you're not contagious? You're spending a lot of time with those sick folks."

"I'm not contagious. The disease seems to spread by direct contact with an infected person and, as I had it years ago, you're safe."

"Are you still willing to help us?" Cuff asked.

Luke hesitated. "I guess so."

"You don't sound very convinced," Cuff said in a softer tone drawing closer to Luke.

"Maybe it's because I'm a bit conflicted," Luke said.

"Are you conflicted about whose side you are on?"

Luke didn't want to get into this conversation but she was asking him questions he was asking himself. "There's so much need around here," he said slowly, "those poor blacks just outside of town, the hundreds, probably thousands of wounded soldiers who need attention…not to mention what we're doing. I also want to help those men who have lost their legs."

Cuff reached for Luke's hand. "I would be happy to help."

"No, let me work this out on my own. I feel so frustrated."

"Is it that little black girl? We could take her with us."

"With us?"

"Sure. Why not. I could take care of her while you were working at the hospital."

"Sounds like we'd be a family," Luke said slowly.

"Yes, it does, doesn't it," Cuff said.

Suddenly Luke wanted to stop the conversation from going any farther. "I will ponder a bit," he said, "but I really think Posey would be better off with her own kind."

As soon as he said *own kind,* Cuff's face turned red. "What do you mean by that?" She retorted. "You think blacks aren't human? I don't care for that comment."

"You got me wrong…and I think you know it. Why're you so upset?"

Cuff reached up and pulled on her hair and a wig came off revealing Cuff had close cropped African textured hair. "Does this explain anything?"

Luke was speechless. His surprised face relaxed after a moment, then he managed a smile. "One of the things it explains is that I have a long way to go before I'll understand women." He looked around, "but you should put that thing back on before anybody sees you."

A caisson led by a pair of gaunt horses rambled by heading southeast.

Luke inhaled. "Cuff, I need time. I don't care if you're black or white, I like you. I like you a lot. It's just that I have to deal with an obligation I have with another woman. Another woman I met several years ago and made her a promise. I take promises seriously. All of this comes at a time when I have this deep frustration about not being able to do enough. Men are dying and many could be saved if I helped them. You saw Posey. Her folks are all dead. The blacks with the pox. They need help, and I can't think straight."

Chapter 23

"Just the man I wanted to see," John said in greeting as Luke reached the bottom of the steps. "I want you to meet Jim Hanger. Jim, this is Luke Pettigrew. I believe you two have something in common. Luke felt the firm handshake of Jim Hanger and instantly liked him. A tall man, he sported a mustache and perfectly trimmed goatee that pointed straight down making his face appear longer than it was. He had a wide smile and friendly blue eyes.

"My pleasure," Jim said looking down and Luke's foot. "Yes, we do have something in common," and he pulled up his left trouser leg revealing a perfectly shaped wooden leg.

After seeing the fine craftsmanship of his prosthesis, Luke pulled his pant leg up. Mine isn't near that finely carved. You make yours?"

"Sure did, but yours looks mighty fine."

"I'll let you two talk for a while, I gotta get back to work. See you later," John said.

Jim stood rail straight. His manner had a hint of aristocracy. When he spoke, his words were carefully chosen as if he thought about each one so as to convey his exact meaning. He wore a black coat, unbuttoned, that extended to just above his knees. His trousers were gray with a vertical black stripe. Luke wondered if Jim might be a preacher, but he didn't have a preacher's voice. Maybe he was an engineer…concise and thorough.

Luke and Jim walked outside and found an empty bench. "Lost my leg the second day after I enlisted back in June of '61. They called it the Battle of Philippi. Ricochet canon ball. Bounced off the ground and sheared the leg off mid-thigh. Damnedest thing."

"How did you get the shape of the leg? Did you carve it from a block of wood?" Luke asked.

"No. Used barrel staves…had the perfect curve," Jim said.

"Me, too!" Luke echoed, feeling proud that the two of them had seen the exact same congruity totally independent of each other.

"How did you lose yours?" Jim asked.

"Gettysburg. Rode with Stuart. Got shot off my horse and shattered the bones. It got infected and I thought I was going to die. I went into some kind of coma, but woke up with it cut off about the same place as yours."

As they talked, they both discovered they had made their prostheses under similar circumstances. Both were in an isolated upstairs bedroom while healing from the amputation and both sought a way to walk as a way to fight their boredom and, more importantly to avoid the stigma of being an amputee.

They compared their wooden legs. Luke was amazed how similar they were in many ways. His use of a rubber strap to bend the knee going forward differed from Hanger's spring action. Luke thought the spring was better although Jim didn't necessarily agree. One area where Hanger's prosthesis was much better was the ankle because the hinging mechanism had a tighter fit, and conformed to irregular walking surfaces better.

An hour later, they were still talking, thinking about ways to improve their designs. "I have a little factory over in Churchville," Jim said, "and we're so busy, we going to expand and start another one in Richmond. Jeff Davis, himself, gave us a contract to supply our poor soldiers. The demand is huge." He reached over and put his hand on Luke's knee. "I could use a fella like you to help run the place."

Luke thought for a while. "You mean move to Richmond?"

"Just leased an old building on Carey Street down by the river," Jim said.

"Near the prisons?"

"Yes, sir. Mr. Davis suggested we might be able to use prison labor to work assembling our products…He introduced me to a captain…Captain

Alexander, who said he would give me all the workers I needed." When Luke straightened up slightly at the mention of Alexander's name, Jim added, "What? You know him?"

"You could say that," Luke said guardedly.

"You at all interested?" Jim asked.

"Very much so, but I've a couple things to do here and need a little time."

Jim stood and stuck out his hand. "The job is yours whenever you can make it and the sooner the better." They shook hands, and Luke remembered he had promised Posey he would see her first thing that morning and he was very late.

"Thank you for the job offer," Luke said, "I've seen so many soldiers with missing legs and I know their lives can be much improved with a devices like these. Since I made this contraption, and now that I've seen yours, we can offer those amputees another chance in life. Give me a week or ten days and I'll see you in Richmond."

When Posey saw Luke approaching the camp, she stopped stirring the soup and ran to meet him. Her face was streaked from tears, but his arrival made her smile. He picked her up and placed her on his shoulders and walked into camp with her tiny hands holding on to his ears.

"We had to bury two this morning," Posey said, "but six got better and left."

Maude, Jupiter, and Isaac stood by waiting for instructions. He realized he had never told anybody what to do before, except possibly the nurse in the pox ward. Everybody told him what to do. His father always gave him orders, telling him to do things he didn't want to do. Things that interfered with his hunting and fishing. Maybe if he'd seen the purpose behind his father's orders, he'd still be there. It all seemed ages ago.

While he and Maude, with Posey's assistance, made the rounds checking each patient, Isaac and Jupiter gathered firewood to boil water, and generally clean the campsite. Luke took his time with each patient, making them as comfortable as possible. Several hours later, he saw Cuff standing under a nearby tree as if she was waiting for him to finish.

"Looks like the old man knows what he was talking about," Cuff said. "Both armies have moved south. Nobody bothered with this Gordonsville area…looks like neither army thinks we're worth occupying."

"They're much too concerned about defeating each other," Luke said, "Nobody cares about the sick and wounded…nobody cares. It's like once you can no longer fight, you no longer matter."

"The Confederacy is dying," Cuff said. "Their resources all go to Lee, who cares little for the dead and wounded. It's just a matter of time. I hear Lincoln has just requested another one million soldiers and he might get them. The Confederacy has no such luxury. They've drafted every man between the ages of fifteen and fifty. They're even talking about offering slaves their freedom in return for serving. Imagine that. This whole war is based on slavery and now the government wants the slaves to fight. Seems like they're asking them to fight for the right of being slaves."

Luke tried to absorb the meaning of Cuff's words. He could see her passion. He wanted to tell her how he felt about the South being invaded because of their governments' differences concerning slavery and that most of the soldiers under Lee had no slaves, but he didn't want to give away his feelings.

Cuff could read Luke's indecision, or at least thought she could. "If the next battle is going to be around the Spotsylvania Court House area like the old man said, maybe we should get a move on. Maybe we'll find a way to do the same thing we tried at the wilderness." She waited for Luke to respond.

"I suppose you're right," he said finally, "But I need to spend a couple days here to get my patients out of danger before I can leave."

"How much time?"

"The ones who are infected will typically be out of danger in about five days. Most in the camp will have been there that long by then. We've had a limited number of new cases, thank goodness."

Cuff stepped closer to Luke and gazed into his eyes. "Luke Pettigrew, in the short time I've known you, you never cease to amaze me. First, I learn you are a master prosthesis maker, making your new leg from parts of an old barrel. Then, I watch you dig a Minie-ball out of a dying man's rear, as if you'd been doing it all your life. Then, the way you treat these poor blacks with the pox. You not only treat them as patients, but you treat them as if you really care deeply." She came even closer. She placed her hand on his arm. "The way that little girl, Posey, looks at you. She treats you like you were some kind of a god." She turned her head and pressed it against his chest while putting her arms around him and holding tight. "I know you said you need some time to figure everything out," she said, "you can have all the time you need. Just know I am here." She released him and walked away. "Let me know when you want to go to Spotsylvania."

Instead of returning to the camp, he hurriedly walked back to the dormitory and searched under his pillow for his laudanum. The bottle was nearly empty. He downed what was left and marched to the hospital where John was working intently over a soldier who had a gut wound. A bottle of laudanum was always near these procedures, and without anybody seeing, Luke grabbed it and walked back toward the dorm.

There he sat on his cot and stared on the bottle. The last swig from the empty bottle was having its effect and the label on the bottle came in and out of focus. He wondered why Cuff's words had bothered him so much…she was just trying to be nice…give him a compliment or two… nothing wrong with that. What was the problem? The room started to spin. He took a huge gulp from the bottle, lay down, and quickly passed out. The bottle slipped out of his hands, spilling its contents over himself and the floor.

Chapter 24

Nine days later Luke and Cuff searched in the night for a ferry to cross the Po River, on their way to Spotsylvania, where the wizened old man had said the next battle would be. Most of the ferries were being used by Lee's army, and the only one they could find was a small, rickety punt operated by a young boy who said his father had been wounded and was bedridden. The hair on the boy's head was so thin, that in the darkness he looked totally bald. His eyes bulged out and he had a large pointed nose that dominated his pale face. When Luke asked the boy if he could handle the small punt, the boy assured him his father had taught him well.

All except two of Luke's patients at the camp had remained when they left. Thinking he would be gone for less than a week, Luke had left Posey with Maude, Jupiter and Isaac, who promised they would take care of her. Posey didn't want Luke to leave, and he solemnly promised to return as soon as possible.

The punt was a flat twelve-foot square raft made from flat boards nailed to three logs. It was attached to a rope, strung across the river and tied at each end to sycamore trees. The boy had a long pole made from a tree limb that he used to power the craft to the other side. Luke doubted the boy was big enough to pole the punt over, but he did not see an alternative. When they stepped on, the punt dipped severely until they stood in the exact middle. The moon cast enough light to see, and Luke judged the river benign.

They started across, and each time the boy pushed with the pole, the punt tilted, and standing upright was difficult, so Cuff and Luke sat in middle. Halfway across the river, the rope bowed downstream from the force of the current against the punt, which made the second half of the crossing slightly upstream. The boy had to push much harder, causing their little platform to pitch more than before. Then they crossed a large sunken rock and the upwelling from the current caused the little raft to pitch yet more.

Cuff wrapped her arms around Luke to keep from sliding off. "I can't swim," she shouted in a panicky voice.

The young boy, who looked emaciated, and Luke thought must weigh no more than sixty pounds, nonchalantly kept poling, not paying any attention to the tilt of the platform or the strong current. He wore a pair of cut-off dungarees held up by a length of twine around his waist. His feet were bare and he was having difficulty getting enough traction on the slippery deck. When Cuff yelled that she couldn't swim, he looked at her and shrugged as if he either didn't care, or he couldn't imagine anybody not being able to swim. It flashed through Luke's mind that this boy had never poled across before by himself, and possibly by the looks of him, was only risking it because he needed the money for food. Then, just as the boy was trying to exert pressure on his pole, his feet slipped out from under him and he fell crashing into Cuff, causing all three of them to pitch into the river.

The water was so cold it took Luke's breath away. He struggled to find his bearings. He shot to the surface and searched for Cuff. He saw the boy in the dim light swimming toward the opposite bank, but he didn't see Cuff. He was being swept downstream in the current. Treading water, he turned frantically, trying to catch a glimpse of Cuff, knowing she wouldn't survive long submerged in the very cold water. He heard frantic splashing and a gasp for air just behind him. It was Cuff. He turned, reached out and grabbed her. She was panicking and desperately grabbed him around the waist, pinning his arms, in a frantic attempt to survive. They went under together and her grip grew tighter.

Dying flashed through his mind as he tried to contort his body to loosen her grip. His prosthesis was nearly useless in water and flailed wildly when he tried to kick. He could not generate any power with just one leg. His arms were useless. He knew he couldn't hold out much longer and felt an overwhelming fear they were both going to die. Slowly, Cuff's grip slowly loosened and he was able to stroke to the surface just at the very end of his endurance.

As he hit the surface, he took huge gulps of the night air. He was sure the reason Cuff had released him was because she had inhaled water and was drowning. He had very few seconds to find her. He drifted downstream, turning around frantically, searching, and he felt her brush against his foot. He reached down and grabbed her by her jacket and at the same time his foot touched bottom. The river made a sweeping turn and the two of them had been swept toward the outside of the bend. He gained another foothold and found the opposite bank from which they entered.

Luke knew he had to act quickly to get the water out of her lungs. He sat down and pulled her up next to him. He turned her over on her stomach with her head turned sideways and pressed hard on her upper back then released. He pressed and released, pressed and released. He knew time was running out and his movements became quicker, press and release, press and release. Nothing. He didn't know what to do. Somehow he managed to stand. He grabbed her feet and held them up in the air hoping the water in her lungs would be pulled out by gravity. Nothing. He shook her body. No response. He put her back on the ground and started to press and release again. He felt her slipping away…like an invisible shadow disappearing in the darkness.

As her life faded, he realized how much he cared for her. This person who felt passionately about slavery and the Northern cause. This young woman, who had picked him up in her wagon and provided shelter. This girl, who he thought first a boy, and then revealed herself as a black woman.

Slowly, it dawned on him she was dead. The pain caused by this realization was almost unbearable. He turned her over and placed his head on her lifeless bosom and wept.

He felt her body slowly starting to cool and that made him realize he was shivering from the cold himself. He risked exposure if he didn't do something, but he couldn't take his eyes away from Cuff. He thought about the fine line between life and death, Cuff's lifeless body and his. He was able to get to the surface in time and she wasn't. He thought about how, at the hospital, his patients many times came close to that line and survived possibly because of something he did. He cursed himself for not being able to save her.

Unable to carry her, he left Cuff's lifeless body safely on the riverbank, and started to walk, looking for help to bury her. After a short time, he saw a dim light and cautiously walked toward it. As he got closer, he determined it was a campfire and then heard the warning of a sentry. "Halt, who goes there," came a voice with a southern draw.

Relieved, he said, "Name's Pettigrew. From Tennessee. Rode with Stuart. I need some help."

A soldier appeared from behind some brush and pointed his rifle at Luke. "Walk this way," he said and another soldier appeared next to him.

The wooden parts in his artificial leg had expanded slightly because of the river water causing a squeak each time he took a step. The soldiers both surmised he was an amputee and lowered their weapons. "You rode with Stuart?" One asked. "You don't look like you could ride a horse."

"Lost it at Gettysburg. Seems like a long time ago. My partner drowned in the river earlier tonight and wondered if I could borrow a shovel to dig a grave."

"Might be able to arrange that," one said, and he led him to their camp so he could get warm and dry off. Luke decided he would wait until first light before he returned to Cuff's body.

The sun was high in the sky when Luke returned the shovel. He didn't plan to go to Spotsylvania to do the spying he had intended with Cuff. It would be too painful. Instead, he had decided to travel the short distance to Richmond and take up James Hanger's offer. Even though he was offered a ride in a Confederate wagon, he chose to walk. Cuff's death hung over him like a heavy cloud and he wanted some time to think. He had been raised in a religious family, but when he placed Cuff's body in her grave after she had been wrapped in a blanket, he hoped that her life wouldn't just end there in the ground…maybe she would continue living…maybe in a different world…but somewhere. He knew she had loved him and he wished he had told her how much he cared for her. For the first time in his life, he prayed.

About five or six miles north of Richmond, a faint noise that sounded like thunder drew Luke's attention. An azure sky extended from east to west and the noise slowly grew louder. But it wasn't an approaching storm. Luke stood on the north side on an elevated area from which he could look out from behind a clump of bushes that prevented him from being seen. The metallic rattle of cavalry swords portended a huge force of mounted soldiers approaching from the direction of a ridge on his right. As the cavalry broached the ridge, he saw the tips of a wide line of cavalry flags and banners. The thunderous din grew as thousands and thousands of mounted soldiers came into sight, headed to the southeast. The shear number of horses made the ground shake, and Luke could feel the enormity of what was in front of him. The uniforms were blue. The horses were in a coordinated fast trot. However, when the center of the line reached the top of the rise, swords were drawn and an unheard command was issued. With precision, each horse broke into a full gallop and the huge force charged at some unseen target on Luke's left. The thunderous roar grew louder overwhelming Luke's senses as he watched from his position less than a half mile away.

To his left, small puffs of smoke rose from small-bore cannon fire from hidden positions. He could barely hear them over the roar of the Union advance. More puffs of smoke and cannonballs hit several horses, causing them to pitch over directly in the path of the advancing federals. Some horseman were able to swerve to miss the downed horses and soldiers, while others were able to jump over. However many collided and went down, causing a massive pile-up of flesh, both horse and human. Then, a huge number of Rebel infantry counter-attacked from Luke's left, and above all the din came distinctive Rebel yells sounding like thousands of banshees.

Even though Luke was a safe distance away from the clash, he instinctively lowered himself behind the bushes, still maintaining his view. He thought a Confederate force as big as he was seeing could only Stuart's cavalry, and even though his support of the South in the war might have been wavering, he was rooting hard for his old commander. In his mind, he wondered if the battle in front of him might turn out to be the largest cavalry battle ever fought.

The day wore on and the battle ranged from side to side until the Union cavalry mounted a concerted counterattack on the Rebel left. From seemingly out of nowhere, a thousand riders charged, led by a hatless officer with long blond hair. The fighting was intense with both sides yielding ground in turn, but the Confederate line started to give to the overwhelming numerical superiority of the Northern forces. As the Confederate line came close to breaking, Luke, still hidden behind wood sorrel bushes, saw the officer he had been looking for.

Jeb Stuart rode directly into the fray, with his sword held high for all to see. Distinguished by his rakish hat and long plume and the brim turned up on the side, and mounted on a large bay with a long black mane. As the men rallied behind him, Luke was heartened at the sight of his old commander. He remembered Stuart's kind but mischievous smile when they first met, only days before Luke was shot. Stuart had smiled broadly at Luke after seeing how well he could handle a horse and had asked him to be one of his couriers: a coveted position. It was a highlight in his life. Then two days later, while carrying out Stuart's orders, he was severely wounded. The wound that ultimately led to his amputation. If Stuart had asked him to jump into a burning fire, he probably would have.

Stuart's men rallied behind him and the Union advance stalled. Vigorous hand-to-hand fighting ensued. Stuart went down and disappeared in the melee. His men fought viciously, holding the new attack at bay, but then the Confederates began to disengage. In a well-organized retreat they slipped off to the southeast.

Luke, mesmerized by the unceasing action, stayed hidden as the battle wound down. He had lost all sense of time, but when Stuart went down, he felt he had to do something. He didn't know what, but he wanted to offer medical help his old friend. He called him his friend and was not sure he deserved such distinction, but Stuart had had such an impact on his life he chose to consider him a friend. The Union command, while they had clearly won this battle, seemed to be confused at to what to do next. The road to Richmond was open, however, and they gradually peeled off to the north possibly thinking they were not strong enough to prevail against Richmond's defenses.

Luke walked behind the Confederate entrenchments that were now filled with dead and wounded soldiers. He heard the familiar sound of moans and cries for help he had heard so many times before. Again, the losing Rebel army had retreated without any thought for the wounded and dead. He stepped over the bodies and wanted to help those still living, but he desperately wanted to find his fallen friend.

The skirmishing was still going on when Luke spotted a man sitting against a tree. He was not wearing his hat, but he wore a long dark beard that Luke recognized immediately. He was surrounded by some of his staff, one wore a white coat, and appeared to be a doctor. As Luke approached the fallen general, he was heartened to see a horse brought up, and Stuart was able to mount the horse with some assistance. Then Luke saw that the General had a gut wound, and his hope faded quickly. The horse was led to the rear of the battlefield, with the doctor and a few others like Luke following closely waiting for an opportunity to help. The general admonished his attendants in a weak voice, telling them to direct their attention to the battle.

Two Confederate soldiers walked passed Luke. One was helping the other, who had a portion of his right foot shot off. The wound had been field dressed and Luke asked where they were headed. "Away from this hell hole," the unwounded soldier said, as he stopped to catch his breath.

"Any idea who was leading the Union attack?" Luke asked.

"Sheridan. He's been attacking Stuart every chance he gets." The soldier seemed to know Stuart was wounded. "Looks like he finally got him," he said as he continued to the rear.

An ambulance wagon was finally brought up and the general carefully ensconced onto a bunk inside. When the doctor stepped up to get in, Luke quickly approached and said, "Doctor, I'm a medic and I know the general. Could I assist?"

The doctor looked Luke over up and down and said, "Yes, I could use some help." Luke scrambled aboard and the ambulance began its journey toward Richmond.

Chapter 25

The ambulance picked its way south through the fringes of the battlefield, avoiding the wounded and the dead. Stuart was lucid, but his face was contorted with pain. The disorganized ranks of Stuart's retreating men were visible through the rear opening of the ambulance. The sound of sporadic small arms fire blended in with the roar of belching cannon and both sides were in disarray. However, as the wagon drove toward the rear lines, the men in gray seemed to be moving in the same direction. Seeing his men giving ground, in a faltering voice Stuart yelled, "Go back, go back, and do your duty as I have done mine and our country will be safe." His volume faded as he added, "I'd rather die than be whipped." His men didn't hear his voice and probably didn't even know he was in the ambulance.

The ambulance, which was no more than a wagon covered with canvas, with several cots inside, gave Luke an uncanny feeling. As he looked out through the rear opening, he had a view of a defeated army...dead men, dead horses, men leaving the battlefield with their heads down. They passed a horse that had been hit by a cannon ball and a rear leg had been shot off. A cavalryman, evidently the horse's rider, held up a gun to the poor animal's head. He was crying and when he pulled the trigger, the gun did not fire. He reached into his bullet pouch and had no more cartridges. In frustration, he unsheathed his saber and held it over his horse's neck. When he raised the blade to strike a mortal blow, the horse looked at him with panicked eyes, and the man hesitated and was unable deliver the blow. Luke looked on and knew exactly how the soldier felt, because he had had the same experience with his horse, Bonnie.

The ambulance had stopped because of a passing brigade of artillery. Luke jumped off the wagon, grabbed a dead soldier's revolver and shot the horse dead. The owner slowly lowered his saber and sat on the ground overcome with grief. Giving the gun to the cavalryman, Luke got back in the ambulance as it started to move again. Inside the wagon, everybody's attention had been riveted on Stuart and nobody noticed what Luke had done.

The doctor tried to calm the general. "You've been seriously wounded," he said. "Please try to remain calm. We're taking you back to Richmond."

Luke sat behind the doctor, where Stuart couldn't see him clearly. As the general scanned the faces of those in front of him, he put his hand on the doctor pushing him slightly to one side to see the young man behind him. Stuart's eyes showed recognition when he saw Luke's face, but his attention was quickly averted when they went over a bump in the road that caused him to wince in pain.

Luke had asked the doctor if he needed help on an impulse, never believing the answer would be yes. The irony struck him. The general who had ordered him on a mission that resulted in a near fatal wound requiring his own amputation was lying in front of him...with a probably fatal wound himself.

The doctor urged the general to close his eyes and rest. He explained that a bullet had entered his left side, tore through his stomach and exited in the back and that he thought the bullet had missed his spine, which was good news. It was about the only good news the doctor could have told him because everybody in the ambulance knew the wounds were fatal.

"What can I do?" Luke whispered to the doctor. "Can we stitch him up to stop the bleeding?"

"The bleeding has been stopped with his bandages. To move him to stitch up the exit wound would only worsen things," the doctor replied. "We can only keep him quiet."

Luke's mind was reeling. He poured some water from a canteen into a cup and gave it to the doctor to give to the general.

Several slow hours later they pulled up in front of a house on Grace Street in Richmond. Luke recognized the area as being close to Madame

Lew's. He thought of Cuff and how she had hung on to him when the punt pitched on the river. A sad emptiness engulfed him.

Another doctor, who Luke was later to learn was Doctor Brewer and the owner of the house, met them and supervised the movement of the general into a large bedroom on the first floor. Many people, including a minister, gathered around the large four-poster bed. The room had wooden floors covered with oriental carpets. The walls were papered with a floral design that was perfectly matched by the drapes on the two windows that looked out into the back yard. A dressing mirror and a butler's dressing chair between the two windows still had the owner's coat wrapped across the back. Four chairs around a small coffee table at the foot of the bed provided seating for some of the visitors.

Luke looked on from the back of the room. He had the feeling with all the very important people around, he had no right to be where he was, but he wanted to stay out of an allegiance to his old commander. As the others engaged in small talk, Luke wondered what his father would think if he could see him. While his father had never taken a firm side in the war that he knew of, he had always been a fan of bold decisive people like Stuart and Mosby. He recalled a scene from his childhood. His father was trying to clear a field of rocks so he could plow and plant it the next spring. One particular rock seemed immovable. He dug around it and hitched his horse to pull it out which proved unsuccessful. With a rare demonstration of frustration, he slammed his shovel to the ground, looked up to the heavens and screamed, "Lord, if you're up there, why have you chained me to this god-forsaken place." Luke always thought his father wanted to be some-where else other than the farm. He wanted to be more than just a common farmer. Maybe he would approve of his son, now that he was mingling with such important people.

The general was moving in and out of delirium and Luke slipped out of the bedroom and went into the kitchen, where the odor of bread made him realize he was hungry. Food, brought by friends and acquaintances, filled a table and Luke helped himself to several small sandwiches. His hunger satisfied, he left the house and walked to Fort Stuart Hospital, just a short distance away, where he found a mattress on which he could catch some sleep

The next morning Luke decided to check on General Stuart's condition before he searched for James Hanger's new factory. He was surprised to see that Grace Street was already lined with parked buggies, and when he approached the front door, he was challenged by a guard who would not let him in. He walked around to the back of the Brewer house and found the back door unguarded and walked in. Several women were preparing food in the kitchen for the many visitors. One of them recognized Luke from the day before. He asked of the general and the woman shook her head saying that it was not good. She asked Luke to help distribute the food to the guests, and he gladly accepted thinking it would give him something to do and, something to eat.

A sense of excitement prevailed as the morning wore on, and Luke learned that Jefferson Davis himself was coming to visit his old friend, Jeb Stuart. After Luke briefly looked in on Stuart, who was dozing, he stayed in the kitchen, continuing to help. The general continued to deteriorate, and death was eminent. Everybody was hoping he would last until his wife arrived, but nobody knew when that would be.

The ladies assigned Luke the job of slicing loaves of bread and ladling bowls of soup. The soup was ham and bean, with the ham hock still in the large pan. As he was walking from one table to another, a tall, slim man entered the back door. He wore a starched collar shirt, tie and waistcoat and his demeanor was grave.

"Forgive me for coming in the back door," he said as he handed his hat to one of the ladies. "Sometimes, the crowds are overwhelming."

"Why, yes, Mr. President, we understand completely," she said, bowing slightly.

When Luke realized who it was, he saluted and in the process, he dropped the ladle on the floor spilling its contents in all directions, some landing on the president's pant leg. The president looked down at his dark pants and the creamy soup that had splashed on them. Luke leaned over to pick up the ladle and as he stood up their eyes meant. The president could see Luke's red face and his embarrassment. "It's nothing, soldier," he said and started to walk into the next room. As he did, he noticed Luke's artificial leg and stopped. "You're not the soldier by the name of Luke…last name I can't remember…who Jim Hanger was telling me about, are you?"

"Why yes, sir, I am," Luke responded his face still feeling red.

"Carry on, soldier," he said and as he left added, "Hanger said some good things about you." The president walked into the next room.

Luke stood with his mouth open…the President of the Confederacy himself had spoken to him. He seemed so calm, Luke thought. Then he had to spill soup on him. He felt like he wanted to crawl under the table.

That evening he walked back to the hospital where he had stayed the night before. He was over the embarrassing moment with Jefferson Davis, and even felt a certain amount of pride when he thought about Davis's compliment. But, down deep, he did not feel good about himself.

Luke figured Stuart's impending death would only hasten the end of the war. His plan had always been to find Carol when the war was over. That was before Cuff. But, in a way he wanted to see Carol more than before. If she still cared for him, she was the only one. He feared the rejection he might receive. He wondered how she would reject him. Would she pretend to accept him and his prosthesis or would she just slam the door in his face. He imagined the disappointment in her eyes when she looked down at his leg.

His mind wandered to Posey. He had left her at the camp back in Gordonsville, with a promise that he would return. He remembered her sad pleading eyes and her seeming total trust in him. The memory of the little girl haunted him.

Luke woke the next morning with a hangover from laudanum. The bottle he had scavenged from one of the hospital rooms lay under his bed. In the lobby of the hospital, several doctors and nurses were discussing the death of Stuart. Luke was relieved the general would not have to suffer any more. He thought back to the first time they met. It was just before the Battle of Gettysburg. Stuart was on a big raid around the Union lines, completely cut off from Lee. Luke had traveled all the way from Chase Prison in Ohio where he had escaped, to southeastern Pennsylvania. In the freight wagon he arrived in was a huge load of contraband Sharp's rifles that Stuart desperately wanted. Later, when Stuart saw how well Luke could handle a horse, he asked him to be a courier. It was a high point in his life. Then two days after that Luke was severely wounded while carrying out Stuart's orders…it seemed like he was recalling a different life at a different time. He looked down at his prosthesis and cursed his luck. He walked down the hallway of the hospital looking for another laudanum bottle.

Chapter 26

He opened his eyes and saw a dim light shining through the window. His head ached, and he wondered whether it was early morning or early evening. He got up and staggered down the hallway to a toilet. A passing orderly wished him a good morning. Luke drank thirstily from a sink using his cupped hands. He splashed water on his face and looked at his reflection in the small mirror in front of him.

He didn't like what he saw. He hadn't shaved in several days. His hair looked disheveled and ratty. His skin was pallid and ashy. His uniform, having slept in it, was rumpled and tousled. He walked back to his cot, looked at the empty bottle on the floor, sat down and buried his head in his hands. He had slept for nearly fifteen hours. He remembered how much better he felt with his first swallow of the laudanum the night before. He thought if it was better after one then it would be even better after two… after three, he lost track.

The new Hanger factory was an unmarked brick building several hundred feet from Castle Thunder. Strangely, a prison guard stood outside the door, but did not say anything when knocked at the door. While Luke waited, he looked back at the prison and hoped he wouldn't see Captain Alexander again. Then he remembered Cuff and the way they worked together to over-power the guard. When he became convinced she was a woman. Her soft touch. Now she was dead and he still felt the pain of losing her.

When Jim Hanger opened the door, his face broke out into a broad smile, "I was hoping you'd come," he said, "we are in desperate need of help here."

He enthusiastically showed Luke the small workshop. Twenty workers sat at crude workstations making parts for artificial legs. Each worker wore prison-striped clothing, and eyed him suspiciously as Jim showed Luke what each worker was doing. The workers were working from penciled measurements that Jim had made for each amputee. Some of the prisoners worked enthusiastically, while others seemed just to go through the motions of assembling the legs with no enthusiasm.

When Jim saw what Luke saw, he knew what he was thinking. "I know, I know," Jim said, "but my only source of labor is the prison. Our production isn't near what it should be, but a war is going on and good workers aren't available."

Luke's mind flashed back to the time when his father had asked him to dig around a large stump in a field that his dad was clearing to plant the following year. The stump was an old butternut tree that his father had felled the summer before. He wanted Luke to loosen the trunk up enough to be pulled out using a draft horse. Luke hated the job, it was tedious and backbreaking. The soil was hard and full of rocks and after several hours, his progress was nearly nil. He rested sitting on the stump and realized that when he finished, his father would never say 'good job' or give him a compliment. If the job was perfect, he would find something wrong with it. The work wouldn't have been so awful if Luke had even a little incentive.

"Those sketches," Luke said, "are they made from the measurements you took from each patient?"

"Yes," Jim said.

"So each worker never sees the amputee for whom he is working?"

"No. Why do you ask?"

"Incentive. Maybe if each worker knew the person and could talk to him about how he lost his leg and see how much the poor man's life could be improved, he would have an incentive."

Jim was silent for a few moments. "I'm not allowed to take the prisoners out of this building. Captain Alexander would never give permission."

Luke quickly added. "No need. Bring the patient here."

Two things Luke really liked about Jim Hanger. He never took much time to make up his mind, and he was open to new ideas. "Hell, yes, son. Let's try it. That is if you'll coordinate it all."

They shook hands on it, and Jim showed Luke some sketches of how he planned to make improvements in his designs. He had adopted Luke's rubber casing design around the thigh and he had also improved the hinging apparatus at the knee and ankle. Luke spent the rest of the day getting familiar with Hangar's operations.

The next day, Jim asked if he would accompany him to the Chimborazo Hospital on the southwest side of Richmond. The steel rimmed wheels of Jim's buggy rode hard over the pebble stone streets. The rim on one of the wheels had worn through. Jim told Luke that new rims were not available because all metal production was for the war effort.

The hospital was a huge complex of buildings on top of a rise originally intended to be army barracks, and converted in 1861. As the buggy approached, Jim said, "These first three buildings are ours. They're full of soldiers who need our legs." In front of the buildings, dozens of soldiers were gathered around, and all were missing a leg. When Luke sat agog at the sight of so many amputees, Jim said, "Wait'll you see inside."

As Luke and Jim approached, the men started to crowd around them, anxious to be chosen for a new prosthesis. As Jim explained to Luke, even though the Hanger Company had not been paid for the prostheses invoiced to the government so far, as Davis had promised, Jim continued to supply custom fitted new artificial legs to wounded soldiers at no cost to the amputees.

Inside, the former barracks room contained nearly one hundred cots, all filled with soldiers who had lost arms or legs. More were on the floor between the beds, all in various stages of healing from their amputations. Luke wondered if he had worked on any of them. Whenever he saw a legless man's exposed stump, his eyes automatically went to the flap, evaluating the quality of the work. The room had four windows down each side that were open to let fresh air in, however, the room still had a foul oder and Luke guessed that many were infected and some had gangrene. No nurses were present and the patients' sheets needed changing.

"How do you choose?" Luke whispered. "Each one of these soldiers deserves one."

"It's complicated," Jim replied. "First, we look for breaks between the knee and hip. Then, there must be enough bone for us to attach the prosthesis at least six inches below the hip. Of course, we have to consider the soldier's age and health. We'd have only a limited number we can help, so we tend to choose young healthy soldiers. I'm glad I didn't come here when I was wounded, I would have been passed by." Jim managed to crack a smile on his normally stoic face.

Luke did not laugh. He was overwhelmed by the sheer number of men who were going through the very thing he had. He thought about the long time it had taken him to make his new leg and how many men were back at the factory. "How long does it take for one of the prisoners back at the factory to make one," he asked.

"'Bout a week, and I know what you're thinking. We can only make so many and the one's we do make, we want them to be perfect for the poor bastards we select. Let's pick twenty. We won't have capacity for them until next week, but at least we can make the selections."

Jim and Luke examined the patients waiting outside, as they were further along in the healing process. Jim asked them to form a line and he made a brief entry in his workbook for each one.

Several days later Luke accompanied a wagon sent to pick up the twenty they had chosen, and escort them to the factory. He introduced each of them to the prisoner inmate who was to make their prosthesis. Luke and Jim could see a relationship being built between each amputee and prisoner. The prisoners seemed to give special care in taking measurements while sharing war experiences with their amputees.

"I'm impressed," Jim whispered to Luke, "I've never seen so much enthusiasm amongst the prisoners." Jim patted him on the back. "I never would have guessed this, Luke. I thought some of these prisoners were beyond redemption...you've proven me wrong."

"Something good in everybody," Luke said.

By the end of the day, all the measurements had been taken and the amputees were returned to the hospital. The prisoners were marched back across the street to Thunder Castle, leaving Luke and Jim alone. They sat around a potbelly stove in a corner. Jim leaned back in his chair, lit his pipe, and with a thoughtful look as if he was about to say something important said, "Luke, you're just the man I needed. My other factory needs me and I would like to spend more time there. You're the ideal person to manage our little operation here. I'll pay you well and I think you're up to the challenge. What do you say?"

Luke looked dumbfounded.

Jim stood. "Come with me."

They walked to the back of the building and opened a door in the corner. Inside a room was a desk, a single bed, several chairs and a small cot. Another door led to a washroom. "This is where I stay when in Richmond," Jim said. "If you take the job and you can stay here. No charge."

Luke was sure he wanted the job before he was offered the living quarters, but as he scanned the room, his eyes locked on the cot. He stuck out his hand and said, "Mr. Hanger, you're a generous man and I accept." As they shook hands, Luke added, "I need a couple days before I can start, is that okay with you?"

"This is Thursday. How about you start on Monday? If you need a buggy for whatever you have in mind, you can use mine," Jim said.

Chapter 27

Luke left that night in Jim's buggy. The moon shone through broken clouds, and provided enough light to follow the road leaving Richmond. He could see the horse's breath in the cool night air. Passing through the outer defensive positions, he told the sentries he would be back on Sunday night. He wanted to give himself as much time as possible to get to Gordonsville and back before Monday morning, when he planned to start his new job with Hanger. He had to find Posey and bring her back with him as he had promised.

He set the horse at a trot thinking that, including a few rests, he would arrive at Gordonsville sometime in the morning. The road was easy to follow, and after several hours they passed Montpelier, and he stayed on Mountain Road heading northwest. Thinking the horse needed a rest, Luke pulled up to a tavern in the small village of Cuckoo. He went inside, sat at the bar, and ordered a cup of chicory coffee. The bartender said little. He was a huge man with a long black beard and a scar on the side of his face. His nose was bent slightly. His shirtsleeves were rolled up and exposed his muscular forearms. This man was somebody to reckon with.

Two men sat in the corner and eyed Luke as he took a seat. They had discolored gray uniforms on and a nearly empty bottle of whiskey sat on the table with an ashtray full of butts. When Luke was served the chicory, one of the men approached. "You from these parts?" The soldier asked.

"Tennessee," Luke replied tersely.

"I see you lost your leg," the man said. He stood about five feet away and Luke knew he had been drinking…probably too much.

"Gettysburg."

"How?"

"Horse shot out from under me."

The man took another step forward. "You don't talk much, do ya?"

"Not much to talk about."

"Maybe you don't want to talk to us. Is that it?"

Luke took a swallow from his cup. He wished he hadn't come in.

"Hey Joe, this man doesn't want to talk to us…maybe he feels he's too good." The man took another step forward and stood less than three feet away, staring at Luke. Luke could see the man's eyes were bloodshot. His face and clothes were soiled. He was unarmed, but Luke was sure his partner had a pistol in the holster he wore. "I don't think I'm better than anybody," Luke said finishing his chicory and getting off the stool.

"You sure look like you think you're better." The man took another step forward forcing Luke to step back.

Luke felt his face turn red. The men were obviously deserters, because regular soldiers would not be in a tavern at night, as very few leaves were being granted. From the corner of his eye he noticed a near empty bottle on the bar. "You know, now that I think about it, I am better than you. Wanna know why? Because you two pieces of shit are the scumbags of our army. You're deserters! Common chicken shit deserters. You're damn right I'm better than you."

Just as the man reached back to hit Luke with his fist, Luke grabbed the whiskey bottle and smashed him on the side of his head. The bottle broke and cut a large gash in the man's cheek as he fell to the floor. Blood spilled onto the floor and mixing with the whiskey, mud and grime, forming a rivulet that disappeared through a crack in the floorboards. He lay inert on the floor. When the man's partner reached for his gun, Luke froze. Then a loud explosion came from behind the bar. The man's head shot back as a bullet blew through his forehead spattering blood on the wall behind him.

"God damned deserters," the bartender said, "this country is crawling with them. Get 'em every night. I'd shoot 'em all if I could. All I need is a good reason." He set his Henry .44 caliber on the bar making a reassuring clunk. The muzzle was still smoking.

Luke was a bit wobbly. He shook his head to clear his thoughts, the gun blast was still echoing in his ears. "Thanks," he said, "don't know what they were going to do, but I'm sure it wasn't good."

The first man was starting to come to. "Best you get going. I'll handle this," the bartender said grabbing his Henry again, and chambered the next round.

Luke walked toward the door. "Name's Luke Pettigrew. Thanks again. I owe ya." He looked at the sign above the bar that said *Cuckoo Tavern* and smiled. "Guess you're the only one not '*cuckoo*' around here...remember, I owe ya." The door shut as he left. He took several deep breaths, got on the buggy and pulled out onto the road again. Shortly, he heard the Henry discharge again.

––––––––––––

When Luke pulled into Gordonsville, the early morning light was just enough to see that the little town was nearly vacant. He drove the buggy down to the little creek where the pox camp was located looking for Posey. As he had neared the village, he was hoping against hope that Posey was okay, but he had a gnawing feeling she wasn't. He jumped off the buggy and as he approached the campsite, he saw only Isaac and Jupiter sitting by a small fire. The pox victims had all gone leaving the area strewn with paper, rags, trash and detritus.

"Where's Posey?" Luke yelled as he drew nearer. The two men looked up and when they saw who it was, Isaac exclaimed, "Masta Luke! We thought you were gone."

"Where's Posey?" Luke said again in a pressing, urgent tone.

"She's gone, Masta Luke. We haven't seen her for the past few days."

"Where's she go?"

"Lord sakes, Masta Luke, we don't know. Each day after you left, she's sit right here by the fire and wait for you, but then, she just left," Isaac said.

"She just left? She just left? Is that all you can say?" Luke said.

The two men could see the emotion on Luke's face. "Sorry, Masta Luke, that's all we know," said Jupiter. Both men were standing, looking sympathetic, and wanting to help.

Luke stared at the two men saying nothing for several moments. He pictured Posey waiting for him by the fire. Then he turned and ran in a fast hobble, back toward the village. "Take care of the horse," he yelled, "I have to find her."

He'd gone no more than a hundred yards when he realized he was out of breath and had to stop. He was standing near the center of the village panting and saw a familiar woman approaching. He stared at her trying to remember her face. She recognized him, "Doctor Luke," she said with a smile extending her hand. When she saw Luke couldn't place her, she added, "I worked with you in your pox ward."

Then he remembered. "Why, yes of course." He shook her hand, out of breath.

The nurse could see Luke's agitation and being winded. "Anything wrong?"

"I'm looking for a little black girl. About ten. Large brown eyes. Wears a gunny sack. Have you seen her?"

"No. Most of the darkies went north looking for Grant's army after Lee retreated."

"Anybody at the hospital? Could she have gone there?" Luke asked.

"You might try there. Doctor John is still there. He's treating some of the patients needing more time to heal."

Luke thanked her and walked as fast as he could to the hospital. He cursed himself for having left her. He should have known better. He hobbled up the front stairs and sure enough, John was making his rounds on the first floor.

John saw Luke approach. "Luke, I was wondering. How you been? Where did you go? We missed you," he said.

"You seen Posey? She's missing. I have to find her."

John saw the emotion in Luke's face. He smiled. "Try downstairs. The dormitory."

Luke went back down the stairs so fast he fell on the last step. His momentum was faster than his artificial leg could handle. He fell forward skinning his knee and his prosthesis came off. Luke lay on the ground, reached for his leg and strapped it on. He walked into the dormitory where he had previously slept. His heart skipped a beat when he looked at his cot and saw Posey sleeping with a blanket covering her body and only her head showing. She opened her eyes and saw Luke, but she closed them again. Luke nudged her. "Posey, it's me," he said.

Posey's eyes opened again. She realized she wasn't dreaming and it was really Luke. "Masta Luke!

Luke put his arms around the little girl. "I'm back," he said, "and I missed you."

Her body convulsed in his arms as she sobbed.

Luke had never felt so needed in his life. He held her away. "Let me look at you." Tears were flowing down her cheeks like rain on a window-pane. "I see you've grown since the last time I saw you."

She smiled and wiped her eyes.

"I have some good news…," he said softly.

Her eyes asked the question.

"We're going back to Richmond. You can stay with me."

They left for Richmond the next morning. Luke wanted to be sure the horse had plenty of time to rest for the long return journey. Posey was hap-py. They had walked together to the old camp together to say good-byes to Isaac, Maude and Jupiter. The morning was bright and breezy, but high clouds from the west portended a change in the weather. Luke was glad the buggy had a landau top, which he opened to give them some protection should it rain. Posey hung on to his arm as they left Gordonsville. He looked down at her he realized she was totally reliant on him. She needed him and to a certain degree he needed her.

He thought of Carol again. How would she react to Posey? He hoped she approve because he had no idea what he would do if she wasn't. He decided he would write another letter to her when they got back to Richmond.

Shortly before noon, they reached the Cuckoo Tavern and Luke decided to give the horse a rest even though the wind was picking up and the sky was getting dark. They entered the tavern and took seats at a table in the corner. The cook came over immediately and told Luke that they did not serve darkies. Luke started to raise his voice in objection when the big bartender from the previous visit came to their table.

"What's the problem here," he said to the waiter.

The waiter pointed at Posey. "We don't serve blacks," she said simply.

"I'll handle this," he said to the waiter and she left leaving just the three of them.

The bartender, who Luke now surmised was the owner, told Luke to have a seat. "I took care of the second deserter the other night," he said.

"I heard the shot."

"The two of them had some money in their pockets." He plucked two twenty dollar gold pieces on the table. "I'm splitting it with you."

"Thank you, but I'm the one who owes you," Luke said.

"You owe me nothing. I probably would have shot those two anyway. Now tell me. I have some beef stew made in the back...want some? On the house?"

Luke winked at Posey. When her eyes lit up, he said, "we'll take two bowls, thank you."

After they had finished and were about to walk out the door, the bartender whispered to Luke. "You'd better get used to some poor treatment if you're going to keep that little girl around. I'm originally from Ohio and I harbor no ill feelings with blacks, but it sure ain't that way around here. Just sayin'"

"Got the message, and thanks for everything." Luke offered him his hand. By the way, what's your name?"

"Herb Woolford. You're welcome here anytime...both of you.

Chapter 28

Six weeks later, Luke and Posey sat on the edge of Luke's bed in their room behind the workshop as he read aloud from *Uncle Tom's Cabin*. Reading before going to sleep had become a ritual, and Posey especially looked forward to it. Luke did not know how much of what he read she understood and he wasn't sure he understood it all himself, but he looked forward to it, also.

He had found the book under the cot in their room left by Jim Hanger. Even though the book had been banned in the South as abolitionist propaganda, it was widely read.

After returning to Richmond from Gordonsville that storm-filled night nearly six weeks before, their lives had settled into a normal pattern. Work at the factory progressed, and Luke was able to add ten more 'craftsman', as he preferred to call them, to the line that now totaled thirty. They were able to produce thirty highly individualized prostheses per week and while Luke wanted many more, he was pleased with the results, as was Jim Hanger.

Luke hired a Negro woman to bring prepared meals each day. In addition, she stayed with Posey during the day and was teaching her how to sew. Her name was Jenny and her husband was a servant for First Lady, Varina Davis. Jenny quickly grew fond of Posey and she revealed that she had still-born daughter in 1863.

Luke read from the book: "You would think no harm in a child's caressing a large dog, even if he was black; but a creature that can think, and reason, and feel, and is immortal, you shudder at; confess it, cousin. I know the feeling among some of you northerners well enough. Not that there is a particle of virtue in our not having it; but custom with us does what Christianity ought to do,—obliterates the feeling of personal prejudice. I have often noticed, in my travels north, how much stronger this was with you than with us. You loathe them as you would a snake or a toad, yet you are indignant at their wrongs. You would not have them abused; but you don't want to have anything to do with them yourselves. You would send them to Africa, out of your sight and smell, and then send a missionary or two to do up all the self-denial of elevating them compendiously. Isn't that it?" "Well, cousin," said Miss Ophelia, thoughtfully, "there may be some truth in this."

"What do you think the author is trying to say?" Luke asked Posey.

Posey thought for a moment. "I'm not sure. Maybe he's sayin' what Mr. Woolford, the bartender, was sayin' when we left the tavern."

Luke closed the book and gazed at Posey who returned his stare. After a moment, he said that it was time to go to bed. Posey frowned, but she crawled under her covers. Luke tucked her in kissing her goodnight.

Luke lay in his bed unable to sleep. He marveled at the way her mind worked and readily acknowledged that he was probably learning more from Posey than she was from him.

He reached under his cot for his bottle of laudanum. He pulled out the cork, and as he was about to take a swig, he felt Posey's hand touch his arm in the darkness. "Masta Luke," she said, "don't be like my father."

Luke couldn't see her in the darkness and he was glad she could not see the shame on his face. He heard her little feet return to her bed. Luke re-corked the bottle and set it under his bed. He wasn't exactly sure what she meant, because she never talked about her father, but down deep he knew.

The next day, Thursday, Jenny arrived early, and Luke, having slept very little, headed for Chimborazo Hospital to select patients to be fitted with prostheses the following week. Winter was fast approaching. Luke wore a heavy sweater under his white smock. He always preferred to wear white at the hospital, because the patients paid more attention to those wearing white smocks.

When he pulled in front of the three buildings at the hospital that housed the amputees, the ones who were ambulatory, albeit using crutches, were waiting outside. They all wanted to be selected and knew he would come on Thursday. Today, the number waiting looked like more than one hundred. A hospital liveryman hurried over to attend to Luke's horse.

He took his pencil and paper, got off the buggy and walked toward the group. He saw a big man standing off to the side of the building who looked familiar. The big man started walking toward him, but Luke was distracted by the pleading voices of the men in front of him who were jostling trying to form a line, each one attempting to be in the front. The big man burst through the group and ran right at the now dumbfounded Luke. It was Clyde McCallister.

"You son of a bitch," he snarled through bared teeth, and just as Luke recognized who he was, the big man slugged him, square on the side of his head, spinning Luke around. He fell to the ground, wrenching his leg, and searing pain swept through him. His head hit the grassless ground with a thud. With Luke's leg twisted underneath him, the big man sat on top of Luke swinging his fists at his head. Luke could see rage in his face.

Over his pain, Luke tried to protect himself with his hands. "Clyde, what the hell?" was all he could manage to say.

Clyde punched him in the face. "You low-down scum. I invite you into my house. Feed you. Nurse you. Treat you like a hero. And what in the god damned hell do you do in return?" Clyde punched him again. "You impregnate my wife's poor defenseless sister. Is that how you show your gratitude?" Clyde punched again. "She had your kid for god's sake."

His voice was thick and full of anger. He drew his huge fist back to hit Luke as if he wanted to kill him, but all of a sudden Clyde's head was pummeled by crutches from the amputees standing nearby all at the same time. The amputees were protecting the one person who was providing them with hope for a normal life, and they were not about to stand idly by. Their canes and crutches made sickening sounds of wood smashing flesh. The barrage continued and Clyde slumped, rolling off Luke, who was fighting to remain conscious. He felt somebody pulling on his shoulders and a searing pain up his leg that caused him to black out.

When Luke opened his eyes he smelled ammonia and saw a nurse kneeling beside him passing a cotton wad under his nose. Luke instinctively put his hands up to guard his face from being beaten. "Easy, fellow, nobody's going to hit you anymore. Just lie still for a few moments."

Luke looked side to side. He was not alone. Several dozen soldiers were standing around, staring at him, all leaning on their crutches. He remembered the beating at the same time he felt the pain in his knee. He winced and looked down at his good leg that appeared to be in a normal position. Then the image of Clyde straddling him and hitting him savagely...the rain of crutches turning Clyde's head to a pulp.

"Guess I owe you men," he said as his hand went to his bruised face.

"Your knee has been stretched beyond its normal limits," the nurse said, "you will have to stay off of it for a few days."

Luke sat up. His head was throbbing as he looked around.

"If you're looking for the big man...I think you called him 'Clyde', he was taken to jail. We have laws in this country against brutal beatings, especially if the victim is defenseless and maimed."

The mention of Clyde brought back the realization of what he had said while he was beating him. "She had your kid...", he said. *Kid?* He asked himself. He must have been mistaken...but then, how could he make such a mistake. He remembered the stormy night when Joanie's sister came into his room. He saw her unclothed body on top of him lit up by the flashes of lightning. Her insistence. Then his reluctant submission. "Oh my god! What have I done," he whispered to himself. The realization of what Clyde had accused him of and that it might well be true hit him harder than Clyde's fist smacking his head. "Oh my god," he said again, "Oh my god." If the child was his, he was responsible for her. He would have to keep her. What would Carol think? How could he explain—that he was seduced by a crazy woman? And Posey. If he had to take care of a small child, how could he work? What would Jim say?

Luke woke the next morning to little hands pulling up his blanket. It was Posey trying to make sure he was warm. When she saw he was awake she hugged him. She didn't say a word, she just held him tight with her head on his chest. He felt her curly hair tickle his nose and he put his arms around her. He was in his own bed and the sun shone through the only window casting a bright light into the room that portended a new day. A basin lay next to the bed filled with clear water and some rags folded nearby. Next to the basin was his prosthesis.

"How long have I been here?" Luke asked.

"They brought you last night."

"They…?"

"The ambulance. They said they had no rooms, so they came here." She lifted her head up and looked at Luke.

"Your eyes are bloodshot," Luke said, "have you slept?"

"Not much."

Luke realized that his left eye vision was obstructed and assumed it was swollen because of the pummeling he had taken. His hand went to his eye. "How bad do I look?" he asked.

"You look a little like my mama after my papa come home drunk." She reached down, wet a rag in the basin and proceeded to expertly dab the oozing bruises on his face.

"That's what you meant last night, isn't it?" Luke asked.

"Yes," Posey said. She continued to bathe his bruises on his face.

"Where's Jenny?" Luke asked.

"She was here early, dropped off some food, but had to go home to take care of her husband."

"Her husband?"

"She says he has some kind of head sickness, but she said she will return in the morning."

Luke didn't want to think about Clyde, but he forced himself. If he were in fact the father of the child as Clyde had said, what would he do? He tried to remember Clyde's exact words, but he had to admit it was highly likely the child was his. Should he ignore it and pretend it didn't happen? Maybe the child could be adopted by another family. He wondered if it was a boy or girl...what did he or she look like? What about the mother? Then he thought back to the nurse who woke him up with the ammonia. Something she said...she referred to him as being 'defenseless and maimed'. He never considered himself 'maimed'...only one leg with the other one in question. Then there was Posey. And now a child...surely Carol would have nothing to do with him. He looked around the room for a laudanum bottle, but knew there was none.

Chapter 29

The buggy came to a stop in front of Castle Thunder. Returning from a visit to the hospital, Luke normally would have gone straight to the factory, just down the street. However, he had learned that Clyde was being kept at Captain Alexander's notorious prison. Clyde would have cooled down over the past few weeks, and Luke thought he could reason with him. He asked to see the Captain and was told he was out but would be back shortly. The office was not as neat and orderly as Luke had remembered. A portrait of Jefferson Davis hung askew on the wall. A waste can in the corner was full and overflowing. A chair opposite where he was sitting had a tear with the stuffing exposed. Luke smiled when he saw a painting of Captain Alexander, himself, hanging perfectly straight. *The man's ego was surviving better than the Confederacy*, he mused.

Luke's knee had healed, but his face still showed the bruising from the beating. Meantime, the work at the factory continued at a brisk pace and the demand for prostheses kept increasing, even though fighting had diminished, due to the winter's onset. Word was spreading about the Hanger prostheses, and soldiers were coming to Richmond from all over the South in hopes of being fitted with a new leg.

Grant and Lee were dug in for the winter in two parallel opposing lines twenty-five miles long, south of Richmond near Petersburg. Lee had protected Richmond so far, but the Confederate resources were stretched to the breaking point, and the spring offensive that was bound to come would force Lee to decide whether to protect his army or Richmond, he could not do both. As a result, those civilians who could see what was coming were starting to pack up and leave the city.

From a distance, Luke heard the clacking of a large horse and recognized it immediately. It was Captain Alexander and the sound of steel on cobblestone made by the huge hooves of his black steed echoed with an eerie medieval peel. The door opened and the first to enter was Nero, Alexander's near two hundred pound black dog. Although the dog appeared ferocious, he trotted over to Luke and started to lick his hand wagging his tail as if they were the best of friends.

Luke stood as the captain entered. He was dressed in all black again, this time with a large black cape hanging from his shoulders. He eyed his visitor. "Ha. I wonder what the other man looks like," he said, "or did you come out the losing end?" He walked up to Luke and stood in front of him with his hands on his hips.

"You have the other man here in your prison," Luke responded.

"Justice is being served then." He went into his office and beckoned Luke to follow. He took off his cape and sat at his desk. "Is it true our friend is dead?"

"Yes, she drowned in the Po River trying to cross at night."

"So you were right about that."

"Yep, then I sorta gave up the spying game. Don't think I'm cut out for it. Guess I'm not a good liar."

"Ha…the spying game…won't do much good anymore. Seems like we're nearing the end."

The captain paused for a moment as if he were reflecting on what could have been. Then he said, "You're across the street? Hear your doing some good…my boys helping any?"

"Yes, sir, some are turning into fine craftsmen."

"So, what brings you here? Surely not to see my handsome face?"

"I want to see the man who did this," Luke said pointing to his bruises. "Then I want you to set him free."

"Huh? After what he did to you, you want him to go free?"

"It's a long story," Luke said.

"Who is he?"

"Big man named Clyde McCallister."

The captain wrote the name down and said, "We are over crowded here and usually we don't keep common criminals…why don't you talk to him and then give me a yes or no." He instructed a guard to take Luke to the appropriate cell.

As the guard took Luke up to Clyde's cell on the second floor, Luke was reminded of his own time in Castle Thunder. The hallway floorboards creaking, the smell of a mixture of urine and whitewash, the quietness and the cell doors with small, iron barred windows.

The guard opened Clyde's cell door. Luke walked in and held up his hand to the guard indicating he needed five minutes. He heard the key turn in the door lock behind him. Clyde sat on his cot and looked at Luke. Clyde's head was bandaged leaving only his face uncovered. His nose was black and his eyes open but swollen. Without getting up, he scoffed, "you got some nerve coming in here, what do you want?"

"I want you to know the truth," Luke said taking a couple steps closer.

"The truth is you took advantage of my wife's sister. She's wasn't right which makes it worse."

"Will you listen to what I have to say?"

Clyde spat on the floor and shrugged. A mouse ran along the base of the wall and disappeared through a crack.

"There was a storm one night. I woke up and wanted to close the window, but someone was in my bed. I didn't know who it was at the time, but it was Joanie's sister who I didn't even know lived in your house. She came to me…thought I was 'Paul'. When I insisted I wasn't Paul and my name was Luke, she wouldn't hear it…kept calling me 'Paul'. She was naked. I thought I was dreaming or something."

Clyde had straightened when Luke mentioned 'Paul'. "She called you 'Paul'?"

"Yep…over and over…she wouldn't listen to me."

The mouse came out of the same crack and scurried into another hole.

"Then you screwed her."

"I'm not proud of that."

"On top of that, she died giving birth to the little girl," Clyde said through clenched teeth.

"She died? Joanie's sister is dead?"

"All because of you…and to think, I saved your ass. Hauled you out of that hell hole of a farm house and saved your sorry ass. Believe this, I would never do it again. I'd leave you there to bleed to death. A nice slow death… and even that would be too good for you." Clyde shook his head in disgust.

Luke let Clyde vent his anger…he felt he had no excuse and even if he did, Clyde was in no frame of mind to accept it. The sound of prisoners playing a game outside drifted into the cell. Then, came a distant scream that lasted for a few seconds. Luke guessed torture might be going on in Alexander's prison.

"Are you sure the child is mine?"

"Who else's would it be? Santa Claus? She hadn't left the house in three years." Not a sound could be heard. "Get the hell out of here. I'm tired of looking at your sorry face," Clyde said.

"I'm going," Luke said walking toward the door, "but when this war is over, I'm coming back…I'm coming to get my kid."

Clyde just stared at Luke with hatred in his eyes.

Luke tapped on the door, which was opened by the guard, and walked out. He descended the steps, stuck his head into the captain's office, gave him an affirming thumbs up, and left. After he had hoisted himself up on the buggy, he thought for a moment. What had he just committed to? In a way, he was relieved…he had taken responsibility for his own actions… but then the consequences of so doing weighed on him. He felt like a heavy weight had been placed on his shoulders. He had not even a faint idea what he would do with the child, but his inner sense of right and wrong told him if the child was his, then he would have to be responsible. He thought about what his father would think and he was sure that his father would not have approved of him having intercourse with Joanie's sister, but he had always taught him to do the responsible thing. Then the news that she was dead…dead because he had yielded in a moment of weakness. He harbored no emotional feelings toward Janie, but she obviously was a very troubled woman who deserved better than to die giving birth to his child.

Then he remembered what Clyde had said,…Joanie sister died giving birth…to a little girl. A little girl…

The following Thursday Luke made his weekly trip to Chimborazo Hospital. When he pulled up in front of the three buildings that housed amputees, three other buggies were parked plus a large carriage pulled by two beautiful matched bays. The soldiers who were normally outside waiting for him to select the next thirty men for prostheses were all crowded around the door to one of the buildings. As Luke approached the door, Jefferson Davis stepped out of the building. He had been visiting the war wounded and when he saw Luke, a glint of recognition showed in his eye.

"…It's 'Luke', right?" He said extending his hand, "Jim Hanger's right hand man?"

"Yes, sir," Luke managed to say. Davis resumed his walk toward his carriage. "Keep up the good work, son."

Luke watched as Davis boarded his carriage.

After Luke had picked thirty more candidates for prostheses, he rode back to the factory. The white oak trees that lined many of Richmond's streets had dropped their leaves and the wind had blown them into golden piles along the edges and as the buggies wheels went over them, the noise changed from a cobblestone clack to a muffled sound. It was December and winter was upon them. Luke felt chilled as he pulled up in front of the factory. He saw Jim's buggy parked in front of the building. He hadn't seen Jim in almost a month and Luke anxiously went in.

Jim was warming his hands around the potbelly stove in the corner. He beckoned Luke over. "Your troubled face says something's wrong," Luke said.

"My friend, Jeff Davis, is letting me down," Jim said. "He refuses to pay for our raw materials."

"I thought the government agreed to pay," Luke said.

"Well, you have been so successful that the cost has escalated beyond what I can handle. When I explained this to Davis, he agreed to pay for all our raw material costs. He did for a while, but now he says this war is draining the treasury dry, and he cannot pay. I think we're going to have to close this factory."

Luke was shocked. "Maybe the soldiers could pay?" It was more of a question than a statement. Luke reeled trying to think of a solution.

"Most of our soldiers don't have a dime," Jim answered. "The government pays them sporadically, but they pay in Confederate dollars and you know what they are worth these days. As a matter of fact, if the South loses this war, the Confederate dollar will become worthless. All the money our poor soldiers may have will become worthless.

"But, how does the government pay for the things they need for Lee's army?" Luke asked.

"Gold, if they have to…from the treasury."

"So, the treasury has gold, they just don't want to spend it on amputees," Luke said. "Who makes the decisions?"

"Probably Judah Benjamin, the Secretary of State."

Luke tried to search for a good answer, then said, "How long do we have? I mean, how long until we have to close down?"

"Two, maybe three weeks.

Luke had an idea. But would it work?

Chapter 30

Luke arrived at the Chimborazo Hospital early the next Thursday. In spite of the cold temperature that morning, the amputees were already jockeying for their places in line. But Luke was looking for someone special that morning, somebody with a sympathetic story who would help him convince Judah Benjamin to release payment for more new legs. In addition to using the usual criteria, he asked the soldiers about their families back home.

The next morning Luke pulled up the buggy in front of the Confederate Office Building on Main Street. He was relieved to see the main entrance was on the ground level so that climbing stairs would not be necessary. He stepped down and assisted his passenger out of the buggy. He was Sergeant Josh Edwards. Edwards lost his leg during the Battle of Peach Tree Creek near Atlanta while trying to thwart a counter-attack from General Hooker's right flank. When Luke had questioned him about his family back in Tennessee, he seemed to be perfect for the mission Luke had in mind.

The sergeant was not yet proficient with the use of crutches and when they found out they had to go to the second floor, he had trouble shifting his weight as he stepped up, even with Luke helping him. They finally arrived at a door that said *Office of the Secretary of State, the Honorable Judah Benjamin*. The door was open and they walked in.

"Luke Pettigrew and Sergeant Josh Edwards to see Mr. Benjamin," Luke announced trying to sound authoritative.

"Without looking up, the clerk behind the counter said, "Sorry, you need an appointment."

"Is he in?" Luke asked.

"Yes, but he's much too busy to see you," she said dismissively.

"How do you know the reason I want to see him?"

"You want money, don't you," she looked impatient.

"We'll wait," Luke said as he walked toward two chairs in a corner.

"You're welcome to wait, but you're wasting your time," she said. "You kind of people are always looking for a handout."

Luke bit his lip and the two of them sat.

An hour later, the clerk stood, put her pencils in a drawer and left. Luke assumed she was going to lunch. After waiting a while longer, he got up and walked to Mr. Benjamin's office door and listened. When he heard nothing, he slowly inched the door open. When the door made an unexpected creak, Benjamin's head jerked up from the papers he was reading and stared blankly at Luke. He was a short, stocky man with a sparse black beard. His round face and brown eyes had a hint of kindness that encouraged Luke.

"Excuse me, sir, do you have a moment?" Luke asked. Benjamin put his papers down, took a deep breath and leaned back in his chair, not saying a word, and Luke took that as a sign to come in. He motioned to Josh and together they walked in and stood in front of Benjamin's desk. Benjamin said nothing as he watched Josh struggle with his crutches.

"I'm Luke Pettigrew and I work with Jim Hanger making new legs for our soldiers who have lost theirs fighting for our cause. This is Sergeant Josh Edwards who recently lost his leg at the Battle of Peach Tree Creek. Sir, this man is from Knoxville, Tennessee. He and his family live on a small farm. His father was a lieutenant under General Bragg and was killed two years ago. His mother had to move in with Josh's wife and four young children, three boys and a girl. Josh's soldiering days are over. He will go home and try to put food on the table for his family. But look at him, Mr. Benjamin, how can he possibly provide for his family when he can't walk? He must rely on his already overworked wife. And what more can she do? She is already so busy managing the household and the children. Is she to now also plow the fields? Reap the crops? I think not." Luke waited to let what he had just said sink in. Raindrops splattered against the two windows behind Benjamin's desk.

"Now, look at me," Luke continued, "I have an artificial leg, similar to the ones we make at the Hanger Factory. This prosthesis allows me to continue my life in a productive manner. Our government has been funding the production of these limbs, but has recently stopped those funds and Mr. Hanger cannot afford to continue. Josh is a typical amputee. Mr. Benjamin, there are thousands like him…thousands. Our government cannot ignore these soldiers who have given so much. We need your help." Luke stopped and waited. Josh looked over at Luke with admiration on his face.

"Are you finished?" Benjamin finally said. Luke nodded. Benjamin sat upright in his chair and stared blankly at the papers in front of him as if he were contemplating about his decision. He had a pencil in his hand and tapped it on his desk. He looked up at Josh, and then returned his gaze to his desk with a pondering look. Luke said nothing. Benjamin leaned back in his chair again and folded his arms across his chest. Luke took about ten steps to the side then returned hoping Benjamin would see how well his leg worked.

"I got your message…it's Luke isn't it? Let me dwell on it," Benjamin said dismissing them with a wave of his hand.

Luke shivered in his bed that night after he had tucked Posey in with an extra blanket. Fall was losing its grip as outside temperatures fell and the room where they stayed had little heat. The chimney flue from a potbelly stove in the factory that passed over their room was the only source of warmth.

Sleep did not come quickly as Luke's mind returned, over and over again, to his meeting with Benjamin. If he was unwilling to help pay for further production of artificial limbs, they would have to close down the factory. He wondered what he would do if the factory closed. Maybe he would go home…if only he had had a home. He had Posey and the thought of her total dependence on him scared him. How would he provide a home for her? His thoughts drifted to Clyde, and the child he had fathered. How on earth could he manage? He cursed himself for yielding that stormy night back in Tennessee. Then, there was Carol. An image came to mind. Standing on her front porch, Posey on one side, a baby in his arms, and an artificial leg, and asking her to marry him. She would look first at the child, and then at Posey...her eyes would drift down to his leg. Why would she do anything else but laugh in his face and slam the door?

After several hours and still unable to sleep, he decided to write her another letter. He would tell her of his plight. He lit a candle and with pen and paper tried to compose his woeful story, but he couldn't find the right words. He kept imagining Carol crumpling up the letter and throwing it away in disgust. He decided that he couldn't tell her everything at once and after many tries decided on the following:

> *Dearest Carol, It's well after midnight here in Richmond and I cannot sleep because my thoughts always come back to you. I wonder when we will meet again and I can hold you close. This war will surely be over by spring and I will find my way to you. I am working at a factory that makes artificial legs for our many poor soldiers who desperately need them. These limbs are made of wood and allow the amputee to walk and resume an almost normal life. If you wonder why I am working here, it's because I, myself, lost my leg during the Battle of Gettysburg. I was ashamed to tell you fearing your rejection. Please forgive me. Look for me soon, dearest, I will find my way to you. Luke*

The next day Luke performed his normal duties in the factory. He made sure each worker had the correct materials and also checked their work. He was amazed how much better their products were after his men had met the soldier for whom each prosthesis was being made. Most of the prisoners anticipated being set free as soon as the war was over, and many were considering continuing the work.

Jim Hanger arrived around mid-morning. The weight of having to shut the factory down because of lack of funds continued to wear on him. When Luke described his meeting with Benjamin, Hanger laughed out loud at Luke's boldness. Jim wanted Luke to repeat every word.

As they were talking, a soldier came to the front door. The visitor wore a dark blue uniform with gold epaulets on the jacket shoulders. He struggled to carry an unfinished wooden box that had *CSA* stenciled on all six sides.

"Mr. James Hanger, please," the man said and when Jim presented himself, he said, "you have to sign for this."

Jim signed and looked at Luke in wonderment as the soldier left. There was no note with the box and they both noted it was very heavy and nailed shut. With a hammer and screwdriver they wedged the top off. Inside was a bag full of gold double eagles. Jim reached into the bag, grabbed a handful and Luke reveled to the resonant sound of heavy coins clinking back into the bag. "I don't know exactly what you said to Benjamin," Jim said, "but you really got to him." Jim hefted the bag. "Must be one hundred coins in here…enough to keep us going for at least a couple of months."

"There's good in most people," Luke said. "Now, we can keep on going. This is great news."

That evening when it was time for Luke to read to Posey, she sat on his bed next to him. It was her favorite time of the day and, as Luke read, she would stare up at him instead of the book. Her little fingers would move across his face almost like she was exploring. When he stopped to ask her a question about what he had just read, he always got a prompt answer proving she was listening intently. Near the end of a Chapter he read the following: *It was the first time ever that George had sat down on equal terms at any white man's table; and he sat down, at first, with some constraint, and awkwardness; but they all exhaled and went off like fog, in the genial morning rays of this simple overflowing kindness.*

Luke put the book away signaling it was the end of schooling for the night. He sat upright on the bed, folded his arms and said, "and what do you think that last paragraph meant, young lady?"

Without hesitation, she said, "It's the way I feel every time I'm with you."

Chapter 31

The gold Double Eagles were almost depleted by the end of March, 1865, four months later, and the factory was nearing another halt for lack of supplies.

Lee's army had been in their winter mode, of simply surviving the cold weather, so the fighting had diminished substantially. Both sides were hunkered down in two parallel lines facing the other. The lines extended south from Richmond, nearly thirty miles and severely challenged Lee as his adversary had nearly twice as many men.

It was Saturday, April 2nd, and Luke had promised to take Posey for a walk downtown. Luke wanted to buy her the doll that he had promised himself he would make her, but had not found the time. Saturdays were special for them because Hanger insisted on the workers having both Saturday and Sundays off, and Luke got to spend most of the day with her.

The newly leaved Linden trees glimmered in the morning sun as they left the factory. Warm air portended a beautiful day. "Maybe we could go on a picnic," Luke suggested as they walked toward Grace Street. As they approached the commercial district, they saw hundreds of people nervously milling in the streets. Luke expected the worse when he saw some of the residents carrying boxes and belongings and packing them onto buggies and wagons.

Luke grabbed the arm of a man passing by. "What's going on?"

"Lee's left is under attack," he said, hoisting a heavy box onto a cramped wagon. "A place called Five Forks". The man was out of breath and he stopped to rest a moment. "If Lee's flank gets turned, he might have to vacate Petersburg."

"So, what's the big rush?" Luke asked.

"If Lee vacates Petersburg, then he'll pull Longstreet away from the defense of Richmond and we will be open for attack."

Luke felt Posey's hand tighten her grip. He knew the day would come when Richmond would fall, and his plan was to stay in the factory and wait until the Union army arrived. He was confident they would see the value in the production of limbs for their own army and therefore spare it of any damage. At least that's what he hoped.

They walked on and the street became more crowded. Horses neighed, whips cracked as wagons and buggies vied for right of way. They approached a street corner, and Luke asked a bystander, "do you know if President Davis and his cabinet have left?"

The bystander started to walk across the street and then yelled back, "they're still here, but they're packing. Mrs. Davis left on a train last night."

Luke hoisted Posey up on his shoulders, and they walked toward the state house. Immediately across the state house was St. Paul's Episcopal Church. As he strode past, they could hear the congregation singing *What a Friend We Have in Jesus*. Even though Luke was not a churchgoer, he enjoyed hearing hymns, and they stopped in front to listen. The words wafted out.

Jesus knows our every weakness.

Take it to the Lord in prayer…

Luke looked down at Posey, the young daughter of enslaved parents who had been taken against their will and subjected to the iron will of others. He wondered how Jesus, if he knew their every weakness, could condone slavery.

A soldier on horseback rode up and dismounted directly in front of the church near where they were standing. He hurriedly entered the church and after a few moments, the singing tapered off and stopped. Just as the singing stopped, the erect figure of Jefferson Davis walked out the front door, followed by two soldiers in crisp, clean uniforms. His face showed no emotion as he bowed to several strollers on the street, climbed onto his carriage, and left, his horses at a brisk trot.

Luke approached the two soldiers. "Is Richmond in trouble?" Luke asked. A carriage passed by with the horses at a gallop. A buggy went by going the other way, also in a hurry. "Davis is leaving by train tonight," one whispered.

Luke immediately turned around and headed back the way they had come. Posey, who sensed something was amiss asked, "Masa Luke, what will happen? Are we still going on a picnic?"

"Posey, big trouble is coming. Do you remember when we talked about the Union Army coming into Richmond?"

"Yeah. I remember."

"It's gonna happen very soon. Maybe tomorrow or even sooner. I'm taking you back to our room. You'll be safe there."

"But, we'll be together…won't we?" Posey asked.

"Yes, Posey. But I have an important errand to run. Don't you worry, I won't be gone long."

After they arrived back at their room, Luke told Posey he would be back as soon as possible.

When he was about to leave, Posey, sensing something unforeseen, ran to him and clasped her little arms around his legs. She looked up at him. Tears were welling in her pleading eyes. "Don't go," she said.

He put his hand softly on her head. He always marveled at her hair. Her dense curls were kitten soft and would tickle his nose when he held her tight. Posey had given him a purpose. A sense of responsibility. If he had to kill a man to protect her, he would do it.

Luke lifted her up to eye level. He wiped away a tear flowing down her cheek and smiled. "I'll be back in a couple hours. I have to try one last time to get funding to continue our work," he told her. "Don't you worry. I'd take you with me but the crowd out there could become a mob." He slowly put her back down and walked out afraid to look back because he feared he would lose his will. He felt guilty about leaving her but he felt this would be the last chance for him to attempt to get more funding for the factory.

When he reached the corner at Ninth Street, his fears were confirmed. In front of the Central Hotel, which had become the offices of the Confederate auditors, were several huge fires. The smoke rose straight up into the still air and formed a huge cloud that shaded the area from the sun creating a dark ominous shadow. Men ran back and forth into the hotel as they heaped more and more boxes of documents on the flames. To all the people of Richmond, upon seeing the crystal clear evidence of the government vacating their city, the reaction just added to the furor and chaos in the streets.

Luke thought his only hope was to appeal again to Judah Benjamin, the man who had helped him before. If the Confederacy was about to fall, the money in the treasury could be put to good use and help those who had suffered so much. He stood on a bench across the street from the hotel and searched for Benjamin, hoping he would be making his way to his offices. After a half an hour of frantically trying to catch a glimpse, he saw a short man approaching the hotel. His face looked familiar and his identity was confirmed when Luke saw the man with a large cigar in his mouth twirling a gold-headed cane. It was the same cane he had seen in Benjamin's office. Luke stepped down from the bench and tried to make his way through the throngs of people to the other side of the street. About half way across, he saw Benjamin climb the steps to the building. He yelled his name but his voice was lost in the din of the near-panicked crowd.

The front door was guarded by three young men dressed in uniforms he had never seen before. The uniforms were gray with horizontal rows of gold braiding across the chest. When Luke tried to enter one of the boys boldly stepped in front of him. "Unauthorized personnel are not permitted to enter," he said. His voice had an intonation of teenager who was unsure of himself.

"I have urgent business with Mr. Benjamin," Luke said, "let me pass."

The boy brought his rifle up to a horizontal position to block Luke from entering. "I have my orders, sir, nobody enters without authorization."

Luke looked at the rifle and smiled. It was an old muzzle loading flint-lock that looked like it had been used in the Revolutionary War. The young man's hat was oversize and fell down over his ears. His eyes were almost pleading as if he hoped Luke would obey his command and not embarrass him in front of his fellow soldiers.

"Okay, okay," Luke said, "I'll wait outside to talk to him when he leaves."

The young soldier's chest expanded as he looked back at the other soldiers with a sense of accomplishment.

Around mid-afternoon, a wagon loaded with ten more young men, in uniforms similar to the first two, came to a stop in front of the building. The wagon was pulled by a team of horses that Luke thought would be more suitable for pulling a plow. The soldiers immediately went inside the building.

"May I ask what company you are with?" Luke asked the guard.

"We're all from the Naval Academy," he replied proudly, "we've been summoned to protect the Confederate treasury."

"Naval Academy?" Luke said.

"Yes. The Confederate Naval Academy. We train aboard the *CSS Patrick Henry*. Stephen Mallory assigned us our duties, sir."

Luke recognized Mallory's name as being the Confederate Secretary of the Navy. "What's the wagon for?" Luke asked.

"We're supposed to take the treasure to the train. President Davis is leaving for Danville."

Luke stood aghast. The soldiers at the church were right, but he could not believe Davis would take the money belonging to the Confederacy and simply leave. Surely, if Richmond fell, the war would be over. Why would he leave? Either he was keeping the money for himself or he had some grandiose idea he could continue the war. But how could he ever expect to win?

A few moments later, the young soldiers started to carry out bags of coin and loading them onto the wagon. They worked continuously for almost an hour going back and forth with what Luke assumed was either gold or silver. Then came stacks and stacks of paper Confederate currency that was nearly worthless. Then came stacks of United States currency and finally gold bullion bars. When the soldiers finished, a driver drove the wagon away. The horses struggled to pull the heavy burden and the wagon creaked as it slowly moved off toward the train station.

Luke continued to wait by the front door. Finally, Benjamin came out having just lit a fresh cigar. "Mr. Benjamin…," was all Luke could utter before Benjamin with a wave of the hand dismissed him.

"I cannot help you again," he said, "Davis prohibited any unauthorized cash disbursals and I'm sorry…"

"But, what about all of those soldiers with no legs…" Luke asked. "What will Davis do with all that gold?"

"I can't talk about that," Benjamin said walking toward the street, "I only know he thinks the South has not been defeated."

After Benjamin's buggy pulled away, Luke decided he had to give it one last try. He headed for the train station. The closer he got to the station, the more crowded it became. Many Richmond citizens wanted to leave on the Danville train scheduled to depart at 8:00 PM. Luke speculated that those associated with the government in particular were the ones trying to get out. The line outside the ticket office extended several hundred feet, however Luke counted only six passenger cars behind the antiquated locomotive that was to take them to Danville. One car was guarded by the young soldiers from the Naval Academy, and Luke assumed the treasure was aboard that car. The car in front of that was only half full, but guarded by regular soldiers. That would be Davis's presidential car Luke reasoned.

The number of seats on the train quickly sold out and the people waiting became loud and restless as darkness approached. When the train engineer pulled the lanyard and blew the whistle, some citizens climbed on top of the rail cars. But the train did not leave. Soon thereafter, the carriage carrying Jefferson Davis arrived and the crowd started to cheer for their leader. Slowly he worked through the throng of people, boarded the presidential car and was joined by several members of his cabinet.

As the train started to very slowly chug away, Luke became desperate. He thought if he could get a glimpse of Davis and Davis saw him, he might, as a last minute gesture of good will toward his faithful soldiers, grant him the funding to continue. He put his foot up on the step to the back door of the presidential car, but his foot slipped and, losing his grip fell, rolling down an incline and coming to rest in deep grass. The fall had taken the air out of his lungs and he gasped. The train continued to pick up speed. Luke felt water seeping into his clothing. Unable to see in the darkness he realized he was lying in a small stream. When he tried to get up and gain his footing, he noticed his prosthesis had fallen off. He felt around in the shallow water, but could not find it. He started to panic. He had become so used to his prosthesis that the thought of not having it made him feel completely helpless. Sitting up, he yelled for help, but his pleas were drowned in the pandemonium that broke out when all the people left milling at the station came to the conclusion that the departure of their government meant that there was no law and order.

When nobody responded to his pleas, Luke crawled out of the water using his hands to pull him through the grass, then leaned his back against a tree, all the time searching for his prosthesis. His shoulder ached from the fall, but he was sure that there was no further damage. He tried to crawl back up the incline back to the railroad tracks, but with only his hands couldn't find anything to grab onto to pull himself up. He realized how dependent he was on his prosthesis. In the darkness he felt alone and totally powerless. He yelled for help again. His voice was lost in the din of the uproar going on at the station, only one hundred feet away.

He managed to pull and squirm his way to a nearby tree, where he was able to stand on his good leg. He looked around for a tree limb or large stick he could use for a crutch, but couldn't see anything in the deep grass. He yelled again for help, but nobody heard him. The area was so dark, he couldn't see his hand in front of him. He thought of Carol and was certain that if she saw him now, with his one leg, unable to help himself, she would certainly be revolted. The factory would no longer have money to continue. He had failed. He imagined what his father would think if he could see him now. Surely his helplessness would only exaggerate his father's lack of confidence in him. He brought himself back to the present.

A breeze blew against his wet clothing combined with the cooling night temperature and he started to shiver. He smelled smoke, like a burning campfire. The crowd at the station had moved toward the city center, but he could still hear the distant shouts of rioting people. Feeling even more alone than before he shouted for help again. Hearing no response, he yelled again, "Anybody! Help me! I'm over here in the trees!"

Then, a faint voice. "Masa Luke? Masa Luke?"

Luke knew immediately it was Posey. "Posey, over here in the trees by the railroad track." She quickly found him. Saying nothing they hugged each other for a long time, each realizing how dependent they were on each other. Able to move easily, she located Luke's prosthesis and together they went back to the factory avoiding the riots and the fires occurring downtown.

Later, as Luke tucked Posey into her bed, Luke asked, "I told you to stay here when I left. But you left anyway. Why?"

"I jus' knew, Masa Luke. I jus' knew. My mama always was able to know when something was wrong...guess I got it from her."

"But, how did you know where to look?"

"The soldiers at the church. They said Masta Davis was going to leave by train."

Luke kissed her on the forehead and blew out the candle.

Chapter 32

The next morning Luke was awakened by a familiar tickle on his nose, Posey's hair. When Posey felt scared she would sometimes crawl in bed with Luke. He did not object. He got up and donned his old uniform that had dried from the night before. They had watched through the factory window before going to bed, seeing the glow of huge fires over the top of the buildings that separated the factory from downtown.

Later in the morning they began to hear a soft chant of people outside. The noise did not sound threatening and they walked outside to see what was happening. Hundreds of Negroes were in the street outside that led from the docks of the James River directly downtown. Luke could clearly make out what they were saying.

"Masa Lincoln. Masa Lincoln," the crowd continued to chant. Upon leaving the factory, Luke hauled Posey up on his shoulders and they approached. The chant was almost a song as they continued to chant, "Masa Lincoln, Masa Lincoln."

Luke could feel Posey tense. A stovepipe hat could be seen bobbing slowly along the street. Luke moved closer hoping to see what Posey could see. The crowd parted as a tall man continued through, then came together again. As he neared Luke, a black man knelt down in front of the visitor as if to kiss his feet. The man, who by now everybody knew it was Abe Lincoln, shook his finger at the prostrate black man and said, "Kneel only to your God and thank him for the liberty you will hereafter enjoy."

Lincoln continued his walk to the center of Richmond, and the number of Negroes increased. Luke marveled that anyone would risk their life in that loving way. Luke knew that behind each shaded window a sharp-shooter could appear at any time, but Lincoln was willing to risk it. "All slaves are now former slaves," Luke said. "All Negroes are free."

They walked back toward the factory. Luke thought about fighting for the South, and after seeing the hordes of former slaves and the adoration they had for the man who effectively freed them, he wondered why he made that decision four years ago. His mind went back to that fateful day when his father told him he had to leave. Luke standing in front of the post office with the two banners, one for the North and the other for the South. Perhaps he picked the South because his father preferred the North. He knew then that he'd made a mistake.

All the prison doors were open when they passed it, and the entire building was empty. No soldiers and no prisoners. They walked on, and when they got to the factory, a group of the prisoners were standing around the front door. They were some of the regular prisoners who had worked there for the past months, and all were skilled at making prostheses. All of them wanted to stay in Richmond and continue to work. Luke was proud that they wanted to stay but he told them he had no money to pay. He asked each to write down their names and addresses and he would contact them if and when he found the money to continue.

Luke sat on his bed after they returned to their room, and tried to think what he to do. After a while he made a decision and started to pack his things. When Posey saw Luke do this, she began to put her few things into her old burlap bag dress that she had kept under her bed. Luke stopped what he was doing. Posey was sobbing. He went over, picked her up, and sat on the bed with her on his knee. Tears streamed down her face and started to trickle off her chin. She wouldn't look at him and only stared at the floor with her feet going back and forth. Luke used his hand to turn her face toward him, but she resisted looking with her eyes. Slowing, however, her eyes met his and she saw he was crying also.

"I will never, ever, leave you," Luke said, "never." He held her close until she stopped sobbing. "We will leave in the morning," Luke said, "together." He felt her little arms tighten around him.

While she was finishing her packing, she asked, "Where're we going?"

"We're going to Tennessee."

"Why?"

Luke waited to answer, as if to select the right words. "To see your little sister."

Posey thought about what Luke had said. "I have a sister?"

"Yes, Posey, she's around two years old now."

"Is she your daughter?" Posey asked.

"Yes."

"And she's my sister?"

"Yes, she is."

She repacked her things again. "Does that make me your daughter, too?" Posey asked slowly.

"Yes, Posey, it does…that is if you want to be."

Posey was silent for several moments. She continued packing and re-packing her few things. "Yes, I want to be," she softly answered.

───────────

Six days later, Luke and Posey crossed the James River and headed west, out of Richmond, on board Jim Hanger's buggy. Their departure had been delayed because of the heavy fighting west of Richmond, but with Lee's surrender at Appomattox the prior day, Luke felt safe to begin the journey. He estimated the trip to be over five hundred miles, and he hoped to arrive at McCallister's homestead in three to four weeks. He had no idea of the reception they would get. The buggy was loaded with the basics they would need on the journey: oats, blankets, some food, a tarp to stay dry, extra grease for the axles, a spare buggy wheel and a rifle that Jim always kept handy at the factory. He had left a long note to Jim detailing his plans and when he might return. He also left the list of prisoners who wanted to work when they had the money to continue the production of prostheses.

Luke planned to take a well-traveled road to Roanoke, and then join the Wilderness Road crossing the mountains through the Cumberland

Gap into Tennessee. A fair-weather wind from the west promised good weather as Posey sat next to Luke, both excited about the trip ahead. Luke set the horse at a slow trot and they made good time on a road that showed the sign of heavy usage by two opposing armies during the prior week.

Remnants of Lee's defeated army crowded the roadway. Soldiers milled in groups as if they didn't know what to do. Their uniforms were tattered, and the men were gaunt. None had weapons. All the soldiers were free to go home, but most lacked horses or other means of transportation, so they walked.

"If the war is over, will these soldiers go home?" Posey asked.

Luke thought of his own home. "Yes, they will if they still have one to go to."

"What will they eat?" Posey asked.

"Hopefully, some food will be provided by the Union army."

Luke had an uneasy feeling. Men would do anything if they were hungry enough. He eased the horse into a faster trot. They passed a wagon headed the opposite way loaded with wounded soldiers. From what Luke could see the wounds had been field dressed, but some needed more attention. He felt the urge to stop and help, but he knew their needs were far greater than anything he could provide. He looked over at Posey. Her safety was the most important thing he could think of.

After the next ten miles, the stragglers were fewer and more strung out. When they came to a small creek, Luke decided it was a good time to water and rest the horse. After letting the horse drink they parked under an old sycamore tree. They sat in the buggy eating some bread and corn meal.

"Is my little sister white?" Posey asked.

Luke smiled. "Well, I think she is."

"Is her mother going to be my new mother?" She asked.

Luke shook his head in amazement. "No, her mother died giving birth."

"So," she said slowly, "I have a sister, but no mother?"

"You ask too many questions," he said laughing. She scooted closer to him. He took the reins and set the horse at a trot again. Again, Luke thought about how, while she had definitely lost her parents and he was nearly certain he had, too, she seemed to have adjusted to her loss better than he had. But then, maybe she didn't talk about it.

Days later, they made their way through the Shenandoah Valley, where they saw the devastation wrought by the Union army the previous fall. Barns and granaries had been burned leaving only the charred skeletons of the structures standing like black ghosts of pillage and destruction. What fields that weren't scorched were unharvested. Cotton, wheat and oats lay fallow, while spots of voluntary growth in the burned fields created a stark contrast to the old and the new.

As sunset apprached, Luke saw a small group of blacks camping under a copse of loblolly pines by the side of the road. He steered the horse over. "Mind if we join you?" Luke asked.

"Sure, masa, but we have little to eat," one of the men said. There were six in the group, four men and two women.

Luke could see no threat from these people so he got off the buggy and lifted Posey down. "This is Posey and I'm Luke," he said as he reached into the wagon and fetched his rifle.

All six eyed the rifle as a threat and their eyes got big with fear. "I might be able to help with the food and this will come in handy," he said holding the gun up. He turned to Posey. "Please stay here, I'll be back in a half hour." He continued to look at her to see if his leaving was okay. She smiled and seemed at ease with the group. "We'll need a fire," he said to the men and he walked off through the pines.

Luke had seen an area as they had approached near a burned- out barn with fresh dirt turned over by a rooting animal. Luke reasoned the animal had to be a hog missed by the Federal troops the previous fall. With his rifle held in a horizontal ready position he softly treaded over the pine needled ground. Walking slowly, he exited the woods area and approached the old barn from the rear. When he was within about one hundred feet, he squatted down behind a rock pile hoping to see what had caused the uprooted soil.

He waited. He knew the animal would be extremely leery of humans, so he remained hidden. The sun had completely disappeared and with the oncoming darkness, Luke's hopes sank. Just as he was about to give up and go back to camp, he heard a soft noise to his right. The sound stopped, then started again. It was a grunting noise and Luke's heart beat raced. He stood to see into the shadow of remnants of the old barn structure and there it was: a boar pig. When Luke stood, the slight noise drew the attention of the hog, who stared at Luke and grunted. His head came up with roots and grass falling off his snout. Luke shouldered his rifle, aimed, and pulled the trigger. The bullet hit the hog between the eyes and it fell dead. Luke triumphantly approached his prey knowing the hog would be a welcome sight to Posey and the others.

The hog was still twitching, and as he knelt down to inspect the dead animal, he remembered the feeling of pride he had as a kid when he was able to shoot a squirrel that his mother would serve for dinner. Then he remembered his father always found something wrong with the squirrel. It was always something. *Should've shot him in the head not the chest. This one's too old and tough, must've fallen dead from old age.*

Luke was snapped out of his flashback by a scream coming from the direction of the camp. From the euphoria of a kill he went into a panic. He stood to reload his rifle. He tried to do it too fast and the cartridge fell from his fingers and he had to grope around on the ground. Finding it, he wiped the dirt off, loaded the gun and started running toward the camp. He took three steps and tripped over a unseen stump. He took a deep breath and realized how panicky he was becoming. Getting up, he walked as fast as he could to the camp. Maybe it was just a yell he tried to convince himself. Then he held another scream…a child's scream. It was Posey. Somebody had Posey. Luke's fear of somebody harming Posey turned to rage. He charged forward making the most speed he could with his artificial leg. When he reached the pine trees the needles on the ground softened his foot noise and he snuck up on the camp.

From the darkness of the woods, he could see the silhouette of the six Negroes outlined in dim sky. He did not see Posey. Then he heard the crack of a whip. "You god damned niggers think you're better than us already," a deep southern voice yelled, "I'll teach you." The man cracked the whip again and Luke heard one of the women scream. Then again and one of the men cried in pain.

Luke stepped out of the woods into the clearing. The Negroes were cowering against a large tree to Luke's right and the man with the whip in front of them. Luke had his rifle shouldered and aiming directly at the man. Luke's whole body quivered with rage. "Drop the whip," he yelled. "You crack that thing one more time and I'll splatter your face all over the next county."

The man turned in surprise but sneered and quickly drew back his whip as if to hit Luke. Luke could just see the end of his barrel and that the man was clear of the blacks, but there was enough light from the fire to see the man's face. His face was full of hatred. His eyes looked wild and his teeth showed through his sneer. Luke lined up and pulled the trigger. The shot hit the man's face, spewing blood all over one of the black men behind him.

Posey ran to Luke from behind the tree and hugged his leg and Luke ruffled her hair. He took several deep breaths and walked toward the dead man. Something caught his eye on the deceased man's chest…a silver star with the word: *Sheriff.*

Chapter 33

The four black men were scared and wanted to run. Luke told them they were freemen and not subject to the rules of slavery anymore. However, they believed that the hangman would find them if they didn't start running. They did not want to listen to Luke's assurance that the world had changed when Lee surrendered. Finally, he convinced the two men to carry the dead man back into the woods and bury him with his whip and pistol while the four women butchered the hog he had shot.

They all arrived back at the camp several hours later. The hog had been cut into quarters and they agreed the blacks would take most of it with them on their journey north. Luke was satisfied with the work they had done, but something was missing. Something was gnawing at him. Then, it came to him. "Where's the dead man's horse?" he asked.

One of the men looked around, scratched his head and said, "guess he ran away when he heard the shot."

Luke knew that the horse would return to his home stable, at which time a search for the sheriff would start. "We need to get out of here," he told the group, "I suggest you head straight north and stay off the roads," he told the six blacks. "Posey and I will leave as soon as we can harness the horse."

Immediately after Luke warned the freemen, they panicked and all six ran off into the woods leaving everything including the pork. Luke wrapped one shoulder of the pork in canvas and put it in the wagon. Then he harnessed the team and left with Posey. By mid-morning Luke and Posey had made good time and were five miles from Salem, Virginia.

Luke slowed the horse to a trot. From a rise in the road several hundred yards in front of them appeared a band of horsemen coming the opposite way. As seven men rode passed, Luke could hear the horses gulping air through their bridle bits. The men were armed, wore badges, and were towing a riderless horse. Luke stopped the buggy and watched the posse disappear around a curve.

"This could be trouble." Luke said to Posey.

"Why? We did nothing wrong."

"The man I shot was a sheriff."

"But he was using a whip on the freed men…"

Luke looked directly at Posey. "Just because the North won the war and all slaves are free does not mean the hate goes away."

"Because we are black?" Posey asked.

"Unfortunately, yes. Because you are black. But most white folks don't feel that way…just a few." He gave her a one armed hug. Posey smiled, and Luke set the horse off at a brisk trot. He guessed the dead man was the Sheriff of Salem, and he wanted to get as far west as he could by nightfall. However, by the time they reached the town, one of the wheels of the buggy started making a grinding noise, and Luke knew they would have to stop to pack grease into the wheel hub. He thought the fastest way to fix the wheel would be to take the buggy to the local livery, and after asking directions, found it near the center of the town.

When Luke drove up in front of the livery, a middle-aged man wearing a tattered Confederate campaign cap, walked out of the barn. "You need somethin'?" he asked as he leaned on the pitch fork he was carrying.

Luke's eyes went to the man's right leg. He had a peg leg sticking out from beneath his trousers that appeared to be new without much wear and tear. The man, when he saw where Luke was looking, said, "Battle of Hanging Rock, last year."

Luke stepped off the buggy and the man saw Luke's leg and his eyes got big. "And you?" he asked.

"Gettysburg. Got shot off my horse," Luke replied instantly feeling comfortable with the old veteran. Luke pointed to the rear wheel of the buggy. "We need to get this hub packed," he said.

"No problem," the man said, pull it inside and just take a couple hours."

Luke did as the man asked, then helped Posey down from the buggy. As the man began to block the wheel up off the ground, he asked, referring to Luke's artificial leg, "Where'd you get that?"

"Made it myself," Luke said then pulled up his pant leg.

"Made it yourself? I've seen some before but never like this." He looked at the ankle hinging mechanism. "Nice."

"We make 'em in Richmond," Luke said, "...or at least used to."

Luke put a wood block underneath the rear axle as the man levered it up. "Where you off to?" the man asked.

"Tennessee. Hope to be there in a couple weeks."

As the man worked on the wheel, Posey ambled outside. "Don't go far," Luke warned, and she smiled back at him.

A while later, Posey came running back into the barn. She had fear on her face. Her eyes were big and her voice had an urgency to it. "Those men are back," she said.

Luke and the man both looked up from their work, which was almost finished. "The posse?" Luke asked.

"The men said the sheriff is missing and they hung a bunch of niggers back up the road." Posey said, her voice quivering.

The man seemed to understand that Luke and Posey were somehow involved in whatever had happened. He let the wheel back to the ground. "Let me see what's going on. You stay here."

Posey and Luke waited in one of the livery stalls. Luke knew the posse would probably assume the sheriff was dead. The fact that they hung the six Negroes made him sick in the stomach. He realized there was no law in Salem and, if anything, prejudice and hatred were worse than before the war ended. If only he could get themselves safely out of town and across the mountains, things might be better in Tennessee.

Minutes later, the liveryman came back into the barn and found Luke and Posey huddled in the stall. "They're assuming the sheriff is dead," he told them. "And they also assume the blacks didn't do it. They hung 'em because they wouldn't talk." He watched Luke and Posey's faces for reaction.

"They found a butchered hog in a pine woods," he continued, "all the meat was lying on the ground except a front quarter. The blacks didn't have it nor did they have any weapons, so they're assuming somebody with a gun may have shot the sheriff and that person may have a large piece of pork."

Posey eyes nervously shifted to Luke. The man saw it. "When they mentioned the missing pork, I became pretty sure you are involved. I smelled it under your tarp in the buggy," he said.

Luke stood up. "He was whipping the Negroes with a bull whip. They had done nothing wrong. When I told him to stop, he tried to whip me... that was as far as it went."

"Listen, I know the sheriff is...was...a dirty rotten son of a bitch," he man said glancing at Posey because he had used profanity in front of a small child, "He deserved to get whatever he got. He used that whip freely on anybody he didn't like...If anybody protested, they would mysteriously come up missing." He looked over at the buggy. "You need to get rid of the evidence. If they catch you with it, you're probably both dead, and probably me too."

Luke took a pitchfork and started to muck a stall next to the one they had been hiding in. He pitched a pile of manure to one side of the stall, then took the tarp from the buggy, placed it in the hole and covered it. "That should take care of the smell," he said as the stench from the up-turned manure rose from the pile.

After discussing with the liveryman what to do next, they decided the only thing to do was quietly ride out of town. They further decided Posey should hide in the back of the buggy until they were a safe distance from town. Before they left, Luke shook the man's hand. "It's good to see there are a few good men left in this country. I'll be back in Richmond in a month or two," Luke said, "if you stop by the James Hanger factory down by the river, I will personally make you a new leg and foot."

Luke set the horse at a leisurely walk and left town heading west with the rise of the distant Appalachian Mountains clearly visible miles away. On the other side was the McCallister's, Maryville and Carol.

Chapter 34

Five days after leaving Salem, Luke and Posey still looked back. They knew the chances of being apprehended by a posse diminished with every mile but they still worried. The road had become rocky in places with steep climbs and descents, and Luke thought slow and steady was the safest way to get through the Cumberland Gap. The two dangers he was most worried about, besides being apprehended for the shooting, were broken buggy wheels or a tossed shoe on their horse. Either one would mean a long wait, which would give a posse a chance to catch up with them.

Luke thought back to the shooting. What if he'd known the man with the whip was the sheriff? Would he have shot him anyway? He remembered the look on the sheriff's face as he wielded his whip against the blacks…an angry, anguished look with a hint of satisfaction…like he was mad because he hated so much, but pleased to inflict the pain his whip was causing. He was pretty sure if he had it to do all over, he would do it again.

He wondered what his father would have done in similar circumstances. When he saw the man whipping the Negroes, would he have done the same thing? Maybe he shouldn't have shot the sheriff. Maybe he could have blunted the strike of his whip by holding his rifle up in front of him. But then what would he have done. The sheriff could have easily out maneuvered him. Then he would not have been able to protect Posey.

He glanced over at Posey who was busy scanning for a posse. It seemed to him that many times when he thought about Posey his mind wandered back to his father. Posey's parents were both taken by the pox and she was alone and would never have their love again. He remembered how alone he felt as a kid. While he was sure his mother loved him, she never told him so. He had never seen his parents hugging or demonstrating any affection toward each other. As a kid he would have done anything to gain his father's approval. He never remembered any sign of approval...a nod, pat on the back, kind word. He was not aware of it at the time, but he couldn't even remember his father ever touching him...*Maybe, somehow the way I feel about Posey is the way I wished my father felt about me,* Luke thought.

Luke discovered the little buggy was not well-suited for the difficult passage over the mountains. The trail was full of deep holes, large rocks, and scattered debris causing stress on the buggy's fragile wheels. The last time he had crossed, two years before, he was riding in a heavy freight wagon built for rough terrain. Now, each time the road became uneven, their little buggy would creak and strain, and Luke had to slowly ease over each obstacle to avoid damage. As they climbed out of the foothills, they encountered steep inclines and their horse had to work hard. Luke frequently had to get off the buggy and lead the horse over the more difficult terrain.

Their progress was much slower as they continued to climb than Luke had anticipated. He had hoped to make good time so they could stay well ahead of any possible posse that might be searching for them. Posey's job was to keep a sharp eye to the rear and warn Luke if she saw anything move. She took her duty seriously, however Luke knew that if a posse were chasing them, they would have little or no chance of escape.

For that reason, he always tried to find a place to spend the night that was off the trail where they could hide from anybody passing through one way or another. Luke espied just such a place on their tenth day. The trail curved to the left and a cove of trees to the right well away from any traffic looked like it was ideal to set up camp for the night.

When setting up camp, they had fallen into a routine. Posey would gather fire wood while Luke would tether the horse and scout the area for small game they might prepare for dinner. Two nights before, Luke had shot a rabbit and then cooked it on a small fire using a spit. The fresh meat was a welcome change from the cans of beans and hardtack they usually had.

Luke checked the rifle, making sure it was loaded. "If you hear a shot, you'll know we'll have fresh meat for supper," Luke said as he started to walk toward another grove of trees. Posy smiled as she continued to gather wood.

Luke always thought his best chance of catching game was in the late afternoons when animals would start hunting for their own supper. He slowly walked around some bushes then made a zig-zag pattern combing the area. Time went by and as the sun went down, he realized they might have to settle for just the canned beans. Then he heard the neigh of a horse. It came from the direction of the camp and Luke realized he had walked farther away than he intended. Luke immediately started back toward the camp as fast as he could.

When he got to the bushes near his camp, he heard men's voices. Luke checked his rifle and cautiously stepped forward. Two men were standing near the place where Posey had piled wood for a fire. Their backs were to Luke, and Posey stood to the side with a worried look on her face.

Luke took a few more steps toward the men and shouldered his rifle. "One funny move and you're dead," he said.

The two men, surprised by the realization somebody was behind them, jerked around to see who was talking. The men both wore Confederate uniforms. "Whoa there," one said raising his hands into the air. "Take it easy now. We mean no harm."

The other man's hands went up also as he moved away from his associate. "We're just crossing over these mountains heading for home. Don't shoot."

Luke stepped forward and did not lower his gun. He looked at Posey, who was unharmed but continued to look worried. The men's uniforms looked new and clean. "You soldiers?" Luke asked.

"Yep," the first responded, "we just came from Appomattox. The war's over. Lee surrendered."

Luke lowered his rifle, but only slightly, keeping it aimed in their direction. "Mind telling us what unit?"

"Not at all. We were with Longstreet…Second Corps."

"Yep," the second man said, "Longstreet, Lee's old war horse, Second Corps."

Luke knew this was a lie. He stepped closer, his rifle still ready. "Posey, come over by me," Luke said. "You two mount up and get out of here. You're not welcome."

The first man dropped his hands and one hand went behind him.

"Pull that gun and you're dead," Luke said as he shouldered his rifle.

"You gonna shoot us both?" the other said dropping his hands, also. "You ain't gonna be able to do that with that single shot rifle."

"You might be right about that...but one of you will be without a head... have you ever seen what a forty-four caliber cartridge does to a skull? The brains blow out the back through a hole about six inches in diameter." Luke moved the gun back and forth. "Either of you willing to take the chance? Go for a gun and I'll guarantee one of you will have a bloody ending."

The two men glanced at each other. Both appeared doubtful. "Look, mister, we're just looking for a place to camp for the night and we thought you were friendly...guess we were wrong about that, so we'll be moving on."

"You might want to keep your hands up while you mount up," Luke said.

As the two walked toward their horses, Luke followed closely to keep them in easy range. They mounted never taking their eyes off Luke and his rifle.

"Thanks for the kind hospitality," one said as he spurred his horse and the two of them rode off.

When they were out of sight, Luke lowered his rifle and when he turned to go back to camp, Posey was right behind him. "Put everything in the wagon," Luke said. "I'll hitch up the horse, so if they come back we can move fast."

Darkness had settled in when Luke and Posey crawled under the wagon to sleep. Neither said anything for some time when Posey said, "Masah Luke, how did you know those men were bad."

"Three reasons. First, Longstreet was in charge of the First and Third Corps at the end of the war, but never the Second. Then they had guns. All Confederate soldiers who were not officers had to turn in their weapons, so they were lying. The third was those uniforms…they were new. No soldier under Lee had a clean uniform except maybe his general staff. And they weren't general staff, so they were, or are, up to no good."

"Would you have shot one of them like you said? He didn't have a whip." Posey asked.

"You should go to sleep young lady. Might be a long day tomorrow." Luke said giving her a hug.

Posey was silent for a while, then asked, "would you?"

Luke stared up at the bottom of the buggy and answered in almost a whisper. "Yes."

———————

Weeks later, the little buggy began the long, slow descent onto the Cumberland Plateau that would take them directly to the McCallister homestead. With each passing day, Luke thought with more trepidation about his meeting with Clyde and Joanie. Would Joanie even speak to him? Was Clyde over his anger? What would his daughter look like? What would he do with her? How would they live?

A soft evening breeze blew against their little campfire, throwing sparks into the air as the two of them roasted pieces of a fresh rabbit upwind. "We'll be at the McCallister's tomorrow afternoon," Luke said.

"Will I see my sister tomorrow?" Posey asked.

"Yes, I hope you will," Luke said.

She thought about that for a moment then changed the subject. "Mr. McCallister's the one who hit you, isn't he?"

"Well, you could say that," Luke said, "but he didn't really mean it."

Posey hesitated. "But he must've been very angry at you."

"Maybe he had good reason to be, Posey, but sometimes people can get angry because they don't understand things completely."

"Then, why was he mad at you?"

Crickets chirped nearby. "Mr. McCallister thought I took advantage of his wife's sister, but he really didn't understand."

"Took advantage? What does that mean?" Posey asked.

Luke chose his words carefully. "Mr. McCallister thought his wife's sister and I did something she did not want to do. But that was not entirely true. We may have done something we shouldn't have done, but nobody took advantage of the other."

"So, now I have a sister?"

Luke signed. "Maybe when you're older I can explain it better…now, eat your rabbit. It's probably overcooked."

Chapter 35

The lane leading to the McCallister homestead was recognizable due to the deep ruts left by Clyde's heavy freight wagon. Luke recalled how well he liked late spring days in eastern Tennessee and the cool, dry air. He had taken his time getting there, keeping the horse at a moderate walk.

He felt like he needed time to prepare for his meeting with Clyde. Even though he was fairly sure Clyde knew Luke was responsible for him being released from Castle Thunder, he was anxious. Clyde was a big man, and Luke feared he would be easily overpowered. Clyde might not be expecting him to come and claim the child, even though Luke had told him he was coming. Luke hoped by doing so, Clyde's anger would be soothed.

He wondered what the child might look like. Her mother's face, while the image of the rest of her unclothed body remained vivid, was illusive. He had only been able to see her when the lightning flashed. He believed she had blue eyes like him, but her skin was ruddy and her hair reddish blonde. He wondered if he could, or would love her, as he did Posey. Thinking about Posey, Luke speculated that maybe after two years, Clyde and Joanie had become attached to his child much like he had with Posey. If that were the case, what would they do?

The barn doors were open and the big freighter was gone when they finally arrived. It was Thursday and Clyde frequently didn't get home until Fridays. Then he remembered the last time he saw the freighter. It was in Chattanooga where it had been confiscated by Union troops. Luke drove on up in front of the house. Stepping from the buggy, he was greeted by Nanny, the goat, with a head butt that hit him so hard he lost his balance and fell. As Luke picked himself up off the ground he saw one of the twins looking out the window of the house.

With Posey in hand, Luke lightly knocked on the front door. He did not know how Joanie would react to him. He hoped she would be friendly, but that was before the baby and Janie's death. He looked out into the front yard where he had spent time with the twins. That was almost two years ago. Shortly, Joanie opened the door, but not totally. "Oh…Luke… it's you" Joanie said opening the door half way.

"Joanie, it's been a long time." It was all Luke could think of.

Joanie looked back into the house as if something was distracting her and seemed to be at a loss for words.

"Clyde home?" Luke asked.

"No, but I expect him sometime soon. He rode off to visit a neighbor."

"Joanie, this is Posey," Luke said trying to break the ice.

"Hello, Posey…"

Joanie still did not open the door completely and after a few silent moments, Luke said, "Look, Joanie, I know about the baby girl…Clyde told me. I'm sorry…"

"Then you also must know my sister died giving birth," Joanie said.

"Yes, and I regret it," Luke said, "I've regretted it every single day since."

Joanie pursed her lips and her fingers gripped the door tighter as she tried to decide what to do. She looked back again and Luke assumed she was looking back for Tommy and Timmy, who he was sure Joanie had told to stay hidden.

"Then tension in Joanie's face relaxed. She shook her head slightly as if she was disgusted with herself for what she was about to do. "Oh, hell," she said, "you might as well come in."

As soon as those words were out of her mouth, Timmy and Tommy appeared both with smiles on their faces. Luke left Posey standing in the doorway and took a few steps inside, then squatted down to greet them. The boys had grown in the two years since he last saw them. Their childish enthusiasm was slightly diminished and replaced with awkward bashfulness. They came to Luke and when they both offered their hand, Luke pulled them to him and hugged them, then introduced them to Posey.

The aroma of beef stew wafted from the kitchen as they all stepped into the parlor. Luke sat on a sofa with Posey next to him. Luke commented about how much the boys had grown and Joanie made small talk about her garden. Posey sat quietly but kept looking around the room. Luke didn't know if it was because she had never been in a parlor before, but when her eyes lit up he saw what she was looking for. A two-year-old girl came running out of the dining room and ran to Joanie. She was dressed in a calico dress tied at the waist with pink ribbon. Her hair was curly blonde and outlined her pink cherubic face. When she reached Joanie, she looked over at Luke then at Posey as she stayed close to Joanie. "Mummy, who are they," she asked with her finger in her mouth.

Joanie took a deep breath.

Luke was aghast. The first sight of his child…her sky blue eyes were the same as Joanie's…her blonde hair had curls that hung loosely over her ears…Luke tried to take it all in.

The little girl's gaze shifted directly to Posey who got down off the sofa and took a few steps toward the little girl. "I'm Posey," she said, "what's your name?"

The little girl looked up at Posey with a quizzical expression, then her face broke out into a big smile, "My name is Samantha and I'm two," she said proudly holding up two fingers.

Posey sat on the floor. "Are you really only two?" Posey asked, "you look like you might be three or four."

"Tell me, Luke, how is your leg?" Joanie asked.

"Well, I learned it floats," Luke replied. "Lost it swimming in the Tennessee. It also doesn't stay on when falling down a railroad embankment, but all in all, it works pretty good. Of course, I wouldn't even have this contraption if it wasn't for the boys."

Timmy and Tommy beamed.

"Sounds like you've been on some adventures," said Joanie relaxing a little, "care to tell us about them?" She looked at Posey, "I'm sure there's a big story about Posey."

The girls continued to play and Luke told how he avoided being shot crossing the Tennessee, meeting Forrest, and the prosthesis factory. The boys were intrigued and the afternoon went by quickly. As the sun started to set, the dogs barked and the deep voice from Clyde saying hello to his dogs.

Luke stood. "Excuse me, might be best if I talk to Clyde outside,' he said. "Posey, I'll be back soon."

Joanie looked relieved.

Posey smiled. She seemed to be enjoying playing with Samantha.

Luke walked out of the house and toward the barn where Clyde was busy unsaddling a horse. Without looking up, he said, "Been thinking you might come around one of these days."

"I trust the Captain treated you well?" Luke said.

"Well, I shouldn't have been in that god damned prison in the first place, but I reckon I owe you thanks for getting me out." Clyde busily shook his saddle blanket and hung it on a rail.

"It was the least I could do," Luke said. "I still owe you."

Clyde stopped and looked at Luke for the first time. "Why are you here?"

"You told me I fathered a child borne by Joanie's sister, and I'm here to do the responsible thing"

"And, how the hell would you take care of her? How would you feed her, clothe her and provide a home?"

"I've a got job back in Richmond," Luke said, "I hope to get married and move back there."

"You've got a job?" Clyde glanced at Luke's leg. "What kind of job?"

Luke didn't like Clyde's tone. "That's my business, not yours." He could feel his face turning red.

Clyde stood directly in front of Luke. "Don't get snippy with me or I'll rap you up the side of your head like I did last time."

"Is the child mine or not? If she is as you said, then I've come to claim her."

Clyde's face softened. "Look Luke, I think you're an okay fellow... and I respect you for coming...a lot of young men wouldn't have." Clyde leaned over and pulled a timothy seed blade and stuck it in his mouth. "You want to know how you can repay us for saving your life and leg?"

Luke hesitated not knowing what was coming. "I guess so."

"Get on your buggy and ride out of here, that's what you can do. We've raised Samantha from day one as our own. She's a fine little girl. She's the girl Joanie and I have wanted for the last ten years. Joanie loves her and so do I. We want her here with us."

It was the second time that afternoon that Luke was dumbfounded. He remembered Samantha calling Joanie *Mummy*. He felt a little weak in the knees and sat down on the grass. Clyde squatted down, also. Luke thought about how he felt about Posey having been with her for just a few months. Clyde and Joanie probably felt the same way about Samantha. So, what would he do if somebody out of the blue claimed to be Posey parents?

Joanie came out of the house. She was wiping her hands on her apron. When she saw that Luke and Clyde were having a peaceful discussion, she asked both of them to come in and have supper.

Clyde stood and gave Luke a hand to help him stand and together, all three walked to the house. The dining room table was set for six plus a high chair for Samantha. Joanie had put a pillow on Posey's chair and Luke took the clue and lifted her up. Luke sat next to Posey, across from Joanie and Samantha. Clyde sat at the head of the table, and before he began to ladle portions of stew he said a brief prayer of thanksgiving.

Above the table was a small chandelier with candles that provided light. Luke, sitting directly across from Samantha, studied her face. He had trouble comprehending that she was really his daughter. He looked for physical similarities. Her little nose had a curve up at the end as his mother had. It gave her a haughty look and made her look independent. He smiled at the shape of her ears. She had the same little notch on top of her lobes that Luke did. Occasionally her eyes wondered over from Posey to Luke. Initially, she seemed distant and uninterested, but as the evening progressed, possibly because Luke was always looking at her, she smiled and Luke beamed.

As Joanie helped her cut pieces of the stew to smaller sizes, Joanie's love for the child was obvious. The little girl was happy. The McCallister home was the only home she had ever known. Luke felt like an interloper.

Clyde was aware of Luke studying Samantha, and said little during the table conversation. However, when Luke talked about the factory and the room where Posey and he were staying, Clyde asked about the size of the room.

Luke got the message.

As the evening wore on, and after Samantha had been put to bed, Clyde said to Luke, "It's too late for you and Posey to leave, why don't you stay the night and you can depart in the morning."

Luke, happy to sleep with a roof over their head, agreed. "Do I get my old room back?"

Joanie replied, "nobody has slept in that room since you left." Then she told the twins it was time for bed. They protested.

Tommy said, "tell us about ole' Abe again. Is he really seven feet tall?"

"Maybe he is," Luke answered with a smile, "if you add on the height of his stovepipe." He talked about the danger Abe was in while he walked nearly unguarded through the capital city of a near defeated country. He explained to them how tired and weary Lincoln looked and expressed concern about his over-all health.

They discussed the lawlessness in the South and how order needed to be restored. Slowly, the boys grew weary and Luke asked that he and Posey be excused and thanked Joanie for the wonderful meal. Luke needed time to think and he was anxious to be alone.

Posey and Luke went up the steps to their room. Luke was reminded of the first day he dared go down these same steps with his new prosthesis.

Luke decided to sleep on the floor, and as he tucked Posey in, she asked, "Is my sister coming home with us?"

Luke took a deep breath. It was the exact question he was asking himself. He blew out the candle, "I don't know," he said, "She seems very happy here. I just don't know." He sat on the edge of her bed, "do you want her to come with us?"

"Oh, yes," she said, but after a few moments she added, "but only if you think she'd be happy."

Luke kissed her on the forehead. "Thanks a lot," he said with a tinge of sarcasm, "let's sleep on it."

For a long time, Luke lay awake with his hands behind his head. He thought over and over about Samantha. She would require full time care until she entered school. Would Carol agree to that? But rightfully, Samantha was his daughter. It didn't seem right for a girl to be separated from her real father. Then again, it didn't seem right for her to be separated from the only family she'd ever known. Although he did not love the child, he knew it would be extremely easy to do so. In a way, he was thankful his emotional attachment didn't cloud his judgment on the decision he had to make.

Hours later, and after very little sleep Luke woke up to the call of a rooster from the barn. Then he heard the back door downstairs open and close. A bleating demand from Nanny to be fed told Luke Clyde had gone outside to do the chores. Luke quickly got up, dressed and quietly snuck out to the barn.

Inside Luke heard the hollow sound of milk being stripped into an empty pail as Clyde hunched behind their cow on a stool skillfully pulling on her teats. Clyde watched Luke as he approached, picked up a second stool and sat. When Luke seemed to be searching for words, Clyde kept stripping.

The cow munched corn. Luke said, "I'm going to leave this morning to go to Maryville, where the girl I told you about lives. I'm going to ask her to marry me."

Clyde looked skeptical.

"I would like to leave Posey here for a couple days until I return." Luke hesitated. "Then, I'll come back here and I want you to agree to two things."

Clyde was getting impatient. "What are they?"

"I want visiting rights, number one…and, number two, I would like Samantha to come visit me every once in a while."

Clyde stood abruptly tipping the pail over with the milk spilling onto the ground. He stuck out his hand, "DEAL," he said, and shook Luke's hand vigorously with a broad smile of relief on his face.

Chapter 36

After three hours of easy riding, Luke steered the horse and buggy into the little town of Maryville. Three large mountains to the south were clearly visible as Luke drove to the center of town. A burned-out courthouse and several damaged buildings were signs of the damage the Civil War had inflicted on Maryville as it did most other Tennessee towns. Stopping in front of a water trough near the center of town, Luke gave his horse an opportunity to drink. With a bit still in its mouth the horse made a loud slurping noise as he drank thirstily. The late spring day was exceptionally warm and the horse hadn't had any water since he left McCallister's.

"Looking for the Perry house," Luke asked a passerby.

"Elijah or Samuel? We have two Perry's...not related." The man took off his derby hat and wiped his brow.

"The one that has a beautiful daughter by the name *Carol*," Luke replied sheepishly knowing the passerby probably guessed his ambitions.

The passerby gave him an understanding smile. "That'd be Elijah Perry. They have a house at the edge of town," he said pointing. "Their farmhouse burned down in '62. Just one block, then the second house on the right." The man placed his hat back on his head and started to walk away. "If I figure right, there might be somebody there who's been waiting for you," he said and then, walking away, he added, "though you might not want to show up with a dirty unshaven face. There's a barber across the street."

Luke was thrilled. He climbed down from the buggy and looked down at himself. His uniform looked like he hadn't washed it in weeks. Patting his pant legs, clouds of dust rose into the still air. He walked to the barber-shop and twenty minutes later walked out feeling more presentable.

The Perry house was a white, one and a half story bungalow with a porch across the front, and a swing hanging on one side. All the doubts Luke harbored about his prosthesis disappeared in his anxiousness to see Carol again. He remembered the love letters he had sent her telling her he would return for her. Now that he was about to see her, he thought those letters had been too gushy and he became embarrassed. He mused that his lonely thoughts as he lay in bed far away thinking about her might have been overly sentimental. Would she have laughed at him when she read them?

Overwhelmed with the emotional expectation that he had been wait-ing years for, he stepped up on the porch and softly knocked on the door. Looking back in the front yard, he smiled as two robins played as the male robin ruffled his feathers trying to seduce the lighter colored female.

The door opened and Luke took off his hat when an attractive mid-dle-aged woman appeared wondering who stood on her porch. Luke straightened and threw back his shoulders.

She looked at Luke. "Yes...hello, can I help you?"

Luke had no idea what to say. "Is Carol here?" He blurted out.

A spark of understanding spread on her face. "She sure is." Then her voice became excited and higher pitched. "Are you Luke?" She exclaimed opening the door wider.

"Yes'm," Luke said smiling.

The door opened wide and the woman greeted Luke with open arms. "We've been waiting. She knew you would come...Carol!" she yelled, "it's Luke. He's here!"

"Oh my god, oh my god," came Carol's voice as she bounded down the stairs carefully lifting her crinolines. She rushed into Luke's arms just as her mother stepped aside and smothered Luke as she stood on her tip toes kissing his cheeks one then the other. "I knew you would come...I just knew it." Her smile was radiant and her happiness spilled out and flowed over him like a wave.

Luke stood dumbly overwhelmed and inhaling that same rose fragrance he remembered from almost three years ago. "I was worried you didn't get my letters," he said, "I didn't know."

"You'd better offer Mr. Pettigrew a chair, young lady," Carol's mother said smiling, "He's come a long way."

As Luke walked to a sofa and sat down, Carol noticed his irregular walking. "You've been injured?" She asked sympathetically. "Oh. Is that your new leg?"

Luke inhaled deliberately. This was a moment he dreaded. "Yep, I lost it at Gettysburg," he said, "but, I've got this new prosthesis…"

Carol sat next to him first looking at his leg, which was hidden by his pant leg, then up at Luke's face, "you poor thing," she exclaimed, "the torture you must have had to go through…" She put her hand on Luke's. "You boys are all such heroes, I feel so bad I wasn't there when you needed me."

Luke searched her face for any sign of repulsion. There was none. He smiled thinking how lucky he was to have her accept him so openly. Without taking his eyes off her face he remembered the day several years ago when he first laid his eyes on her. Carol, accompanied her uncle when he visited him as a prisoner at Camp Chase in Ohio, and the minute he saw her, he knew there was a special attraction. She was dressed in a simple toile fabric cotton dress with short puckered sleeves, tight bodice and full skirt. The neckline swept low and a beaded necklace hung between her breasts. Her long brown hair was combed back and emphasized her graceful neck. Then, those emerald green eyes, how could he have forgotten?

The obvious attraction between Carol and Luke was not lost on Carol's mother who was closely watching her daughter's reaction to Luke's sudden return. "Carol, maybe you should introduce us," she said. "Although I already feel like I know this young man very well."

Carol did so and then asked Luke to tell them about his life since they last saw him. Luke started his story with his adventure crossing the Appalachians and finding Stewart. He normally was not fond of talking about himself, but when he saw Carol and his mother's enthusiasm hanging on to every word, he went into more detail. Keeping to a chronological order he told of his injury and his journey back to his parent's farm only to find it destroyed and waking up at McCallister's in an upstairs bedroom, only to discover his leg had been amputated. He told them how he designed and made his wooden leg and the trouble he had learning how to use it.

Tea was served and Luke talked until late afternoon, answering their questions. Carol was totally absorbed and whenever Luke related something he had accomplished, she beamed with pride. He did not tell them about two things: Samantha and Posey. He felt he would tell Carol at an opportune time when they were alone.

Carol's mother stood. "Luke, you'll eat with us and stay the night?"

Luke looked down at himself appraising his filthy clothes. "Well yes, that's mighty kind of you, but I need to clean up. My uniform is filthy."

"We could give him some of dad's clothes," Carol said to her mother. Then she looked at Luke, "Dad's away a couple days. He went to Memphis to buy some farm equipment, you know, a plow, a set of harnesses and some other tools. All were burned during the war."

"Your uncle told me about the fire when I was in Columbus…must have been terrible," Luke said. "Anyway, I'd appreciate the clothes, make me look at least human."

Her mother left to get the clothes. "You look plenty 'human' to me," Carol said kissing him on the cheek with a coy look. She put the back of her hand on his cheek. "Smooth," she said. "You must have stopped at Sam's."

"Sam's?"

"Sam, the barber," she giggled.

Luke remembered how he loved her forwardness. It was an endearing quality that he thought was perfect. It took away all his awkwardness and made him feel at home. She was so easy to be with. He thought about last time he stayed overnight in the same house with her. She had brazenly crawled into his bed and promised him the next time she would completely undress. He knew better than to think too hard on that, so he walked around the room looking at a pictures hanging on the wall.

One painting was a schooner on heavy seas with a weathered captain at the helm. In front of the captain on the deck were two square heavy wood latticed openings used to gain access to the ship's hold. Luke had seen a similar schooner docked down by the wharf on the James River in Richmond. When he looked closely, hands were reaching up from the hold through the lattice. Black hands. Luke realized the ship in the painting was a slaver.

Carols' mother came back into the room carrying some clothes. "Lucky my husband is about your size," she said. "Try these and then we can wash what you have on." Luke's eyes were riveted to the painting and when Carol's mother saw his interest, she said simply, "that's my husband's father, Captain Horatio Perry...handsome isn't he?"

Carol grabbed the clothes from her mother and unfolded the top item, a shirt and held it up to Luke for size. "Not perfect, but it'll do," she said. "My daddy won't mind at all, now you go upstairs, clean up, change and come down for dinner. We'll make you something special."

Luke went up the stairs. "First door on the right and hurry," Carol said.

The bedroom was on the backside of the house with a window looking out onto the backyard where a small white gazebo under which a wind chime was tinkling in the light breeze. The room was small with a single bed and dresser on which was a washbasin, soap and towel. He looked down at himself and his dirty clothes, and that made him promptly get up and start working on getting clean. He undressed and washed. He donned his new clothes and looked at himself in the mirror. His dark hair was full and curly and he was glad he took the time to have it cut. He combed it back and walked downstairs, where he smelled chicken frying. He walked into the kitchen where Carol's mother was preparing the meal.

"Look at you," she said stirring a pot. "I can see Carol was right about how handsome you are. Sit down," she glanced at the ceiling as if Carol was upstairs. "This'll give us a chance to talk a little."

Luke sat. He had a notion what she was going to say was important.

"My dear daughter Carol, as you well know, can be impetuous at times. She probably gets it from me, but she always jumps head-first into things without a lot of thought or planning." Mrs. Perry had a wooden spoon in her hand and held it in such a way as to emphasize the words she was using.

"When she came back from staying with her uncle in Columbus, all she could talk about was you. Luke this and Luke that."

Luke felt a warm glow come over him with those words but remained silent.

"Her father and I thought it would wear off and she would forget and move on. But it didn't. Then, she started to receive your letters. I must admit those letters were beautiful and we started to feel more at ease. We didn't want our daughter to fall head over heels to a man who might snub her or hurt her. Down deep under her outgoing facade, she is very vulnerable. So, without Carol here, I will come right to the point…what are your intentions?"

"I want to marry her," Luke blurted out without hesitation. "With your permission of course. I will ask her and if she accepts, I'll take her back to Richmond where we will live together. I manage a factory making these things," he said pointing.

She looked at him intently trying to read his face. "Luke, are you sure? You've only been together a few hours up to now. How do you know?"

"From the first time I saw Carol, I think I knew. She was the most beautiful woman I'd ever seen. She's all I thought about these last couple years."

Carol's mother smiled and returned her attention to the stew. Carol came in and Luke breathed easier.

Several hours later, Luke sat on his bed thinking about the evening. Carol had come down to dinner dressed in a simple white dress edged with lace with pink ribbon woven through. She didn't say much and kept her gaze mostly on Luke with an air of expectation. Her cheeks were lightly rouged and Luke remembered it was the same shade she had used years prior up in Columbus when they first met. Carol's mother had retired after they ate and the two of them washed the dishes.

After they were finished, they embraced. "You must be all done in," Carol said, "it's a long way from Knoxville to here. You poor dear, why don't we turn in?" She kissed him on the lips, then turned and walked toward her bedroom with her eyes following him as she disappeared behind her door.

He watched the door close and walked upstairs thinking the night couldn't end that way. In his bedroom the moonlight filtered through the muslin curtains giving the bedroom a warm glow. The window was cracked open and he could feel a faint, cool breeze on his body as he undressed and crawled under a comforter. He lay on his back with his hands behind his head and hoped the door would open. He felt his heart beating in anticipation for what he thought was coming. He even felt himself aroused. He inhaled deeply trying to relax. After a while, he wondered if she wasn't coming. *Maybe she wants to wait until after we marry*, he thought. *Maybe she wants to delay until the first night. Did she really think he was too tired?*

Within minutes, the door opened with a faint creak and closed again. Carol walked toward the bed and Luke could see her clearly. She wore the same sheet-like garment that had buttons down the front. The same buttons she had made him promise not to undo the last time at her uncle's house several years ago. She stopped next to Luke and the bed. She had a faint smile on her face and her dark hair hung down covering her shoulders. She reached down and slowly pulled the comforter off Luke exposing his naked body. His hands were still behind his head as her eyes went from his face and moved slowly down stopping at his mid-section when she saw his arousal. With the same coquettish smile, she unbuttoned her cover, one button at a time, gradually exposing her breasts that, in the moonlight, looked better than anything he could have imagined. The gown fell to the floor and she lay down facing him and he turned to face her and their bodies met. He pulled her tighter and they kissed. He inhaled her fragrance. He felt like he wanted to consume her and knew he could never get enough. She felt his urgency and her simple words were, "go slow, let's go nice and slow," as she rolled on top and his eyes devoured her.

The next morning, Luke and Carol, unable to sleep and unwilling to incur her mother's disapproval for sleeping together, decided to go for an early walk. Luke had lost count of the number of times they made love, but as the sun rose flooding Carol's flushed face, he wished they could do it again.

Luke had suggested a walk because he wanted to ask her to marry him. He wanted to marry her that very morning, but knew they would have to follow the rules and go through the ritual like most other young couples.

"Remember, I told you about the camp of coloreds who all had the pox?" Luke asked. "Yes, Gordonville...I believe," she said.

"That's right." Luke was impressed she remembered. "Well, there were dozens of patients and some got better and some died. One married couple were dead when I got there and they had this little girl who was stranded and had nobody to take care of her." Luke hesitated, searching for the right words. Their pace had slowed.

Carol sensed Luke was trying to tell her something important. "Go ahead," she said cautiously.

"The little girl's name is Posey. She's about ten years old. She's cuter than a button and smart. And..." He hesitated again. A wagon loaded with grain pulled by a team of beautiful Belgians passed on the way into town.

She waited...then said, "and what?"

"And I adopted her. I couldn't leave her to die." Luke realized he was being slightly defensive and he didn't know why.

"You adopted her? She's a darkie, right?"

"Yes, she's a Negro...a very sweet little girl and I'm sure you will like her."

Luke felt the conversation not going anywhere near where he wanted it to go, but he persevered. "Carol, I want to marry you...will you marry me?"

With a stern look on her face, Carol said. "Of course I want to marry you, Luke, but let me get this straight, when we get married, am I to understand your adopted darkie child will live with us?"

"In so many words, yes," Luke replied, "and I know you will grow to love her as much as I do."

They had stopped on the walk. Carol gazed at Luke with a puzzled look. Her brow furled as if she was trying to understand something. She turned and slowly started to walk back toward the house. He did too. She didn't say anything for while as if she was trying to figure out what she was going to say. She stopped again and faced him. "If we have children, would this darkie be their sister...their equal?"

"I wouldn't phrase it that way," Luke said, "but yes...equal."

"How would you 'phrase' it?"

"From your tone, it seems we have a difference of opinion concerning black and white issues. But, I do not believe there is any difference between black and white and I have no qualms about a mixed race family."

"Well, I'm sorry, but I do." They stood facing each other seemingly at an impasse. After a few moments, she took a deep breath and said, "Luke, for these past four years, I have waited for you. I could have found somebody else and I had chances, but I waited. Everyday I hoped for another letter or some word of you. It was difficult, staying at home all the time. I was lonesome, but I waited for you. I gave myself to you all this time… now you come back to me and I've learned you were not faithful. I don't mean you found another woman, but you found another love. You've fallen in love with this little darkie girl and you are asking me to share you with her." She hesitated, and then almost whispered, "and I can't do that." She took Luke's hand and looked into Luke's eyes. "I just want Luke Pettigrew and no one else."

Luke felt himself yielding to the power of her words. He pictured Carol checking the mail every day and most days being disappointed. He visualized a young Confederate officer knocking on her door and Carol graciously saying no. The fact that she loved him, Luke Pettigrew, made him feel warm inside…it was everything he dreamed about over the last several years. Then, he thought of Posey. He saw himself standing on Carol's front porch with Posey. The cold weather was causing them to shiver. The door opens and the warmth from the house spills out onto the porch. Carol invites Luke in to get warm and he wants to, but Posey has to stay on the porch. She cannot come in.

And Luke had not mentioned Samantha yet.

When they arrived back at the house, Carol's mother met them in the living room and saw their dour faces. Luke sat on the sofa while Carol and her mother went into the kitchen. He could hear them whispering. Then he heard Carol weeping.

As Luke sat he looked again at the painting on the wall of Carol's grandfather piloting a slave ship. Maybe a casual observer would not see the black's hands reaching for freedom from their crowded hold, but to

Luke it meant that Carol's grandfather had little love for black people and that feeling must have been passed on down through the two generations. He tried to see her point of view, but slavery went against every bone in his body. The Negro and the white man were both human beings in his opinion.

Maybe her love for him would overcome her disdain for Negroes and they could live together with Posey. But he was beginning to think that her intolerance was a mortal blow to their relationship. He wondered what would happen several years hence if Carol and he did not marry. She would definitely find happiness with another, but what about Posey? She had no-body. She would be left out in an intolerant environment with no means to sustain herself. As much as he loved Carol, he would never be able to live with himself if he left Posey stranded. He would always think of her and wonder if she was suffering. The very thought that somebody might treat her cruelly was horrific and totally intolerable. He set his jaw. No way would that happen.

Leaning back in the chair, Luke realized he really didn't know Carol.

Chapter 37

Luke stood in front of the Crossville Post Office. It was the same spot on which he had stood nearly three years before, the day after his father asked him to leave the farm. The same war posters were still pasted on the sides of the building. The Union poster was faded and said something about staying united. The Confederate poster, which had been slashed and mutilated, read: *WANTED: 100 GOOD MEN TO REPEL INVASION.*

During the last several weeks after he had seen Carol, Luke had been waking up at night with nightmares about his father. His recurring dream was after his father had kicked him out, his parents decided to adopt a son who they thought would work better and harder than Luke had. In his dream, he would always wake up after he had gone home and his father confronted him with a bullwhip. The dream was so real he could feel the whip lash burning his back. He thought that by facing down his fears and revisiting his old place he might be able to overcome them.

Luke also wanted to check out the old place because, if in fact, his parents were dead, the farm would be his. Posey had wanted to come along with Luke to visit his old place, but as she seemed comfortable at the McCallister's, especially with Samantha, he asked her to stay behind. He reflected again about the relationship between Posey and his father. He was sure that somewhere in the back of his head was an unconscious connection. He didn't know exactly, but he did know he loved that little girl and would do anything to protect her, keep her safe and make sure she knew she was loved.

The weather was good and he decided to walk the short distance to the old homestead, so he hitched his buggy to a post and started out. The little town showed the scars of war. Luke remembered how divided the community was between the North and South, and he believed renegade bands were responsible for the burning of his parents' place back in '62. This was the same town where Clyde McCallister had left him to walk home, four years before. Those four years seemed like a lifetime.

Scott's Tavern was in the center of town, and he decided to go in on a whim. The building was long and narrow with a bar along the left side and a single row of tables on the right. The old wood planked floor creaked as Luke walked through the open door and approached the bar. The bartender was a woman and Luke guessed she was about the same age as his deceased mother. She wore an apron that showed food stains and when she saw Luke approach, she smiled while wiping the bar off with a towel.

"Can I help you?" She asked.

"Just passing through," Luke said, "I'm Luke Pettigrew. Used to live just outside of town," Luke said.

From a back room a man came out also wearing an apron. "Did I hear you say 'Luke Pettigrew'?" he asked.

"Yep, that's my name."

"Knew your dad," he said, "after you signed up, he came in quite regularly."

"Didn't think he drank," Luke said surprised.

"Oh, no. Not to buy a drink. To buy the paper. He used to buy only the Sunday paper, but then, after Shiloh and the stuff written about you, he bought one every day."

"He did?" Luke said incredulously.

"That's a fact. Our paper came from Nashville and usually it would get here around four o'clock. Sometimes, he get here early and wait for it. He'd buy the paper, then rush back home. He was a man of few words."

Luke stared at the man looking for a sign he was joking, he never knew his father read the newspapers. "Are you sure you're talking about my dad?"

"Gospel truth. What can I get you?"

Luke was shaky and felt like all the air has escaped his lungs. He thought the bartender must surely be mistaken. He turned toward the door. "Nothing, thanks," he said and walked out in a daze.

As he headed out toward his old place he didn't want to believe the bartender. It was a defense mechanism and he thought if he didn't believe what he had said, then it wouldn't hurt if it turned out to not be true.

He passed the McGraw homestead where he used to play as a kid. He heard the singing of their now rickety windmill in the breeze and recalled it was the first windmill in the area. The old road he was walking on was dusty, and when he looked back and saw his tracks, he remembered how he had to drag his wounded leg the last time he traveled this way, leaving a deep bloody groove in the dirt. The image was sharp as if it happened yesterday.

His mind came back to what the bartender said, but he refused to think about it.

Next came the Bricker place. He assumed it had been ransacked because their son had decided to fight with General Johnston. He peered through the trees, and saw that the farmhouse was being rebuilt. Luke had explored all of this area with his horse many times when he was young. He knew the area well, yet strangely it was all unfamiliar. He knew it but didn't, like the first time you see a very close friend after a few years. Everything's the same, but isn't.

His pace slowed as he rounded a curve in the road that would give him a full view of his family's place. He stopped. *Do I really want to do this?* he asked himself. Maybe it would feel like taking the bandage off an unhealed wound. It could start bleeding again. He decided he couldn't stop and walked slowly on.

And there it was. The burned out house with the chimney still standing. The barn totally destroyed. The stream still flowing in the rear. Except for overgrown bushes and weeds everything looked exactly as he remembered.

The path that led from the road to the front door was full of overgrowth and didn't look like a path at all if Luke hadn't known it was there. As he started up the path, he glanced back toward where the barn used to be and stopped. There were two mounds he had never seen before.

He walked over and realized the mounds were the graves of his parents. On top of each were small wooden crosses. He bent down to read them. The first read simply: *MaryAnn Pettigrew 1815-1862.* He took a deep breath and read the second: *Jonas Lucas Pettigrew, 1813-1863.* Dumbfounded, Luke read it again this time aloud, "Jonas Lucas Pettigrew: 1813-1863." He wondered if *1863* was a mistake. If it was true, that meant his father had not been killed in the raid in which his mother was killed, when the place was torched and burned to the ground. He shook his head in disbelief and read it yet again. This also meant his father may have been alive when he came last. Maybe he just wasn't home.

Luke picked his way up the path that once led to the front door. Where the front door used to be was shaded by the old elm tree he used to climb as a child. Its green leaves whispered in the soft breeze as if nothing had ever happened. The front room of the house was like he last saw it…strewn with the burnt skeletons of their old furniture. Ragweed had gained purchase in the ashes and stood three feet tall. He came to the stone fireplace where he had laid down to rest three years ago, and where he was found and rescued by Clyde. He stared at the spot and was sure he wouldn't be there alive today if Clyde and Joanie hadn't nursed him back to health.

He walked back to where the kitchen used to be. An old water basin was turned upside down on the floor, the one his mother made him use to wash his hands before dinner. When he looked outside across from the kitchen he was surprised to see their old out-kitchen building still standing. The same out-kitchen where they had butchered meat, made sausage and where his mom canned vegetables for winters. The door to the little building was ajar and creaked loudly on rusted hinges as Luke pushed it open.

Luke's pulse quickened when he saw an old bed in the corner and a table pushed against the wall with a chair. Somebody had lived in this little room. Everything was covered in dust, so whoever lived there hadn't been there for quite some time. The bed had a rumpled up old blanket on it and looked like somebody had gotten up in a hurry and forgotten to make it. He stepped toward the table on which there was a softbound journal and old newspapers whose pages had yellowed. On the wall behind the table was a board and tacked to the board were pieces of brown newspaper that fluttered slightly with the breeze that came through the door. Luke slowly sat down at the table. He put his hand on one of the fluttering pieces of paper so he could read it. It was an old newspaper clipping from the *Nashville Whig* and read:

Crossville Soldier, a Hero at Shiloh

Private Luke Pettigrew rallies retreating Rebels at the Battle of Fallen Timbers…

Luke stopped reading and looked at another. He could feel a lump in his throat as he wanted to believe the significance of the saved articles. He wanted to believe more than anything. He tried to focus and blinked back the welling tears in his eyes.

Private Luke Pettigrew, one of our own from Crossville distinguishes himself in Medical Corps…

Luke could feel his pulse quicken and his throat constrict as he read another:

Local Soldier, Luke Pettigrew escapes from Chase Prison in a daring daytime foil of the Yanks…

He opened the journal. His hands were shaking and he wiped his eyes on his sleeve. Carefully pasted on every other page were more clippings of news about him, and facing each page of clippings was a hand-written account of Luke's activities. The handwriting was his father's. He recognized the irregular scrolling. The realization that his father had lived here briefly and had kept the journal crept up on Luke like a silent wave. He wept…. his chest heaved as a sense of fierce pride swept over him.

Moments later, as the fact that his father not only approved of him, but also was proud of him sunk in further, his euphoria turned to sadness. He had misjudged his father, who may have been trying to be the best parent he knew how to be. He felt the sting of that misjudgment like a slap in the face. He had gotten it all wrong. He thought about how hard his father had to work to keep the farm going and to provide for the family's meager existence and the effort that that had demanded. There was a reason his father's hands were callused and his back always ached. He recalled how his father's hand would always go to his back when he got up from sitting. It was because he was working so hard. He realized his father didn't really have the spare time to devote to his son as other fathers would have. Luke further realized how selfish he had been always thinking about himself and not seeing the hardships his father was enduring. Tears freely flowed down his cheek onto the old newspaper like drops of rain turning the sepia colored paper to a dark brown.

He leaned back on the chair and thought about what could have been. He wondered why his father had never expressed any approval to him, but Luke realized that demonstrating affection was not his father's way. He realized that his father had demonstrated his approval by trying to make his son a better person. His father had shown by example what he wanted his son to be and the values he wanted his son to have. He realized the burden his father had carried, trying to eke out a living for his family all by himself. The soil was poor and marginal at best for crop production. As a farmer, his father had a certain sovereignty that isolated him and threw the entire onus of success squarely on his shoulders. Luke's chin quivered thinking about how he could have made it easier for his father.

As Luke read a couple more of his father's entries, he thought about his new leg and his accomplishments during the war. Even though his family never openly showed affection in any way, he thought he would gladly give up his one good leg just for the chance to put his arms around his father and thank him. Thank him and tell him he was sorry.

Sometime later, he reread some of the news clips, then got up and walked back through where his old home's front door once stood. He walked down toward the little steam that flowed in the back yard. The same little stream where he had fished so many times with a cane pole, a hook and a bobber. He took the flask out of his rear pocket and flung it as far as he could into the water, then watched it bob its way downstream and slowly disappear out of sight. He straightened his back and started to walk back toward the village. His spirits had never been higher. He felt an inner peace and freedom he had never experienced before. Free of the past shackles that weighed heavily on his mind.

Lost in a cloud of his own memories and unaware of his surroundings, he arrived back in Crossville, stepped up on his buggy, slapped the reins on the horse's back and headed back to the McCallister's.

When Luke arrived, Clyde was in the barn repairing an old harness. The barn looked empty without the big freight wagon and Clyde's team of horses in their stalls. When Luke approached Clyde continued reaming a hole in a strap with an awl.

"Suppose you're here to pick up Posey," he said.

" Yep. Yankees never returned your horses and wagon?" Luke asked.

Clyde continued to work. Timmy and Tommy were yelling while tossing a ball around in the front yard. Then Clyde sighed. "No team, no wagon, no work."

"I just returned from our old place near Crossville," Luke said. "Everything is the same except the buildings are mostly gone, and the graves of my mom and dad."

"That wasn't a surprise, was it? I mean about your mom and dad?" Clyde said.

"No, I suspected it, but the graves confirmed it."

"This war has changed everything," Clyde said. "Sorry. What will you do with the farm?"

"You mean, what will *you* do with the farm?" Luke asked.

"What will I do? You're not making any sense," Clyde stopped working.

"The farm is yours, Clyde, I'll get the papers drawn up." Luke said. "You can either work it or sell it. But it's yours. Consider it payment for mistakes I made. Maybe it'll help you get a new team and wagon."

The big man looked the other way. Luke turned and walked to the house to find Posey.

Ten minutes later, Luke had said good-bye to Joanie and the boys, and had Posey ready to go in the buggy. Samantha was standing behind Joanie and Luke squatted down and waved to his daughter. She smiled and hid behind Joanie's skirt. After Luke had climbed onto the buggy, Clyde came out of the barn and up to the buggy. His eyes were red.

"Visiting rights any time you wish," Clyde said offering Luke his hand.

Five weeks later, with Posey next to him, Luke turned the buggy down Grace Street, a short distance from the factory. The sweetbay trees were in full bloom and the street was rife with fallen white and pink petals giving the impression they were riding on clouds. A group of men were standing outside in a line to get in the factory door, and when Luke and Posey approached, he recognized some of them as prisoners who had worked there before the funding ran out. Only they were now all free men. Inside, applications were being taken by an attractive young lady Luke had never seen before. Jim Hanger walked up from the back and greeted Luke. "You're just in time, Luke, we have our funding and we're going to start production again next week," he said. "You'll run the operation, of course."

"I'd like that," Luke said putting his hand on Posey's head and fluffing her hair.

"That's my daughter Caroline behind the desk," Jim said, "she just graduated from Otterbein College up in Ohio…and she's looking for a job. Maybe…"

She looked up and smiled warmly at Luke her eyes lingering briefly, then resumed her work.

"I think we can arrange that, Jim," Luke answered, his eyes not leaving the girl.

THE END

Author Notes

James Hanger died in June, 1919 but his company lives on today as a world-wide leader in the development and manufacture of prosthetic devices with branches around the world. During WW1, the company received contracts from the U.K. and France and vaulted them to the top of their field where they remain today.

Bedford Forrest died October 29, 1877 of complications from diabetes. Before the war started, Forrest was a cotton farmer, slave owner and slave trader. He was a brilliant cavalryman and was truly a thorn in the side of Union troops. He may best be known, however, for his actions at Fort Pillow, where his men surrounded the fort and demanded its surrender, then easily over-ran it. Upon seeing Negroes in blue uniforms, his men executed many of them, according to eyewitnesses. An inquiry into these atrocities was conducted after the war, but there were no convictions. Forrest later became the Grand Wizard of the Klu Klux Klan, something he denied in a Congressional inquiry.

George W. Alexander was the infamous commandant of Castle Thunder Prison during the war. He was accused of extreme cruelty and tried by the Confederate Congress. While the evidence against him was strong, his flamboyant personality and devotion to the southern cause got him off the hook. After the war, fearing reprisals, he fled to Canada leaving his huge dog, Nero, behind. Nero was captured and sent to New York City were he was auctioned off at a soldier's charity event. Bidders were told not to wear blue as Nero was trained to attack anybody wearing a Union uniform.

Judah P. Benjamin: Toward the end of the war, Benjamin advocated freeing and arming the slaves, but his proposals only met partial success. When Davis fled Richmond, Benjamin went with him and while Davis was ultimately captured, Benjamin escaped, ending up in Great Britain where he became a successful barrister. He died in 1883.

Disclaimer by the author: For the purposes of story, I have taken a couple liberties with established historical facts, of which I loathe to do. First of all, there is some doubt Forrest was in Northern Georgia at the time Luke met him while escaping from Chattanooga. It's a stretch at best. Emma Edmonds did not die during the war and she was not an African American. She did take nitrate pills to darken her skin, however, because she disguised herself as Negro spy numerous times so she could easily move between lines. Other times she disguised as a man and she was very successful at funneling information to General Benjamin Butler, who in turn, gave it to U.S. Grant. Also, doctors and orderlies did not wear white smocks in the Civil War, they wore regular clothing.

Book Club
Discussion Questions

1. Luke is driven to construct a prosthesis so he can walk. What do you think are the factors in his determination to walk again in a normal fashion?

2. What would be Luke's responsibility for Samantha in today's world?

3. How would you describe Luke's relationship with Carol?

4. Name one thing you learned about the Civil War that you did not know before reading this book?

5. Why is the novel titled 'The Thin Gray Line'?

6. Luke's character goes through a number of development changes throughout the story. How, in your opinion, does Luke change and what are the forces behind the change?

7. What role did Janie's character in the novel play in Luke's emotional development?

8. Name Luke's principle demons.

9. Luke and his father had a difficult relationship. How did it develop through the novel? Do you think Luke loved his father

10. Describe Luke's relationship with Cuff?

11. What responsibility did Luke feel toward Posey? And why did he feel that way?

Made in the USA
Coppell, TX
15 June 2022

78860633R00132